E. Allen Wood

Tancredi : A Tale of the Opera

a novel

E. Allen Wood

Tancredi : A Tale of the Opera
a novel

ISBN/EAN: 9783337026356

Printed in Europe, USA, Canada, Australia, Japan

Cover: Foto ©Andreas Hilbeck / pixelio.de

More available books at **www.hansebooks.com**

A Novel.

BY

DR. E. ALLEN WOOD.

NEW YORK:

G. W. Dillingham, Publisher,

SUCCESSOR TO G. W. CARLETON & CO.

MDCCCLXXXVIII.

CONTENTS.

TANCREDI:
A TALE OF THE OPERA.

PART FIRST.

LEX TALIONIS.

CHAPTER I.

> "Our acts are our angels, or good or ill,
> Our fatal shadows that walk by us still."

"It is Jarl, the Miller's Boy."

"Good for him! served him right! It'll learn him to sneak in another time where he's not wanted!"

"How cruel of you to say that! Poor boy! See his arm all torn and bloody!"

"Let him stay where he belongs, and the dog won't bite him."

"How do you know but what he came on business

with Mr. Rellim? And even if he didn't, its wicked to have him bitten by that nasty **brute.**"

"That's what the dog's for."

"Well, I don't want any savage dog about our house to tear harmless children who may come into the yard."

"Children! **Why,** Jarl's as old as I am; he's fifteen, at least."

"Humph! And what are you but a **lad?** I'd like to know."

"Well, I'm old enough to know better than **to go** where I an't wanted."

"And *I'm* old enough to know that it is **a** cruel shame to have a boy bitten by a dog as Jarl is; and it's wicked **in you to say** 'served him right.'"

The young **people who carried** on this conversation **were** Caspar Liftal, aged fifteen, and Charlotte Duval, aged twelve.

The occasion was a children's lawn party, given at the residence of Frederick Rellim, on the thirteenth anniversary of his daughter's birthday.

In the midst of the juvenille festivities, a terrible **cry** was heard,—a cry of distress, accompanied by the angry barking of a dog,—in the direction of the front lawn, where the curious children ran in time to see the gardener dragging and beating off the large house mas-tiff, which ferociously attacked a lad that had stepped inside the front gate. The fortunate rescue by the gardener saved the victim from being torn to pieces.

The wounded youth, Jarl the Miller's Boy, as he was called, was raised to his feet, and it was found that his right arm was frightfully lacerated.

His face was ashy pale, but he uttered no word of distress. There was something wicked and startling in the proud bearing of his compact, graceful form, blemished though it was by torn garb and mangled arm. There was a look of mingled hate and defiance in his pallid face as he glared on the fierce brute now being dragged away by the servant,—a look so striking in its wild brave beauty that would attract the attention of the most indifferent looker-on.

His head was uncovered, and the black hair fell in tangled curls over eyes dark as night. His dress was torn away at the throat, leaving the bosom bare, and through the pallor could be seen that dusky hue peculiar to natives of Southern climes.

Jarl the Miller's Boy, was a notorious character in the neighborhood. He was noted for his wonderful beauty, for his wickedness, for his courage, and for the mystery connected with his advent into the settlement.

"Are ye mooch hurted, lad?" asked the gardener. "Better coome to the 'ouse un 'ev yer arm tied hup."

The wondering children gathered into a following group as the servant, leading Jarl, went to the house.

Charlotte Duval and Caspar Leftal fell in at the rear of the advancing column, while they carried on the conversation narrated at the opening of this chapter.

It was the custom, as it was felt to be the duty, of the good people of the community to speak ill of Jarl. His spirited and combative ways gave them abundant pretext and occasion for saying evil things of him and for treating him shamefully also. There were few persons around who did not conscientiously believe that he merited all he got—avoidance, frowns, kicks, and a bad name.

Jarl was accordingly used as a standing moral text, somewhat as Satan was once used, to instil into the minds of all children a wholesome dread of evil doing. He was a social beacon flashing out the red lights of sin and folly, warning good boys and girls to steer clear of his dangerous soundings.

Hence it was that Master Caspar Liftal took sides against the unfortunate youth.

Caspar was not at heart a bad boy ; he was not better or worse than the average boy, but he was, what his surroundings made him, an enemy of Jarl. The opinion of Caspar's parents, as well as that of the neighbors, was that the Miller's Boy should be howled down the winds, and accordingly Caspar felt it his duty to raise his voice in denunciation of the wicked youth.

Why Charlotte Duval did not join in the chorus of the villifiers is a mystery. Her action in this belongs to the anomalous class of instances wherein a child will not always walk in the beaten way! Why she took up the cudgel in his behalf deepens the mystery. She herself could not have accounted for her behavior at the time; she could not have even justified her course, for had she not, time and again, heard of Jarl's wickedness?

When they reached the hall entrance, they were met by Mr. Rellim, who inquired what the trouble was.

"The lad been hurted by Blucher, Sir. See 'is arm; and he needs summat to tie it hup."

"Where did this happen?" asked Rellim.

"On the fronten lawn, Sir."

"What business has he on my lawn? Poaching, I suppose; stealing flowers? eh! Or, maybe he was cheeky enough to join the children's party! Let him go home and get his arm tied up."

Charlotte Duval had instinctively crowded her way to the front while Rellim was speaking, impelled by sympathy for the suffering and abused boy. She begged Rellim not to act so unfeelingly.

"O let him rest before you send him off, Sir, please. See his arm how it is torn and how it bleeds! See how pale he is! Have mercy! Please, Sir, allow

James to dress his arm," cried the sympathetic maiden.

"I want no beggar's leavings about my premises," exclaimed the host in a passion. "James, lead him to the gate and drive him off."

After giving this brutal order, Rellim turned and entered the house.

Jarl raised his sound arm as if to salute Charlotte, and looked at her the thanks his tongue was unable to utter. He then turned in the path, took a step forward, his head fell on his breast, his legs bent under him and he fell to the ground in a swoon.

"He has fainted!" cried Charlotte, kneeling at his side. "Bring water, some one—quick!"

One of the boys brought cold water from the near spring, which was dashed in the face of the unconscious lad, when he opened his eyes and was once more raised to his feet.

One of the children had recovered his cap, and now handed it to him. From its lining he took a note addressed to Frederick Rellim, and gave it to the servant. Jarl uttered no word, but with a bewildered stare, seen in sleep-walkers, he slowly went out into the public highway. Charlotte Duval followed close after him, begging that she might render him some assistance.

"I want a drink of water, please," he gently said, after he reached the public road.

She brought him the drink, while he sat on the roadside and waited.

These attentions of Charlotte toward one who was looked on as an outlaw, again brought the young people around Jarl, some of whom seemed inclined to second Charlotte's kindness, while others, like Caspar, sneered at her work and insulted the miserable boy. She paid no attention to their jeers, but took from her shoulders a scarf and wound it about the boy's arm and neck, improvising a dressing in which the injured limb was comfortably supported.

"He'll keep your scarf! You'll never see it again," exclaimed Caspar.

Charlotte's face flushed with anger as she turned and frowned on the cruel speaker.

"Would you like to keep the scarf, Jarl?" she asked, turning toward him with kindness in voice and face.

"And will you give it me?" he replied, while a pleased smile lit up his wan face.

"Why should you like to keep my scarf?" asked Charlotte, tenderly.

Jarl made no reply. He hung his head, while the tears welled in his eyes and flowed down his pallid cheeks.

"Keep it, Jarl.   Yes, keep it; I give it you," cried the girl, touched by his distress.

"His mother taught him to beg; that's his trade," said Caspar.

Some, not all, laughed at his malignant witticism.

"Your mother has not taught you to be a gentleman," cried Charlotte, now throughly aroused with anger.

"My mother's as good as yours," retorted Caspar.

"Quick as a flash, Jarl was at Charlotte's side, and terrible was the look he gave Caspar Liftal, who slunk away like a whipped cur.

The brutal taunts of Caspar affected one thing—they dispersed all regret at having parted with her scarf. She was glad to see it on the boy's neck, proud that it became him so well, and exultant because all could see him wearing it.

The brutal treatment of Rellim toward the wounded boy had aroused her compassion; the jeers of her companions had aroused her indignation, and Charlotte Duval, the tender maiden, took the first step which woman takes when she follows man into crime or exile.

Jarl lifted his cap to her, and, oblivious of others, walked slowly away.

Charlotte, the inchoate woman, followed him with her eyes until he was lost to view, when she, too, departed unceremoniously for her home.

The scarf which Charlotte gave Jarl was unique,

and, as it may possibly require identification hereafter, the reader's attention is directed to a crimson silk scarf with a heart and anchor in white silk embroidered in either end. It was a present from her aunt, and which she admired with all a girl's passion for any beautiful article of dress. It was yielding much when she wound it about Jarl's arm; it was parting with a toilet idol when she bade him keep it.

CHAPTER II.

"Chance rules all above,
And shuffles, with a random hand, the lots
Which men are forced to draw."

THE note brought by Jarl was carried by the servant into the house, but the master to whom it was addressed was gone, no one knew whither. It was two o'clock in the afternoon before he came in from the back fields of his farm. He then read the note. From his actions it must have been an exciting note. He was so strongly moved by its contents that he siezed his hat and rushed off to the stable, yelling for his coachman at every jump. In a brief space he was mounted and galloping toward Pittsburgh, four miles away.

His daughter was curious to know the contents of that note, which he dropped in his mad haste, and read what follows :

PITTSBURGH, June, 28th 18—.

FREDERICK RELLIM.

SIR: The Plow and Anvil bank will suspend this day. This information is authentic and reliable. Get your money out as quick as you can.

AARON FULMORE.

When Rellim arrived at the bank he found an excited crowd gathered about its closed doors, on which was placarded the stereotyped explanation usually pasted on recently collapsed financial institutions. The assemblage surged and jostled each other in their frenzy to get near enough to read that notice; and those who did read it swallowed the statement with as keen a satisfaction as though it really meant anything honest, or was an endorsed and secured promise to pay all liabilities whatsoever. Rellim was furious, nor was he appeased by reading the hope-inspiring placard.

"How long has the bank been closed?" he asked a bystander.

"Not over an hour."

Rellim had on deposit in the broken bank about twenty thousand dollars. The amount was not large for a man of his reputed wealth; at most it would not have been large in ordinary times. But at this special time it was likely to be a very critical sum. He had recently purchased an immense tract of coal lands, and this money was held in reserve as a part of the final payment of the same, and which payment came due on the first of the ensuing July, a few days from that time.

He met a director of the collapsed bank, Mr. Fulmore, one of his most intimate and trusted friends.

"What is the matter with the Plow and Anvil?"
he asked the director.

"It's gone up, I fear, for good. We had a heavy
run on us yesterday, but thought to squeeze through,
until the Baltimore Company went for us this morning, wicked. But I'm glad you got your money out,
old fellow."

"But I did not get my money out."

"Not get your money out! What do you tell
me? Why, as soon as I got an inkling of the Baltimore's game I wrote you a note of warning, and
posted it off to you in haste."

"Yes; well, I got that note, but I didn't get it till
two o'clock."

"The very minute the bank closed its door!
What happened that you did not get the word earlier?
I started it off at ten this morning. I gave it to Jarl,
the Miller's Boy, who was going your way."

"Well, he brought the note all right, but, curse
my luck, he was met by my watch dog and pretty
badly used up. I didn't know the young vagabond
had a letter for me, and so I ordered him off my
premises. I'll thank you to send your letters by a
trusty messenger another time."

"How came it that he did not deliver the note at
the time you drove him away?"

"Oh, that wouldn't be Jarl! I suppose the young

beggar was offended at what I said.   When I told my servant to turn him out the gate, I left the house and went across the fields to the back of my farm, and did not return till two.   Then I read the note."

A brief investigation into the affairs of the Plow and Anvil disclosed the fact that it was hopelessly insolvent,—it would not pay one per cent.

Of course, as usual in like cases, many attempts were made through many years in the courts to squeeze blood out of the shrunk turnip,—and some blood was drawn from other sources, but it all went into the veins of constables and lawyers.

It has already been remarked that the peculiar crisis in Rellim's affairs at this particular time was likely to make the loss of his deposit embarrassing; but it was not feared that it would involve him ruinously.

The adage, " Misfortune comes not singly," is generally painfully exemplified when a bank breaks. Rellim felt all the force and bitterness of the saying after the collapse of the Plow and Anvil.   A large amount belonging to his debtors was likewise lost by the failure, some of his heaviest debtors were driven into bankruptcy thereby, and it turned out that, directly and indirectly, his loss in the aggregate was enormous.   But even then he might have weathered the storm, were it not for a fresh misfortune—the

oppression by the Baltimore Company. Active com-
petion in buying coal lands was at that time lively in
Allegheny county, and when the Baltimore Company
learned of Rellim's straightened circumstances, that
company saw in it the opportunity to drive an active
competitor to the wall. Accordingly, that powerful
corporation brought up his paper wherever it could,
got possession of some heavy claims against him,
refused to extend his obligations, and the result was
that Frederick Rellim, who was considered one of the
most substantial capitalists of the county, was driven
into bankruptcy and into financial ruin.

In four months from the time when he branded
Jarl a beggar and thrust him from his gate, he himself passed out that same gate a beggar.

CHAPTER III.

"I love everything that's old. Old friends, old times, old manners, old wine."

JARL lay for weeks at the Old Mill waiting for his wounds to heal.

The Old Mill stood on the river bank, and was driven by the current of the creek which flowed into the larger stream at that point.

The old mill ! Not solely the appellation of age, not the measure of time, but the title of endearment, of wonder and sympathy ;—the name we bestow on familiar objects where romance steps in to invest them with sentiment, and breathe into them the spirit of poesy.

We call a familiar friend our old friend ; the natal spot our old home; the years that have flown the olden time, and the mill from whence we brought the grist, the old mill.

The old mill stood like a huge cornucopia emptying its plenty into the lap of the smiling valley. Its ponderous driving wheel, creaking and groaning as it turned with the rush of waters, was more wonderful and less fickle than the wheel of Fortuna. The crunching stones of flint and granite turned out flakes as soft and white as the new fallen snow. It was Titan battling against famine.

Society lost one of its household deities when the old mill was dismantled. No more trips on old "Fly," with a bushel of corn in one end of the bag and stone ballast in the other. No more we watch with distrust the miller paying his toll, never again shall we see the warm stream of yellow meal pouring from the trembling hopper. These incidents are numbered with the lost arts. And the Indian pudding our mother's were won't to make, it, too, is gone with the mill that ground the golden grain.

The miller himself was a conspicuous character in those days of the olden times.

The miller who drew the floodgate and tolled the grists at the old mill was named Nate Jackman. He was about sixty, was hale and hearty, with the rose-tinted skin flushing through the coating of flour dust, like the bloom of the peach glowing through its down.

Nate was attached to the old mill, from which he had not been absent a day since he had followed his wife to her last resting place ten years agone. His cottage stood in the mill yard, and was presided over by his daughter and only child, Miss Prudence, now a trim and tidy woman of five and twenty. Nate had never been blessed with other children, but had adopted Jarl when he was only three years old. Accordingly Jarl had been the miller's boy for twelve years.

Jarl was the mystery of the neighborhood; but the miller loved the boy with all that corner of the heart left empty when there is no boy to fill it.

Mrs. Jackman loved and petted him for the two years preceding her death, and Prudence loved him fondly and devotedly. The public, as we have seen, held him at arms length as they would a gypsy outlaw.

Who was Jarl?

This question puzzled the curious neighbors until the unsolved problem became as painfully mysterious as the enigma of the Sphynx, or the Man with the Iron Mask.

CHAPTER IV.

"A millstone and the human heart,
  Are ever driven round,
If they have nothing else to grind,
  They must themselves be ground."

IT was one of those days peculiar to October in North America. The lack-lustre sun glimmered low in the smoky sky, and sluggishly swung round the horizon all day long. As it sank towards its nebulous couch, aweary with its ineffectual effort to dispel the murky atmosphere, and willing to draw the curtain of night over the melancholy desolation, brooding over bronzed fields and seared leaves, a woman leading a child, entered the miller's gate and sat on the porch steps evidently well nigh exhausted.

Mrs. Jackman who saw the approach of the strangers, went out and invited the forlorn creature to enter the house.

"No, no, no! Michele says I must go away," she replied in a sad voice and foreign accent. "But once more to hear him sing, I must—just once more."

"Why, good woman, the child's asleep, see! Besides he's only a babe, and cannot sing; come in,

come in, poor soul, do?" said the matron sooth-
ingly.

"But I tell you he's going away—far away to
Italy—far away; and him to behold I never shall
again."

The miller's wife now saw that the stranger was
not quite right in her head, and her sympathy for the
wretched being was made keener thereby.

The scene was one of pensive beauty as it was of
touching interest. It was a rare picture, felt perhaps
by inspiration, but never seen on canvas; a picture
where joy and beauty blended with misery and distress, and where nature complemented human sadness
with its spirit of melancholy. Imagination, glowing
as it maybe, will not quite invent that grouping on
the miller's porch. The grassy yard was strewn with
the faded leaves of autumn; in the distance the dim
hills lost their bold outlines in the commingling dim-
ness of sky, while the brazen sun paled in the smoke
of the Indian summer. In the foreground sat the
strange woman with the sleeping child on her lap,
while the tidy housewife bent over them with pity
and solicitude.

The bared limbs of the child were of the most
beautiful proportions, while the skin was so dark as to
evince that it was a stranger to the clime as it was to
the neighborhood. The complexion of the woman

was darker still. She was young and still beautiful, despite the haggard despair which settled on form and feature. Her form was slight though elegant, and clad in what had evidently been rich material; but her dress was stained and disordered as if from travel and exposure. Her face was startling in its expression, every lineament of which betokened lurking passion and despair. The weird black eyes looked the agony and insanity to which her speech gave utterance.

Her behavior was sad and subdued, rather than violent, and she seemed to invite pity and protection by her gentle demeanor. Her forlorn condition would have melted hearts more obdurate than Mrs. Jackman's, who tenderly took the child in her arms and led the pliant mad-woman into the house.

The hostess plied her guest with many questions, to some of which she gave rational answers; but all inquiries relating to her home, or friends, or name, were evaded or responded to irrelevantly.

The resemblance which existed between her and the child was alluded to, but she persistently denied being its mother, while Mrs. Jackman as persistently held to the belief that she was caring for a mother and her child.

She talked much of music and the opera, all of which was the vagaries of insanity to the simple miller's family. She sometimes addressed a familiar friend in a strange tongue, or sang songs in the same unknown language.

Her attachment to the child was something wonderful as it was pathetic, and confirmed the wife in the belief that the woman was really the child's mother. She would hold him to her breast and caress him in the most affectionate manner, call him the most endearing names, or sing him to sleep, when she would hold him for hours, careful not to awake him. She called him Carl, which, with the accent she gave it, sounded like Jarl to the family, the name they bestowed on him.

On the first night of her stay at the cottage she persisted in taking the child from the soft white bed where it slept, and holding it in her arms; but when Mrs. Jackman protested by replacing the lad in bed, she would stand over him rocking herself to and fro, talking to him in a coaxing, cooing voice, or singing to him in a low, soothing strain. Mrs. Jackman was so moved at the sight that she pushed the demented woman into the rocking chair and placed the child in her lap, which employment completely satisfied the poor creature.

But she did not sleep. Days and nights went round, but she ate none nor closed her eyes in slumber. She drank almost constantly large quantities of water, as if for an unquenchable thirst. When asked if she felt ill she would shake her head and place her hand over her heart.

A crisis of some kind was evidently drawing nigh. One morning, after a more than usually restless night, she suddenly fell in a violent fit, when the physician was sent for. She was placed in her bed and remedies supplied her, but she refused to swallow anything but water. She never rose from that bed.

She sang no more; her speech was affected by the fit, but her concern for the child abated not. She noticed no one but it, and was only satisfied when the little fellow was resting by her side. He seemed best pleased to be there, and, though imagination may have unduly worked on the wife's feelings, yet she said the child seemed to know that its friend was about to leave it forever.

The little thing would prattle to her in its caressing way, play with her dark tresses, or fall asleep with its dimpled arms around her neck, when she would lie still as death, lest she might disturb its slumber. The terrible, despairing black eyes were ever on the watch; no sleep, no rest came to the lorn worn woman.

Her weakness increased day by day until another epileptic convulsion siezed her and left her unconscious, breathing hard and fast, harder and faster, until even that organic function ceased, when she lay calm and still with her cold face turned toward the stars. Two staring eyes gazed away off into the great beyond, where the parting soul fled from passion, disease and sorrow.

The body was laid away under the tangled elder bushes of the lonely country graveyard. Jarl, the disconsolate, raved as if it, too, were struck with madness when they carried away the body of its friend.

The Father of the orphan saw the exile sparrow falling, falling, and he inclined the hearts of the miller's family toward the homeless waif. Basking in the sunshine of their affection the child soon forgot the shadows and ceased to mourn for its lost companion.

Among the few effects left by the dead woman there was little which gave promise of clearing up the mystery, and nothing that would lead to the discovery of the boy's name or parentage. Three miniatures were found, one on the body of the woman. It was the portrait of a very distinguished looking man; on its back was the single written word " *Michele*." A locket suspended around the boy's neck contained two miniatures; one of these was the portrait of the same man as seen in the single miniature; the other was the likeness of a woman, but so defaced, apparently designedly, as to be almost undecipherable. These, and what few other effects that might lead to indentification, were taken charge of by the Jackmans and carefully preserved.

And this was all that was known of the name,
family, or nativity of Jarl, the Mi'ler's Boy.

From the time when the woman and child were
given refuge at the cottage the neighbors took a lively
interest in what they deemed should be the proper dis-
posal of the vagrants. Wives and widows, matrons
and maids, and females of all grades, many of whom
had never before visited Mrs. Jackman, or were even
unknown to her, now honored her with calls, and with
advice, too, prompted by their sense of Christian duty
toward their neighbor and their neighbor's charge.

Out of respect for the consciences of these duty
hunters,—deluded though they were by a false scent,
—this history will not suggest motives far from commendable. It is true that in their conduct there lurks
a suspicion of Phariseeism, moral demagogry, and pru-
rient curiosity, but at present these people shall, un-
questioned and unmolested, indulge in their similation
of philanthrophy, regardless of motives or results.
There is no other way left. It must be taken for
granted that their intentions were praiseworthy,
viewed at least as they viewed them.

And they believed themselves sincere, and in so
far were sincere. They desired to reward virtue,
comfort the afflicted, relieve the oppressed, and feed
and clothe the impoverished. This was the still

small voice of their minimum faith—their everyday religion

But they possessed a heroic faith wherein the louder voices of wrath and vengeance outthundered the small voice of common duty and shook the moral Sinai on which they rested. It was the loud thunder of Retribution—the decree of death to the sinner.

By that heroic fiat the woman and child were doomed. She was the scarlet woman, bereft of her reason as the penalty, and Jarl the child of sin, with the rod of wrath in pickle for him. Hence respectability gathered up its undefiled robes and moved out of their contaminating influences.

The unanimous opinion, voiced like hounds in full cry, was that the vagrants should be sent away.

Where ?

To the poor house.

The woman is too ill to be removed ; besides we are willing to take care of her.

But she is a wicked woman.

Poor soul ! she is crazy. If she is bad it is not right to punish her now.

But the child,—it is the child of sin.

We know not; we will not turn it away.

The sparrow fell not to the ground.

The miller gave the body of the maniac a decent

burial; the miller's wife made soft raiment for the sparrow; the miller's family, in spite of the jeers and protests of their pious and indignant neighbors, found themselves as strongly attached to Jarl as if he were of their own flesh and blood.

CHAPTER V.

"Feared, shunned, belied, ere youth had lost its force,
  He hated men too much to feel remorse,
And thought the voice of wrath a sacred call
  To pay the injuries of some on all."

RELLIM's watch-dog fell at the hands of the assassin. It was the first industrial act by Jarl on the recovery of his wounded arm.

Don't ask how he did it; the ways of the young Spartan were dark and full of wickedness.

A trait peculiar to boyhood is the inclination and the ability to circumvent dogs. Jarl possessed this trait in an eminent degree. The mastiff passed away peacefully in the solemn midnight hour, or if he died with a howl in his throat it attracted no attention, for howling is expected at that witching hour. The untimely taking-off of the canine caused no commotion; Rellim made no complaint—he took it as a matter of course, and Jarl made no boast of the canicide.

There was one other account squared about this time, by whom it was not generally known, but conjecture pointed strongly to Jarl. Caspar Liftal had

either been badly kicked by a mule about the face, or
he had received a terrible threshing from some angry
antagonist. He lingered about his father's cot until
the black marks ran through the colors of blue, green,
yellow, and back to the normal hue of his freckled
skin. Caspar was as still-tongued as Rellim.

The Miller's Boy's creed was *Lex talionis*. He
squared the accounts with every one who injured him;
and when the dog fell dead at his feet he considered
the covenant filled as far as Rellim was concerned.
In the same way he balanced books with Caspar and
burnt them. With Jarl that was the final settlement,
unless they chose to re-open business with him.

The unfortunate lad had abundant opportunities to
practice his creed of vengeance. *Lex talionis*, as a
creed, is a cumulative industry; vengeance travels
further than mercy, and revenge spreads wider than
forgiveness. The remark is of this world and the
people in it.

Many were the inexcusable insults, and numerous
the flagrant outrages, perpetrated on this lonely child;
and, although it doubtless is a tarnish on our hero's
character, yet it must be plainly stated that he generally squared accounts with his persecutors the day
before or day after the time set apart by him for that
purpose. Whom shall I strike to-day? was the first
question he asked himself on rising every morning.

In this way and because of this way the defiant youth fought back at his neighbors ; and thus it came that, what at first was an uncharitable and unjust prejudice toward him on account of his questionable antecedents, was now become a deadly hatred of him on his own account.

Love a person without knowing why you should love him and you will soon have strong reasons for loving him. Hate him unreasonably and you will soon have solid reasons for hating him.

At the beginning the neighbors disliked Jarl under the pretext that he was the son of a gypsy strumpet ; but now they hated him for the added reason that he was violent, dangerous and wicked.

Had they reversed their opinion and treatment would he have been the reverse of what he was? He *was* violent, dangerous, and wicked—who was to blame, nature or prejudice, Jarl or society?

Society often acts on the presumption that secrecy and mystery must necessarily be associated with wickedness, especially when a woman is in the case. There was secrecy and mystery connected with Jarl's case, and a woman was involved. Society had the right to know the whole story, and the reason it did not know was because the story was not fit to be told. It was— must be wicked, wickedness must be punished, and if the woman had lived she would have felt the ven geance of clean skirted zealots, while the child would probably have been pitied and petted. But the woman had gone beyond the reach of the shafts of orthodoxy, and the next best thing was to impound the vicarious little foundling in the social purgatory to purge away the shame of his disgraced mother.

When the child first felt the punishment of his neighbors he could scarcely realize what it meant. The unsophisticated little fellow in vain sought enjoyment in the company of children about him. He was the bound boy at the husking—always crowded into a back seat. It was touching to witness his ingenuous devices by which he strove to ingratiate himself into the good graces of the children about him.

"Your mother was a gypsy," "Your mother was a beggar," "We are not to play with you," were the constant cries of the trained children of these Christian people.

He would stand among them with the dazed feeling that he was not of them and stare with longing wonder at the barrier which isolated him from the joys of childhood. He saw other children happy, revelling in sport and merry-making, and surrounded with the tinselled community of playthings; there were none for him. He was not permitted to touch their toys, or contribute his own to the general stock. Other boys were caressed and praised; there was none for him. The lone child turned away and crept back to the miller's cottage, where he murmured his heart-burning to the loved ones there, who took him in their arms and wept over his distress.

He bore the social ostracism for a long time—bore it until the instinct of pride taught him that he was a conventional target at which prudery shot its envenomed arrows, when he began to avoid his neighbors and no longer,—never again, sought recognition among the children who should have been his playfellows.

He was naturally kind, light-hearted, and companionable, but the treatment he got repressed his affability and froze up the geniality of his disposition. He saw life in false colors, he felt life that was morbid, and if he was to judge humanity by what he saw and felt, how was it possible for him to be other than he was—violent, dangerous and wicked?

Jarl is not a hypothetical creature given to establish the doctrine of self-immolation, wherein the second cheek is turned to be smitten. No other boy ever did that, unless he was a coward, and for the sake of manhood's promise it is to be hoped no other boy ever will consent to receive the second blow. Jarl is too worthy to be immolated on the altar of an unnatural philosophy; no, not even to point a moral or adorn a tale. On the contrary our hero shall obey the stronger promptings of instinct, which makes self protection more imperative as it is manlier that the stoicism of self-martyrdom. Jarl turned on society and fought it back blow for blow.

He went over the fields and among the quiet lanes singing like a lark, and the power and beauty of his voice were wonderful. The cottage and the mill rang with the glad songs of this light-hearted boy, and whatever the world may have been to him, or he to the world, he was always sure of welcome, and tenderness, and love in the simple miller's family ; and wild and wicked as were many of his acts away from home he never was guilty of one cross word or vicious act in or about his home. He possessed a dual nature and with it two lives—one for home, the other for the world outside ; the former life was Love, the latter Hate.

It would be cheerless as erroneous to believe that Jarl was an Ishmael with his hand against everybody, and everybody against him. It was true he had no bosom friend outside home, true he met no companion when he went abroad, and he had no kindness shown him anywhere away from the mill; but he went among the people, nevertheless, although it was with hate and distrust. He did the miller's shopping, collected his bills, and ably executed his general outside business. This led to acquaintances among the people of the city, where he was treated with that respect accorded a person in any honest business pursuit. But the fact remains that his life had little social pleasure, and many, very many, things were said and done to him which are to be deplored and which confirmed and intensified his hate and distrust.

He attended the district school in winter, where he showed a remarkable aptitude for acquiring knowledge, but which was hindered by what his teachers were pleased to call his insubordination. The real drawback was his spirit at resisting tyranny. If there was a fight or a fracas of any kind, Jarl was almost sure to be involved or dragged in, in some way, and, if no one else, Jarl was sure to get thrashed. He was held to be, and probably was bad—the worst boy in school. More than once he had been sent home in disgrace. But there was no let up with Jarl; he suffered but he made others suffer. In those days no one wronged him without feeling the day of reckoning.

On one occasion he exasperated the teacher to such pitch that, after receiving a severe flogging, he was expelled from the school as an incorrigible. He scarcely winced under the rod, and begged for no mercy—he never would cry at hurt from human hands—but when the master ordered his expulsion, he begged to be spared that disgrace.

"I ask to stay," he cried, "not for my sake, but for the sake of my foster father and sister."

The teacher was unrelenting, and Jarl went. As

he crossed the threshold he turned with anger and defiance in his face, shook his fist at the pedagogue and departed.

Little more was thought of the affair until the next morning when the master and pupils found the schoolhouse door and windows securely barred from the inside. Somebody spoke of breaking down the door, when Jarl's voice was heard inside.

" The first head poked in here will be broken."

The tone carried conviction with it,—the door was not broken down. But something had to be done. They tried threats, the garrison was not frightened thereat. Entreaty was tried, the fortress would not yield. Finally the teacher asked Jarl to name his terms of capitulation.

"I want to come back to school. You may thrash me for this, but I want to come back to school."

The assaulting party accepted the terms, when the gate was thrown open and they took possession.

The teacher did not keep faith, however, but prosecuted Jarl for disturbing the public peace.

The trial never came off. The teacher did not appear against him, and every one else was afraid to prosecute. By some process, known only to Jarl, the teacher himself was brought into disgrace, and sought elsewhere a school less difficult to manage.

CHAPTER VI.

"Pauline, by pride, Angels have fallen ere thy time."

THE Duval family was one of the wealthiest and most respected in the county. William Duval, Charlotte's father, was a gentleman of refinement and leisure, living retired on his beautiful farm, after having acquired a fortune in business. The remainder of his days was appointed to ease and enjoyment.

The Rellins lived just across the creek opposite the Duvals, and the families were neighborly, if not intimate.

William Duval was quiet and unobtrusive in manners, without, however, having the stupidity which too often makes silent men contemptible. He held in reserve a vast contingency of pluck and independence which burst forth when occasion demanded. He was very domestic in taste and habit, and was particularly attached to his daughter, Charlotte.

Mrs. Duval was the extreme opposite to her husband in temperament, taste and culture. She differed most from him in her exquisite aristocratic opinions and aspirations. She assumed, what she held to be,

aristocratic ways, classed herself an aristocrat—a title
by brevet, since she herself had been promoted by
marriage from a country school-teacher, where she
struggled for a subsistence and an extra holiday dress,
to that of the mistress of the Duval household. She
was fond of display, in which *penchant* her husband
indulged her to the top of her bent. She played
court to great people, or to people whom she held to
be great, to which pastime her lord found no fault so
long as it did not interfere with his comfort. Indeed
he was a model husband for an aspiring wife, at least
so far as apathetic indulgence in her innocent vanities.
The only time he ever crossed her was when she said
that Charlotte was too good to mingle with the children of the neighborhood, or, rather, that there was
no society in the community good enough for her
daughter. The husband restrained that bit of snob-
bery in the most peremptory manner.

"Never repeat such a sentiment," he said to her.
"The only standard by which we shall choose companions for our daughter must be respectability."

She repressed her nobility rage, but the venom of
pride turned inward, and poisoned her with disgust
and disquiet at, what she conceived to be, her husband's dangerous social principles. She saw only evil
to come from the low-born associations which surrounded her daughter; but she held her peace.

When Charlotte unexpectedly returned home from Rellim's party, and from which she had so unceremoniously withdrawn, Mrs. Duval saw at once that something unusual and unpleasant had disturbed her daughter.

"What is the matter, my dear?" asked the mother. "Surely the party is not over; it is not midday."

"No, mamma, the party is not over; but I could not stay there after what I saw," answered Charlotte, as if she would be best pleased to cry.

"Why, my child, what did you see there that troubles you so much?"

Charlotte then related to her mother the scene with Jarl, and with which the reader is already familiar.

Mrs. Duval was prejudiced—strongly prejudiced,—against the miller's boy, and the daughter, consequently, brought her grievance before an unsympathizing audience. For her tale she got a scolding, and for her tears she got sneers, all of which intensified the ache at her heart, and she broke down in a paroxysm of weeping.

The mother, remembering the husband's admonition, bridled her tongue on the occasion, and no further talk was had between herself and daughter on the subject.

On the following day a neighbor woman called on Mrs. Duval, and, after the local weather, came the local scandal.

"What do you think, Mrs. Duval? That young scamp, Jarl, the Miller's Boy, broke up the party at Rellin's, yesterday! Yes! He got into a fight with the gardener who caught him stealing flowers on the front lawn, and the dog bit him. Yes!"

"The young vagabond!" added Mrs. Duval, encouragingly.

"Yes! And what's worse, your daughter Charlotte took his part! Yes! And what's worse yet, she tied his arm up in her scarf! Yes!"

"You don't tell me that my daughter was seen talking to that low-born trash! Dreadful!"

"Yes! And what's worst yet, she gave him her scarf to keep! to keep for good! Yes! What do you think!"

"Oh, mercy! Gave him her scarf! That scarf with the heart and anchor! The scarf her aunt gave her as a birthday present! Scandalous! Now what'll her father say?"

When Mr. Duval came home the wife poured into his ear her effervescing mind.

"William, you have always disapproved of my efforts to keep Lotta away from low company. I trust you will now see that I was right, and that your social theory is wrong."

" Why, wife, what is the matter now ?"

"Matter, you ask ?   Why, haven't you heard of the scandal Lotta has got herself into ?"

" I have not; nothing serious, I pray ?   But tell me what it is."

" Why, the whole country is talking of her and Jarl, the Miller's Boy.   That low beggar !   Such carryings on I never heard of before !   It's perfectly disgraceful !"

" What's perfectly disgraceful ?   My dear, you don't tell me what the scandal is."

" Oh, it's awful !   Taking that bad boy's part ; the low-born scamp !"

" Who's taking his part ?"

" Why, our Lotta, to be sure !"

"Is that all ?   Is that the scandal ?"

" Is that all !   As if that wasn't enough !   No, that's not all.   She gave him her scarf to keep !   The one her aunt, your sister, gave her."

Duval then heard related with his wife's peculiar coloring and hyperbole the account of the accident which befel Jarl, and the part which Charlotte took therein.

He said nothing by way of approval or disapproval at the time, but managed to secure his daughter for a walk in the seclusion of the garden, where he adroitly led her to talk of the affair.   The tale as it fell from her lips sounded altogether like a different story from the one told by his wife.

The reader must already see that Duval was not hasty or violent ; and yet he was a man of strong feeling, positive convictions, and great steadfastness. He was sometimes slow at coming to a conclusion, but when he did, his whole soul was in the verdict.   Jarl had never crossed his path, he had not seen the boy. With his characteristic fashion of not meddling with other people's affairs, he held no convictions in regard to the social status of that youth.   If he did hold any opinion in the case it was very crude, and probably tinctured somewhat by the general repute in which the boy was held by those who assumed to know all about him.   But he had formed no opinion that would stand as a judgment in regard to Jarl, because he never had had occasion or opportunity to form an opinion. Very likely had he been asked for an expression of his opinion he would have said the boy's reputation is bad.

But now that the lad was thrown in his way, Duval was not the man to condemn him on the opinion borrowed of his neighbors. The opinion of the neighbors was that Jarl was thoroughly bad ; but they might be mistaken in this.   The lad had never molested him ;

he had not experienced his reputed wickedness, and he was much the same to him as any other boy.

In the light of all this he could not find it in his heart to chide his daughter for having shown a kindness to the Miller's Boy. Indeed her opinion in the case weighed more with him than the sum total of public opinion, plus that of his wife, and, in itself, was prima facie evidence to partially vindicate the boy's traduced character. Charlotte's pity led captive her father's prejudice—if he had any.

"And you did give him your beautiful scarf, my dear?" he quietly asked, after she had told him all.

"Yes, I did, father. Did I do right, do you think?"

"I suspect that it was wrong, but we shall see. Your mother thinks it was wrong. And yet I don't see why it should be very wrong. You meant it to be right, and your act was right in motive. Besides it is always right to treat kindly the oppressed and unfortunate. But I don't understand why you gave him your scarf to keep. His wounds would not heal quicker, nor would the arm feel more comfortable by making him a present of the scarf. It would have been just as kind if you had loaned it to him."

There was a merry twinkle in the father's eye as he ran on in this way about the scarf. Charlotte herself seemed to feel that she could offer no plausible explanation to the last remarks of her father, for she hung her head in silence.

"It is scarcely an article for a boy's dress," continued Duval, bent on teasing Charlotte into some kind of an explanation. "Did he ask you for it?"

"No, father; I gave it to him because they made me angry, and because they—they called him—beggar."

She leaned sobbing on her father's hands reached out to comfort and shield her. He raised up her tear-dimmed face and kissed her tenderly. Tears stood in his own eyes.

The two companions walked into the house holding each other by the hand, and quietly took their places at the tea-table. The mother saw by the action of the amicable pair that the daughter had won the father over to her way of thinking, and that he was disposed to make light of the affair. But she was determined that he should not make light of the affair.

"I suppose, husband, that you quite agree with Lotta and believe that her actions yesterday were commendable?" said she in a voice quavering with subdued anger.

"We quite agree, my dear," replied the husband in his quiet manner.

"You had better invite Jarl to the house," said the ironical woman.

"We'll think of it," was the reply of the imperturbed man.

"William Duval, you'll ruin your child if you continue to allow her to associate with all the low people of the neighborhood."

The usually pleasant table chat was visibly affected by these cross purposes, and the family did not eat with their accustomed hearty relish. The wife occasionally came back at her husband with dissent at what was to her mind his dangerous social democracy. But he would not be provoked into a serious discussion of the subject, and by sufferance allowed the wife to have it all her own way, which should have made her a happy woman, but which same she was not.

At breakfast next morning she returned to the charge with more fervor than ever, determined that, if she could not convince her husband of his error, she would at least wash her hands of all complicity in a course of conduct which she felt sure would terminate calamitously to her child. The quiet man ate his breakfast without saying much on any subject and nothing on his wife's subject. He looked up now and then at Charlotte, smiling on her and apparently paying little heed to his wife's railing.

"I'm determined that the beggar's brat shall restore

that scarf this very day!" exclaimed the scorned woman, as her husband arose from the table.

He stood leaning on the back of Charlotte's chair, and looked at his wife with a serious smile on his passive face.

"I mean what I say, William Duval. That bold, low-bred boy shall not parade that scarf around the country as the keepsake from my daughter. I shall demand it of him this very day."

"My dear wife, you shall do nothing of the sort. I'll settle this affair myself, since it troubles you so greatly, and I don't want the subject discussed until I open it. Come, Lotta, get your hat; you and I will visit the old mill."

Duval and his daughter were on their way across the fields, talking and laughing as they went.

He was disposed, or had been disposed, to treat the affair with indifference, but the persistent complaining of his wife aroused a desire and a prejudice in his favor. His wife's railings, no less than his daughter's sympathy, had won him over to the side of compassion.

It does not argue well for the domestic dignity of the Duvals, yet it is true that the head of that family held the opinion of his child on the case higher than that of his wife. The latter was not a short-sighted woman, she was not stony-hearted, nor was she habitually given to holding dissenting opinions from her husband. She had few faults of judgment or discretion, and this, her aristocrat conceit, was her most serious fault. He had great respect for her opinions on other matters, but in the present case she was too highly tinctured with romance, so he thought, to render an unbiased opinion. And yet she might be right. That was what he was determined to learn.

It was fortunate for Jarl that Duval was a thorough man of the world, who had, himself, come up from the plane of youthful folly. He remembered well what it was to be reckoned a bad boy, for he had felt the sting of that reputation. In his experience the "good" boys grew into stupid, negative men; while "bad" boys cropped out into prominent, influential and worthy citizens. He could not be acquainted with all the circumstances of Jarl's life, but he knew in a general way how easy, nay how common it is, to misjudge and misrepresent a spirited youth sowing his wild oats. His own views were strangely seconded by his pure daughter in her sympathy for Jarl. Thus folly and purity blended, and inclined him to give Jarl a fair show.

Arrived at the cottage they were coldly invited by Prudence Jackman to enter the cozy sitting-room. Duval asked for Nate, the miller, who was summoned from the mill, and who came into the room making excuses for his dusty garments.

"I came to see about Jarl," said Duval, in his brusque manner.

The old man sighed and shook his head, while Prudence turned pale. Never in all those years had a single person called to inquire about Jarl, unless it was to find fault, or charge him with some villainy. And now, they thought, Mr. Duval was there to brand him with some fresh infamy.

"Jarl is very sick, sir," said Prudence, in a humble beseeching voice. "He is confined to bed ; and please, Sir, don't worry him to-day."

"Don't hurt him to-day," echoed Nate, in the same tone of anguish.

"Rellim's dog has bit his arm, and the doctor is attending to him," continued Prudence, encouraged by Duval's silence.

"Yes, he's bit by Rellim's big dog. Bit on the arm. Bit awful bad, too, the doctor says," added Nate, as though he would apologize for the boy's inability to receive company.

"That's what we came to see about," said Duval, bluntly.

"Oh, Sir, it wasn't his fault, indeed it wasn't his fault," exclaimed Prudence, taking it for granted that everybody, including Duval, believed it was his fault.

"People ought to be ashamed of themselves for letting a big dog tear a boy's arm to pieces. I don't see how they could have the heart to drive him away without tying up his torn arm. But for your kind daughter, God bless her! the poor boy might have bled to death on the road," she exclaimed, breaking down in great painful sobs.

"Yes, he might have died, Jarl might," said Nate, taking up the refrain of his daughter's discourse. "Died in the road! Died, and not a rag on his sores to stop the bleedin'! Died, poor boy!"

"What was Jarl's business at Rellim's?" asked Duval.

"To carry a letter to Rellim, telling him to make haste and get his money out of the bank, for it was going to break," answered Prudence, revived somewhat with the hope that after all, Mr. Duval's intentions were friendly.

"Yes; and bekase he was obleegin' enough to carry the letter, he let his big dog chaw up his arm. And it's chawed up awful bad—his arm's chawed up till he's got the fever, the doctor says," exclaimed Nate, winding up his hot charge by coughing and drawing his dusty sleeve across his dusty face.

"Everybody is down on Jarl, and have been ever since he came to us a wee child only three years old," cried the angry Prudence. "Everybody but Char-

lotte," she added in a softer key, while she bestowed a
smile, the sweet smile of a grateful heart, on that
young girl. "No one ever spoke one kind word to
him but Charlotte in all these years. What have they
got against him? I'd like to know. He'll let them
alone, if they'll let him alone."

"Yes; he'll let 'em alone, if they'll let him alone.
But they won't let him alone, don't you see? but they
abuse him every time he goes from home, abuse him
all the time. Who can stand it?" exclaimed Nate,
rising from his chair, and looking about him as though
he would be glad to strike some one on the head.
Resting his eyes on Charlotte, he changed his mind
about hitting heads, while the scowl faded away into
the most benignant expression, and he continued, "All
but your little gal, Jarl likes *her!* We all like *her*,
God bless her! We all like her bekase she was kind
to Jarl—spoke kind to him, *mind you*, when everybody else spoke cross! God will bless her for that!"

He reached across the table to where she sat and
just touched the blue ribbon that dangled from her hat
—touched it with the reverence a martyr might touch
the robe of an angel.

Mr. Duval sat silent and listened while the pathetic
story went on. He was visibly interested in their tale
of woe, and deeply impressed with the spirit in which
these humble people stood up for the outcast whom

they fed and sheltered. He began to see the case in a newer and truer light. He began to believe that his child's behavior toward Jarl, so far from being reprehensible, was impelled by the worthiest and most sacred of all motives—pity for the weak and injured.

He drew Charlotte to his side and whispered in her ear, she then went over to the miller and took him by the hand in the most affectionate manner.

"We came to ask about Jarl," she said, "and to help him, too, if he needs help, and you will allow us. My good father feels sorry for him, as I do, and we both want to be good to him."

"God bless you! God bless the little angel!" cried the old man, while the tears made mucilaginous furrows down his befloured cheeks. He put his arms around her neck and kissed her.

Prudence began brushing the girl's clothes, but the tears blinded her, and she saw only a luminous child's face swimming in a halo of opal light. She covered the face with kisses. Duval himself made believe that something was stuck in his throat which required energetic coughing to dislodge.

Sympathy and confidence placed the miller and his daughter at their ease, and they spoke out unrestrained by fear of unfeeling listeners. The silent man let them talk while he did the thinking. Such men are driving the world at this moment. When

Duval came to understand any subject he was generally found on the right side, and actively on the right side.

Jackman and Prudence poured out tale after tale of wrong and injury heaped on the forsaken child, of persecutions, and sneers, and slights, and blows, and tyrannies that had pursued him even to the very threshold of his home, until Duval the cool, mild-mannered man, actually struck his fist on the table, and swore until the house shook with the former, and his audience trembled at the latter.

"I'll hear no more of this, my friends,—I can stand to hear no more. Take me to Jarl."

Nate led the way to the wounded boy's chamber. What was said there is not important to know at present. When they came down stairs the father and daughter shook hands with the Jackmans and started for home after promising to return soon and often.

They walked along for some distance in silence; Duval with his head drooped on his breast as if in profound thought.

"What will mamma say now? I'm all over flour dust," said Charlotte as she gave her dress a shake.

"You are not to speak to your mother a word about it until I give you leave," exclaimed Duval in a stern voice of command.

"Why, father?" said Charlotte in amazement, as she halted to look up in his face.

"1 mean, my dear, that I will speak to mother about this affair, and she will say that you have acted nobly, my darling," he said, in a gentle and sweet voice.

He took her hand, and thus they sauntered home.

CHAPTER VII.

"Kind words are more than coronets,
And simple faith than Norman blood."

"Wife, you have always aspired to move in an exclusive and aristocratic circle," William Duval quietly said to his helpmate as they sat alone on the evening of the day on which the visit was made to the mill.

"William, I have aspired to a position for myself and family among refined people; I should be seconded by you, not ridiculed."

"Certainly, my dear, if you put it that way; but don't get refinement and aristocracy mixed up. But we'll not dispute about the terms you may use. Now, I have no objection to aristocracy,—I mean the pure genuine article, not to your indulgence in the same when you come across real Simon pure aristocrats. The trouble seems to be in our disagreement as to the meaning of the term, aristocracy."

"In that case the proper thing for us to do is to compare notes, and, if possible, agree on what constitutes true aristocracy. Shall we try to come to an agreement by analyzing the word?"

"Agreed; and, as you have given the subject much study—have made a specialty of aristocracy, you shall open the discussion," responded Duval, pleased to believe that the one skeleton-in-closet was about to be exorcised by the wand of philosophy.

"What is aristocracy?" asked the puzzled woman, with a rising inflection, as though she was in doubt how to begin and yet was in for some kind of definition. She felt at once that, with all her supposed familiarity with the subject, the work before her was not plain or easy.

"Yes; tell us what you know about aristocracy; that's the question before the house," said Mr. Duval, drolly, as he turned his face beaming with good humor toward his wife.

"It is better to be a little choice of one's society; don't you think so?"

"Yes, yes; that's true; I grant that. Proceed."

"Well, the Gossels are low people; surely you don't want me to associate with them!"

"Quite right. All they think of is greed, all they practice is avarice. They are grovelling, ignorant people. Proceed."

"Well, there are the Lunnans; you will admit that they are not fit companions for us?"

"Right, again. They are natural born, hereditary

3*

criminals, with a constant representation in the county jail. Who else?"

"There's that low-born, wicked boy, Jarl; Lotta is too good to associate with *him !*"

"I am not of that opinion. However, we'll speak of him presently. You have named some of those whom you believe are not aristocrats; please give me a few examples from among those whom you hold to be true aristocrats."

"Our nearest neighbors, the Rellims; don't you consider them distinguished people?"

"They are distinguished, yes; but what for? Is it on account of their wealth, and their position as wealthy people? If so, that does not make them aristocrats. Imagine them stript of riches—their money, lands, servants, and equipages, would they be distinguished? And, after all, that is the true test,—do we respect such a person for himself—for his intrinsic merits, or because of his surroundings? If for the latter he is no true aristocrat."

"But you are friendly with Rellim, yourself."

"True, I am; but nevertheless my opinion of Rellim is that he is a cold, exacting and selfish man, void of culture or refinement. He knows nothing, absolutely nothing outside of his business, and his single redeeming trait is he knows his business well, and has been successful in amassing wealth. As he is respectable I tolerate him; as he is our neighbor I treat him civilly; but I have no high regard for him personally, and refuse to class him **an aristocrat on** account of his wealth **or his influence.** Unadorned with riches he would be a **very common** fellow; certainly not an aristocrat, as **I understand** the term. There is no native genuine nobility about Rellim, and the gild of gold that **gives** him polish will not wash. Nature's nobleman and a true aristocrat are synonymous with me."

"Why, husband, I never heard you speak so disparagingly **of any one** before!"

"We never held a **court of inquiry into our** neighbor's character before. **As the advocate of genuine** aristocracy I must **tell the** truth plainly, distasteful though it may be. Besides, my dear, this is confidential talk between you and me."

Mrs. Duval sighed, and went on with her needlework. Duval lit a cigar and watched the curling smoke **wreathe harmless cyclones about his head.** Neither spoke for some time.

"Well, now, William, suppose you take the witness-stand as an expert and tell us what *you* know about aristocracy," she presently said, looking up from her work.

"**You** want to know what true aristocracy is?"

"Yes; that's the question before the house. Proceed."

"Juvenal says, 'Virtue is true nobility.'"

"But what do you say?"

"I agree with him, and with Pope, who holds that an honest man's the noblest work of God."

"These are fine platitudes, which sound well, but are threadbare with long and vulgar use, void of aristocratic ideas, and without the pretense of argument. Why don't you come to the point, and not go about begging the question?"

"Well, then, my wife, any one whom we respect for himself alone is a genuine aristocrat."

Mrs. Duval sat musing for some time. At length she looked up at her husband who had been intently watching her.

"What does all this discussion signify? We are as far from agreeing as before. You have some design in it all, what is it?"

Mr. Duval puffed away at his cigar, which was fast burning to its last ashes, but he said nothing. She laid away her sewing and went over and sat on his knee, where she peered wonderingly in his face.

"I know you too well to believe that you would go to all this trouble without a serious object in view. What is your object?"

"To inform you that you have overlooked some true, genuine aristocrats of this neighborhood," he replied, throwing away the stump of his cigar.

"Name them, my dear. Where do they live?"

"We have a young prince in disguise, living amongst us."

"You astonish me! Who is he, where is he?" she eagerly asked, rising from his knees and standing before him.

"He lives at the old mill, and his name is Jarl."

"Jarl, the Miller's Boy! Noble! Are you in earnest?"

"Jarl, the Miller's Boy, is a true born aristocrat."

"You were at the miller's to-day; what did you discover there?"

"I discovered that Jarl is noble; but go to-morrow and learn about him for yourself."

Duval may have spoken wiser than he knew.

He meant to appeal to the weak side—the aristocratic side—of his wife's nature; he meant that Jarl was possessed of a noble nature; he meant to persuade his wife to pay a visit to the miller's cottage. Once there she would see for herself the handsome boy, learn how bright he was, and hear the tales of wrong and distress as told in the eloquent words of the miller and daughter.

He knew at heart his wife was a good woman, and that her one vanity was the only barrier that kept good out of her heart. He believed that the way to reach her heart was through her prejudice, and he therefore appealed to her pride.

As " the gods of our pleasant vices make instruments to scourge us," so may our frailties be turned into leading strings to draw us back into the path of duty.

Blessed is the man who can lure his wife into the ways of wisdom through the medium of her tender frailties.

More blessed still the wife who inclines her husband back to home and love by the lever of his vices.

The voice of the siren is not analogous; the pigmy leading the giant is a feebler comparison ; the only parallel is the legend of the guardian angel leading a mortal with hand unseen and force unfelt.

CHAPTER VIII.

" A generous friendship no cold medium knows,
    Burns with one love, with one resentment glows;
    One our interests and our passions be,
    My friend must hate the man that injures me."

On the day following the debate on aristocracy
Mrs. Duval, accompanied by Charlotte, visited the
miller's cottage.

Old Nate came in from the mill to pay his respects to the great lady, for the Duvals had wonder-
fully risen in the esteem of the Jackmans. He sat
and chatted with Charlotte while Prudence took the
mother to the chamber where lay the wounded boy.

He was asleep when they entered. His injured
arm, bound up in the surgeon's dressings, lay across
and above his head. The bared breast, head and arm
could not have been more exquisitely beautiful if they
had been carved from marble, under the inspiration of
puissant genius. In physical conformation Jarl
deserved to be the descendant of a long line of kings.
He looked noble as he lay in his graceful repose.

Perhaps it was the contemplation of the superb
picture that most attracted the attention and aroused

the interest of the romantic woman. His appearance
impressed her with the belief that her husband had
not jested when he spoke of a prince in disguise. It
was the romance that exactly suited the turf hunter.

In this interview Mrs. Duval heard quite a different chapter in the boy's history from that told her
husband a day previous. Probably it was because she
led the conversation in a different channel, but at all
events, Mrs. D—— heard what Mr. D—— did not,
and he had heard what she did not hear. Prudence
gave all the circumstances connected with the first
appearance of Jarl at the mill; the mysterious lady
with rich dress, refined manners, remarkable beauty,
and who spoke a foreign language, all of which indica-
cated gentility, perhaps nobility, and certainly aristocracy. The pictures of the distinguished looking
person, afforded the woman additional testimony,
establishing the theory that the boy was really the offspring of distinguished parentage. Mrs. Duval was as
thoroughly convinced that Jarl, if not a prince in disguise, was noble, as she was convinced of the identity
of her own daughter.

Filled to repletion with this opinion and its con-
comitant fancies, she had no room for the tales of
suffering and distress which filled the boy's life with
shame and sorrow. The romance monopolized her
entirely; it swelled and rounded out into all the beau-

tiful proportions of rank and splendor, and stopped her ears to the vulgar plaints of misery. It is doubtful if she ever knew, although she may have been told, that Jarl had been wronged and abused.

"You must take good care of him, young woman," she whispered to Prudence, with a patronizing air.

"Take care of him," exclaimed the astonished girl under her breath. "If we don't take care of him, in the name of mercy, who will?"

"The boy has rich and powerful friends somewhere in the world, I feel sure, and no doubt they will be found some day, when they will reward you for all your trouble," whispered Mrs. Duval.

"Trouble! Reward! We want no reward, only to keep him with us always. God bless him!" cried the half indignant young woman, her eyes swimming in tears.

Jarl awoke and stared in bewildered astonishment at the strange lady.

"This is Mrs. Duval, Charlotte's mother. She is here to see you, my dear," said Prudence going up to the bedside.

He smiled and reached out his uninjured hand to the lady, who took it and tenderly held it in her own.

"My little friend, you must make haste and get well," she said, in a cheery voice. "I want to ask you a whole heap of questions, all about your parents and your home before you came here."

Jarl thanked her, and said he would hasten his recovery in every way he could.

"Can you recollect anything about your name or home when you were a child?" asked the curious woman, with the air of one used to dealing with abstruse problems, and who felt that a few well directed inquires would clear up the mystery connected with Jarl's early history.

No; he recollected nothing clearly. He had a confused remembrance of a big house on a noisy street, and that a large musical instrument (a piano, suggested Mrs. D.) stood in that house.

"I thought so," exclaimed the lady, delighted to find that the boy's memory, feeble though it was, reverted to trappings of wealth and splendor. "Can't you think of more? Can't you remember an illustrious father? Does not memory recall a noble mother?"

The boy shook his head.

"Or even of coaches and horses, and servants in livery?"

The head shook.

"Surely you remember of wearing beautiful garments?"

No; went the head.

"Or handsome playthings?"

" Yes; I remember of having a wheelbarrow."

The pedigree hunter looked disgusted. What at?

Did the wheelbarrow carry Jarl toward a coalheaving ancestry?

If he could only recollect the familiar trappings of place and pride—the crowns, and diadems, and courts, and pageants, it would better have tallied with Madam's wish.

Having exhausted her interrogatories on the subject of Jarl's infantile history the female Socrates took her leave, in the main satisfied with her visit.

When Mr. Duval came home in the evening the wife entered at once into a discussion of the subject uppermost in her mind.

" Do you believe me, William, I think you were right about Jarl, the Miller's Boy. He may not be the prince in disguise you claim, but there is something away above the common about him. Mark my words, he is indeed the child of illustrious parentage."

" Jarl, the low-born wicked boy! The beggar's brat! The bad boy to whom Charlotte gave her scarf, noble? Impossible!" exclaimed Duval, in the most tantalizing manner.

" Why, you said so, yourself, now!" whined the wife, in a rebuking spirit. " You have a bitter memory for my former opinion of the youth. It was to please you I went to see him, and now, after I have learned to know him better, and am disposed to do him justice, you turn around and ridicule me."

" Pardon me, my dear wife, but the temptation to indulge in a fling at your late opinion was too strong to resist; forgive me this time. I rejoice more than you think, to know that you do him justice. It shows how clear and good you can be when you get on the right track. You have my warmest praise. Lotta was right, you see, and that was the main point we sought to establish."

" But seriously, husband, what makes you think Jarl is of noble blood ?"

" I do not think he is, or is not."

" Why, you said so."

" No, my dear; I said that he is noble. I referred to the boy, not to his family. I know nothing of the latter."

" Oh; I begin to understand ; he is one of your nature's noblemen,—your ideal aristocrat."

" That was about my meaning."

But still Mrs. Duval had unlimited faith in the high-born lineage of her new prodigy. Her interest in the boy was begot by pride, that of her husband's by sympathy. Jarl profited by both

Did he prove deserving ?

Jarl began life under new auspices, and with altered surroundings. His feelings and his motives were changed. The change was manifest to all who knew him. New thoughts, better impulses, and fresh hope fired his heart with a desire for a better life. Where defiance and recklessness rankled before now grew up the blossoms of peace and good will. His aspirations were not embittered with the wonted spirit of vengeance. It is true he did slay Rellim's dog, true he flogged Caspar Liftal within an inch of his life, but opportunity impelled the blows which were the last rancorous flashes from the expiring embers of hate.

Kindness had conquered him. A common kindness, which costs nothing, brought him over to peace. The gentle kindness of a pure young girl redeemed the young outlaw.

Nearly every day while he was confined to the house with his feverish arm, Charlotte, often accompanied by one or the other of her parents, visited him. The intimacy thus sprung up ripened into a mutual regard between the proud Duvals and the humble Jackmans. The warmest and most beautiful attachment grew up between the two children. It was not that love wherein sexual instinct is the mainspring,— they were but children ; but it was that love, not less firm, founded on sympathy and devotion, and which is ultimately led captive when passion awakes from its embryotic slumber.

It was as humorous as it was pleasant to witness

the proprietary airs of the child Charlotte toward the child Jarl. She assumed to control his words and actions, and, if possible, his very thoughts. It is not meant that she tyrannized over him, or that he was the worse for being thus subjected to a moral quarantine before admittance into a healthy social atmosphere. His ways were a little rough, she smoothed them down; his words were sometimes harsh, she modulated to a softer key; his thoughts, as sometimes expressed to her, were often wicked, she banished them.

To the boy, long accustomed to neglect and ill-usage, it was a severe struggle to reform. Malignity had engrafted itself on his nature, and would occasionally burst through all restraint and overwhelm Jarl with disgrace and Charlotte with dismay. However, under her patient tutorship he did measurably succeed in conducting himself as a civilized boy should.

But there was trouble ahead. In spite of the patronage of the influential Duvals the neighbors one and all refused to admit Jarl to fellowship. They had hated him too long and too strong for so radical a change as that from hate to fellowship.

In justice to Jarl it must be stated that he neither expected nor sought favor of any of his neighbors; apparently he was as defiant and disdainful as ever. But he was, by his discreet behavior, showing that he deserved some friendly recognition at the hands of his fellow creatures. Mrs. Duval tried hard to introduce her protégé to the favorable notice of society, but in vain.

The major part of the residents of the community had injured Jarl in one way or another, and nearly all had spoken ill of him.

It is common, although unaccountable, for a person to hate any one he has injured. This is especially the case where the wrong inflicted is heinous, unprovoked, and deliberate. The hate is still more intensified when the victim is innocent and amiable.

John Roe causelessly wrongs Richard Doe. Doe never wronged Roe, does not even resent the injury he feels; why should Roe hate Doe that much the more bitter? Why does Roe continue the wrong? Why does he add insult to injury?

There is no sensation that so absorbs a man's mind or so influences his conduct as the feeling he has toward the person who owes him a debt. That debt may be one of money, or gratitude, or hate. Roe feels a peculiar interest in his debtor, Doe,—he keeps his eye on him. What that debtor does or says has a more than ordinary interest. Roe is constantly expecting pay day to come around, especially when hate is the debt. Nay, in the latter case, he urges payment by every provocation that suggests itself.

Society was well aware that it had wronged Jarl.

It knew the boy owed it a debt of hate, and society fully expected that Jarl would continue, as he had done, to pay that debt in installments of revenge. Kindness from the members of society toward him now would be a surrender, and an unequivocable acknowledgment that they had been in the wrong. They were not the sort of people to stultify themselves by such a confession; they were not around for the purpose of exalting gypsy beggars to respectability. No; let him cancel his debt with hate for hate. They defied him; they held him at arm's length.

Mrs. Duval was criticized and ridiculed by her acquaintances for her espousal of the young outlaw's cause; but she was not to be turned aside from her romantic undertaking, and continued to patronize the boy with more zeal than ever.

Jarl was often invited to the Duval mansion, where he often went, but obstinately refused to remain for a minute if other visitors were present. Mr. Duval took a deep interest in the lad, for which the latter was touchingly grateful. But Charlotte was the delight of his eyes. It was a sight of beauty to watch them in each other's company. His handsome face would light up with joy when he came into her presence. They roamed the fields and among the shadowy groves together, and the dales echoed with their glad shouts, and rang with Jarl's bird-like songs. He was supremely, boisterously happy, nor was his bliss alloyed with desire for other society than Charlotte's.

The autumn came on, and with it the opening of the district school, where Jarl was to attend. All dread was gone when he learned that Charlotte Duval also was to attend the same school.

On the very opening day it was manifest that the new teacher was primed with opinions prejudicial to Jarl. By constant guard and patient endurance he went through the first two weeks without great misfortune. He felt that he was watched and distrusted as though he were a wild beast of prey.

One day, during the noonday play hour, some trouble arose among the ball players. Jarl never attempted to join in the games, he had been ruled out long before. On this particular day Jarl was watching the game from a respectful distance with no thought of interfering. Suddenly the ball from the bat fell at his feet, where to let it lie was his first thought; but everybody on the field seemed yelling at him to throw them the ball. He picked it up, but in his bewilderment, threw it to the wrong player. This almost involuntary and unintentional blunder on his part, drew down on his head the fiercest maledictions of the party that lost by the mistake. They called him everything that juvenile brains could invent or boyish tongues give utterance to.

"Keep your hands off what don't belong to you,"
exclaimed a big boy, drawing nigh.

"You're always pokin' your nose into what den't
concern you. I've a mind to break your head!"
shouted others, as a mob crowded around Jarl. The
shouting and jeering crowd attracted the whole school
to the spot.

Jarl said nothing, but his clenched fists, flashing
eyes, and ashen face showed that revenge was almost
bursting from his defiant body. Charlotte Duval was
standing near, he caught her eye; she elbowed her
way to his side. She turned and faced the menacing
and angry crowd of boys.

"You cowards are always imposing on Jarl!" she
cried. "You ought to be ashamed of yourselves. I
heard you call on him to throw the ball, and now you
abuse him for doing so! You're all a pack of cowards!"

"Hello, Lotta! You're Jarl's sweetheart, ain't
you? Better mind your own business, tomboy!"

Jarl stretched the young blackguard on the turf,
and looked prepared for all comers, but no one else
came.

A complaint was made against Jarl to the teacher,
and he was called up before the school.

"Did you strike Richard Smith!"

"I did."

" What for ?"

" For insulting Charlotte Duval."

" Did you know it was wrong to strike him ?"

" No, Sir."

" Are you sorry you struck him ?"

" No."

" Then I shall punish you."

" I think you had better not try that."

" Why ?"

" Because you would be in the wrong with Richard. Besides I'll thrash him every time he insults Charlotte. If you punish me for doing right, you'll be sorry."

" Do you mean that as a threat ?"

" I mean it as the earnest truth, and no warning."

The teacher did not heed the warning, but made Jarl strip for the whipping. The poor fellow then received one of those brutal beatings which were once thought to be a department of learning.

Jarl was barbarously beaten; blood flowed at every stroke.

As each blow fell on his almost naked shoulders Charlotte shrieked, until no longer able to endure the shocking sight, the brave girl threw herself between master and his victim, and forced the brute to desist.

" Your'e killing him ! Stop, for God's sake, stop !

Your'e killing him because he took my part!" cried the terrified girl.

And Jarl, how did he behave?

Like a martyr under the knout, or in the flames. He never winced, but his face was pale as death, and his great black eyes emitted a terrible light as he glared on the brutal master.

The teacher saw murder in that boy's eye, and he laid away the hickory rod, when Charlotte fell fainting to the floor. Jarl caught her in his arms, and sprang for the door, where he stood like a tiger at bay.

"You have beat me for the last time! You beat me for these cowards! I'll get even with you all!"

He was gone. He led and half carried Charlotte Duval, who partially revived on entering the glad free air which played and sang among the trees, or moaned among the gables of the slaughter-pen left behind forever. Mr. Duval returned for Charlotte's books and Jarl's clothing. Flight alone saved the pedagogue from the wrath of the enraged father and friend.

When Jarl reached home, the keen-sighted Prudence soon learned the new trouble, and on seeing his shoulders such a wail of distress went up from her throat as would have melted a heart of stone. When Nate saw the cruel welts and blood-stained excoriations, he struck his ponderous fists together and swore like a trooper.

CHAPTER IX.

"Know how sublime a thing it is
To suffer, and be strong."

THE evening of the day on which Jarl received the unmerciful beating was a memorable one in the history of the Jackmans, for it was the time when Jarl first spoke of running away.

The occupants of the cottage sat around the blazing fire after the miller's work was done. The November winds moaned among the pines, and whistled around the gables, and the sleet rattled at the windows.

Prudence had anointed Jarl's wounds with oil and to the great comfort of his external hurts, but there was an ache at his heart which oil and lint could not assuage.

"I want to go away," said Jarl, interrupting the silence which had fallen on the group.

"Go away!" exclaimed Nate, in surprise. "Did you say go away, Jarl?"

"Yes, I shall go away from here."

"And why do you want to go away, my boy?"

"Oh, I can't stand the abuse of the people any longer. I thought maybe it was mostly my fault that everybody is so cross to me, but it an't that. The better I behave and the harder I try to deserve their good opinion the worse they treat me. I'm tired of being fought at and beaten and abused, and I'm tired of fighting back. The only way to end it all is for me to go away from here."

"But where can you go, Jarl," asked Prudence, in alarm.

"Somewhere, anywhere, so it's away from here, and far enough away where I an't known."

"Poor boy! But what's to become of us? what's to become of me and Prudy if you go away? Think of that, Jarl, what's to become of me and Prudy after you are gone?"

Jarl arose and stood beside the old man seated in his arm-chair, and gently and so lovingly put one arm around the miller's neck.

"I think of that, my good father, and my good sister, I think of that every day. I thought of it long ago, and because I thought of you I stayed and suffered."

"Oh, Jarl! We can never let you go!" cried Prudence, taking his disengaged hand in both hers.

"No, Jarl," said Nate, shaking his gray head very emphatically, "we can never let you go. Stay with us, Jarl, we'll be good to you; we love you, Jarl, if other people don't; you needn't go where they air. All, except Miss Charlotte and her father and mother—Charlotte 'll be good to you—they'll all be good to you, all of 'em. They like you Jarl, but not as we love you. You'll stay with us?"

"But, my kind father, listen; I can't always stay at home. I'll be a man some day, and must leave you then; why not now? Besides, I am not going away for good—not going to desert you. I don't mean that. I will come back home often and often, for this is my dear home, and you are my dear father and sister. Why, I'll write to you every day, and it'll be nearly the same as if I were with you all the time."

The three remained silent for some time, and they all looked straight into the fire.

The proposition of the foster child was new and startling. Long as he had suffered, and long as he had wished to fly from the cruel neighbors, he had never before given them a hint of his desire, nor would he now if there was any other course left open for him to follow.

He was fully determined to go. It was bad enough to remain when he could fight his enemies back; there was a degree of satisfaction in that. But his case was different now. The Duvals entered largely into his life, and fighting back was out of the question. To practice his creed of vengeance would

frighten Charlotte and displease her parents. Gratitude toward them was a part of his religion, and
going away was his salvation. Not that he was less
brave or self-reliant, nor because revenge was less
sweet, but because his few friends would be constantly
shocked and mortified were he to continue his life of
retaliation.

As he could no longer fight he must retreat.
Staying meant war, going meant peace.

"Where will you go, my boy?" asked Nate, still
looking straight into the fire, as if addressing it.

"I should like to go where I can get a little more
schooling, and where I can learn a trade," answered
Jarl, speaking to the fire.

"Jarl, my boy, why not be a miller? Why not,
indeed! I could turn out good work when I was
your age. I could, that! I could turn it out with
the best of 'em. The mill's mine; it'll be yourn
some day, if you'll only stay. Some day when I'm
gone the mill 'll be yourn. I have done well here in
the old mill; I have, indeed. You can do better nor
even I did, bekase you're a heap smarter nor even I
was."

The great log at the moment turned over in the
fire, and a brilliant shower of sparks filled the chimney
throat.

"Don't you see how the people hate me, father?

The old mill would rot down with idleness before they would send their grain to my mill."

A gust of wind sent a puff of smoke down the chimney and into the room.

"Maybe so! Maybe so! God pity them all! God pity them as drives my poor boy away from me."

Again silence fell on the sad group. Jarl was standing between the seated father and daughter, with one hand resting on the old man's shoulder, and the other hand in Prudence's hands. They all looked into the fire, their conversation was directed to the fire, and from it they received responses. Their musings were flame girt, their thoughts branded with fire. It was a scene that could only be enacted around the domestic hearth.

"Father," said Prudence, in an absent, dreaming-like voice.

Nate heard not, heeded not, he gazed into the fire.

"Father," repeated the girl.

"What is it, Prudy?" asked the old man.

She made no answer. What is it she sees in the live embers? Is it the face of the dead, fresh risen from the tomb?

"Father; why don't you speak," she exclaimed, impatiently.

4*

"Are you crazy, girl?" asked Nate, reaching around Jarl, and giving her a shake.

"What is to hinder us from going away with Jarl?" she asked, rising to her feet, and turning to her father, with a look of alarm on her face.

The old man also arose to his feet with no less frightened look—a look compounded of dread, terror, and sorrow.

"Go away with Jarl! Leave the Old Mill!"

"Yes, father; go away with Jarl. I, too, am tired, have long been tired, of the life we lead here—the life we have led ever since the poor child came to us."

New thoughts and startling emotions were crowding each other fast and painfully in the minds of the miller and his daughter.

"You are getting old, father, and need more rest than you get. You have saved enough to keep you the balance of your days. Dickson has been at you for a long time to sell him the mill; why not let him have it, and go away from here and take us all with you?"

"Sell the Old Mill! My father owned it before me. I was born here. I was born and bred a miller, and don't know anything else."

"Oh, yes, father, you know what is good for Jarl, and you can help him learn something outside the mill."

"Go away from here and leave poor mother all alone in her cold grave? Leave her all alone!"

"My mother loved little Jarl, too," she said, sobbing, after an interval of silence.

"So she did! So she did!"

"It would break her poor heart to see the way the poor boy is abused around here. It would kill her to see him go away among strangers. It would kill her! And it will kill me."

"I expect it would. I expect it would. Well, I must sleep on it. I must have a talk with Duval; what he says to do, I'll do. So, there, now; that's all I'll promise."

They retired for the night.

CHAPTER X.

"Stand not upon the order of your going,
But go at once."

If divinity shapes our ends, what, then, is the subtle agency through which it operates? Is it by some imponderable and inscrutable dynamics reflected from a world unseen? Is it the faint glimmer that streaks life's gloom with faith and hope?

Perchance the shadows of the dead wife and maniac woman bent over the couch of the sleeping miller, and stamped on the register of his brain their desire.

"I must tell you about my dream last night," said Nate Jackman, smiling pleasantly on his family at breakfast the next morning after Jarl's declaration.

"I dreamt that my wife was a livin' and that me and her and Prudy started to go away—far, far away from the old mill, a leavin' Jarl behind. Just as we were a goin' over the far hill we halted to take a last look at the old spot, when we saw the mill on fire, with Jarl on the roof a wavin' for me to come back and take him out of the fire. We could see the mob of mad people a pokin' up the fire to make it hotter and hotter to burn Jarl. My wife started on a run back to help Jarl, and I run too, but I beat her a runnin'. When I got to the mill the mob ketched me and held one of my feet in the fire to roast it. That waked me up, when I found one of my feet a stickin' out from under the bed-clothes, and cold as ice."

Jarl laughed at the tale of the dream, and more particularly at its queer ending, which, he said, was as ridiculous as the ending of his own dream of the last night.

"I dreamed," he went on to say, "that the witches caught me, and, after saddling me, rode me away through the skies of the night. I cantered along very spiritedly—was what you might call a prancing steed —until the saddle began to gall me, which presently became so painful that I awoke with the smarting, and from a horse with a galled back, was instantly changed into a fidgety boy who had rolled over in his sleep on his sore back."

"What a lucky dream," said Nate, who, like all the old stock, was not quite sure but what witches were real beings. "To dream of witches is a sign of money. To dream of them a ridin' you through the air, is a sign you'll git pooty high up in the world. In fact its lucky it was a dream."

“Why is it lucky?”

“If it hadn’t been a dream, it would ha’ been real, wouldn’t it?”

“I hadn’t thought of that.”

“Did they ride you a straddle?”

“How would a horse know that?”

“’Cause if they did I’ll tell you how to keep them from ridin’ you astraddle another time.”

“How!”

“Don’t go to sleep, and the witches won’t ride you.”

Nate’s loud laughing brought Jarl to gradually know that a joke had been perpetrated at his expense.

“If you don’t want your foot roasted by a mob, you had better stay awake and not take off your shoes,” retorted Jarl.

Nate affected not to hear the last remark of Jarl, but suddenly became interested in Prudence.

“And what did you dream, Prudy?” he asked her.

“I did not dream, father, but lay awake and thought.”

“What was you a thinkin’ about?”

“Of everything and everybody I ever knew. I thought of you, and mother and Jarl. I thought that maybe Mrs. Duval is right—that Jarl has powerful friends somewhere in the wide world who are grieving for his loss, and to whom we should try to restore their lost boy. And then I thought that if ever we do find them, or they us, we must get away from this secluded place and mingle with the great world where they are. And I also thought," she continued in a softer, sadder voice, "I also thought of John Taplan, the sailor, who started for Cape Horn on his way to California four years ago. I remembered his promise, and I wondered if he had kept faith with me, as I have kept faith with him?"

"Poor girl! Poor girl!" exclaimed the father. "Four long years and no word from John! But if he's alive he's true; he's true, I swear he's true, if he's alive! Jarl, when you get your breakfast you must go over to Duvals and tell him I want to see him. I want to have a long chat with him on important business; mind, *on particular business.*"

Jarl met Duval and Charlotte en route to the mill, and turned back with them.

Jackman and his trusted friend were closeted a long time together that morning. The matter between them was the discussion of Jarl's declaration.

Duval listened attentively, and with few interruptions, until Nate had said all he could say on the subject. Jackman concluded his statement by bluntly asking, "Ought I to go, or stay?"

Duval was perplexed, and for a long time sat in

silent deliberation. When he began to talk he spoke very slowly, as if cautiously groping his way along an unknown path in the dark.

"You place a solemn responsibility on me, my friend. The future happiness of yourself and your, daughter, will largely depend on what my advice shall be, and will certainly depend on what course you pursue. We must make no mistake. Let us decide as wisely as we can, since the issue is to be so great. And before I give you my opinion, I must have time to think the subject all over. Let Jarl go home with me; I must have a free and full talk with him. On to-morrow I shall come to you with my answer."

On the following day, Duval, in pursuance of his appointment, returned to the mill.

"Well, Nate," said he, "I have been thinking the matter over and over again; I have talked with Jarl, and the more I study the case, the more I hesitate in shouldering the responsibility of advising you. However I said I would and I will. But, in order that I may be relieved somewhat of the weighty trust confided to me, you shall, with my help, reach the decision step by step."

Nate bowed assent.

"You are getting well on in years?"

"Yes."

"You have looked forward to the time when you could take life easy?"

"Yes."

"You have saved between seven and eight thousand dollars, and your mill and house will bring three thousand more?"

"Yes."

"Neither you nor Prudence can have much regard for your neighbors because of their bad treatment of Jarl?"

"That's a fact."

"You would prefer good neighbors?"

"Yes."

"Jarl can't get an education here?"

"It seems not."

"Nor learn a trade here; or do business, even if he had a trade?"

"No."

"Then it's a sure thing that he must go away, and stay away all his life?"

"I suppose so."

"Then he ought to go soon, the sooner the better."

"Why?"

"In order that he may get an education, and learn a trade. When he's a man it'll be too late."

"That's so! That's so!"

"And he ought to go away so far that the absurd prejudices of this neighborhood will not follow him?"

"That sounds right; I think it is right."

"Prudence wishes to leave?"

"Oh, yes; Prudy's as tired of this place as Jarl is."

"You love her and Jarl, and want to do all you can to make them happy?"

"Certainly! Certainly!"

"Jarl must go, and go he will; there's no help against that. Can you bear to see him go alone?"

"'Fore God, no, Duval!"

"Then in the name of God what do you want to stay here for?"

The old man sat with fingers locked around his knees, and twirling his thumbs over and over each other, as if unravelling a tangled skein.

Presently he looked up with a perplexed air, and said:

"Duval, you've got me so through each other that I don't know which from t'other!"

Nate was bewildered, but it was not the kind of bewilderment he said it was. It was true that Duval had put him "through other," and he was correct when he said so. The truth is, the subject was made as clear to him as the noon-day sun; too clear, for it dazed him with its sudden glare. It was clear to him that Jarl must go, and equally clear that it was his duty to go with Jarl; nay, it was clear to him that when Jarl went nothing could keep him and Prudence from going along. But still the unsophisticated old fellow was puzzled and undecided.

He had trusted that Duval would, somehow, find a way out of the difficulty without Jarl going away; but when the trusted arbitrator spoke so decidedly in favor of going, he was overwhelmed and bewildered.

Nate Jackman was perplexed, but it was that perplexity felt by those who, often toiling in one spot for three score years, are suddenly driven into exile; it was the amazement felt by the recluse when he is involuntarily thrust into the midst of the great world of which he knows little or nothing. Duval's decree was, to the hale old man, like a summons of death for a trifling indisposition.

"You will lose nothing, so far as money is concerned," continued Duval, noticing the painful indecision of his old friend. "You must gain in a social point of view, while Jarl gains everything. It is hard for him to stay here and submit to the abuse of the heartless people; and my word for it, he will not endure such treatment any longer. If you don't go away he will go without you, and he will be justified in such a course. The question is, ought you to let him go to the dogs, or help him begin life anew? I think you should stick to Jarl—he's a grand boy, and will make a grand man. And now you have my opinion—my advice."

"And that says go."

"Yes, go!"

"Well, go, it is," said Jackman, bravely, stepping to the door to summon the children that they might hear the ultimatum.

"That's settled," he continued, with the air of one who has got through with a hard task.

"I have another favor to ask of you, Duval."

"Name, it," said Duval.

"I want you to stand by me, and help me fix up my concerns. I want you to tell me where to go, for I suppose going away from here means going somewhere else. I've heerd of people going away bekase they wanted to go to some place, but I never before heerd of anybody going to a place they didn't know where it was."

The first step was to close with the thrifty German, Dickson, who had long coveted the mill property.

CHAPTER XI.

"What sorrows gloomed that parting day
That called them from their native walks away."

WHEN the transfer of the mill property was made, and after the household effects were disposed of, Nate Jackman began to take on a new character, and display a disposition foreign to his whole antecedent life.

He had been noted for his caution and tact. He knew well how to attend to his own business, which occupation allowed him no time to meddle with that of his neighbors. This trait of character existed, not so much from natural disposition as from commercial inclination and business necessity. It was not constitutional, but was acquired by long and profitable practice. It was a business principle with him to make no enemies, and to avoid even noticing an offence. His whole life had been bent on making the mill a success, while all other aims and objects were made subsidiary to this one central fixed object. This artful, studied, and stubborn line of conduct accounted for his patient, long-suffering demeanor toward those who persecuted Jarl.

But things were altered now. There was no longer the need of commercial stoicism, since patronage was no longer an object. His occupation was gone, and with it went his system of moral philosophy. The natural proclivities of the man now asserted themselves unrestrained by fear or favor.

He not only remembered the bitter tribulations of the past, but he felt that his neighbors were responsible for his banishment from the home of his childhood—the one spot most dear and sacred to him.

His neighbors dropped in to see him and talk over the subject of his going away, with their regrets, for Jackman was universally liked as a miller, and his acquaintances were sincere in regretting his loss to the neighborhood. But he now charged them, one and all, with hypocrisy and falsehood. Those who had been most aggressive in persecuting Jarl were peremtorily ordered away from the premises.

"I hate ye! Git out of my sight or ye'll get hurt!" he roared at them.

Of course the community was shocked. It always is shocked when it meets with merited indignation. The neighbors were astounded at the change in the miller's demeanor toward them, and it is to be hoped they were mortified also. It is certain they were not contrite, but took refuge in charging Jackman with being crazy.

He made a visit to the school-house, and paid his respects to the schoolmaster who had beaten Jarl so unmercifully. He gave that absolute tyrant such a drubbing with his hickory cane before the whole school as will live green in his memory to his dying day.

Nate was hauled up before a country justice of the peace to answer for assault and battery. It was the first and only time the old hero was "sued." He wanted to "fight the case," that is, make a legal fight, but Duval, knowing how plain the case was, and having a wholesome influence over him, persuaded him out of the notion, or, rather, manœuvred him out of it. Nate appeared on the day of the trial, or on the day the docket was to be cleared, and he thought then, and still believes, that he made a fight, and that the trial proceeded in the regular way.

His notion of a lawsuit, having never witnessed one, was that it must be a kind of pitched battle, and, accordingly, he went prepared to pitch in. Figuratively he had on his war paint. He wore no coat and had his shirt sleeves rolled up, although it was cold weather. His suspenders were tied around his waist like a belt, and he flourished his big hickory walking stick, the very one he had used in belaboring the schoolmaster. Thus panoplied he marched to the seat of war.

He took Jarl along with him. "I want to show 'em we ain't afeard. I want to see if the'll lay a finger on you when I'm around," he said, compressing his lips, and tightening his grasp on the hickory.

The entire male population of the neighborhood was assembled at the squire's office in expectancy of fun, for the mad ways of the miller had become notorious. When he saw the crowd, he felt that they were there to oppose him, but he defied them all. It was fortunate that Duval was also present to hold him in check, or his disposition to crack somebody's head might have been indulged in.

"Stick up to 'em, my boy," he said, slapping Jarl on the shoulder. "I'll back you—I'll stand by you. Dang 'em, don't take any of their sass. Dang 'em, its our turn now."

Thus went on the gray-headed hero, dancing about like a belligerent Irishman at Donnybrook fair, egging on some one to tread on his coat-tail.

"Who air you a gapin' at? What air you a lookin' at me for?" he asked, sidling up to Mr. Liftal, and shaking his fist in the man's face. Duval took hold of the rampager, and warned him to desist or the squire would send him to jail for contempt of court.

"I'll mind you, Duval, but I kin lick Contempt and Liftal both put together."

When he had paid his fine for the assault on the

teacher, he took Jarl by the hand, scowled on the court and spectators, and moved off toward home. When he got outside, some one sang out :

"Good-bye, Nate ; if you call that going."

"Yes ; I call that goin'," he said, turning on them. "And maybe it ain't good manners for me to go without sayin' good-bye. I'm goin'. Do you want to know why I'm a goin'? I'll tell you why ; it's bekase I never want to see the likes of you again. I call ye mean. D'ye know why I call ye mean ? It's bekase you *air* mean."

By this time the whole crowd was out of the squire's office to hear the only public speech of Nate's life.

"But d'ye know why I'm goin' away ? Bekase you abused and beat and worried the life out of my poor boy, Jarl. Do you see him ? This is Jarl.

"Mr. Liftel, you know him. You told your son Casper not to speak to Jarl because he was a beggar's brat.

"Bowler, you know Jarl. You wouldn't let your children go to Sunday-school bekase Jarl went.

"Mr. Tobby, let me introduce you to Jarl. You've met him before, do you say? Don't you mind, you blamed him for stealing your watermillions, when you knowed it was your own son, Bob.

"Well, if that ain't Bob, himself ! Why, Bobby,

you great big hulk of an overgrown calf—this is the little boy you blacked his eye. Maybe you'd like to try it on to-day? Eh!

"Mister Rellim, how do you do? You have met Jarl before. Do you think he's grown much since you druv him out your front gate? It was your gate then, it ain't now, is it? Too bad, ain't it? Jarl tried to save you from wrack and ruin, but you wouldn't let him, would you? How do you like to haul coal in a one-hoss cart for a livin'?

"Yes, men, this is my boy, Jarl," continued the red-faced miller, removing the boy's cap, telling him to look up and not be afeared.

"This is Jarl, the boy who is an orphan. He ain't got no father, but I'm his father; nor any mother but Prudy, nor any friend but Mr. Duval, he's his friend. God bless him!

"Ain't you proud of yourselves for abusin' and a beatin' this lone little child, as I took to raise decent, like one of my own?

"Look at him! Where'll you find a better look-ing or a braver boy? You can't, that's all.

"Liftal, how's his nose 'long side of Caspar's pug?

"Bobby Tobby, looke here; this hair ain't red and fuzzy like some folk's—now, is it?"

"Jarl!" exclaimed Bob, sneeringly, wincing under

the old man's coarse sarcasms, "Is that all the name he's got? What do you call him Jarl, for?"

"Bekase that's his name, young man; it ain't Jarl Tobby, nor Tobby Jarl."

"We're agoin' away to find Jarl's parents," continued the old man in a softer, kinder key. "They are great and rich people as wouldn't wipe their feet on the likes of you. The next time you see him he will be rich and great, and he won't know you any more. We don't know you from this time out forever and ever!"

Nate extended his arms and spread out his palms, as if throwing off his enemies for all time to come. He then turned on his heel, and, holding Jarl by the hand, walked rapidly home, where the fire blazed on the hearth for the last time. On the morrow the Jackmans were to depart for their new home.

The proceeds of the sales, together with a sum of ready money on deposit, amounted to over twelve thousand dollars. The major part was invested by Duval in a way that would insure a steady but small income, sufficient, with strict economy, to keep the miller's small and inexpensive family in comfort.

It has already been stated that William Duval had a sister. Her name was Amelia Heron, a childless widow, living in Philadelphia. She was her brother's senior. Her husband had been a produce merchant with a large and profitable trade, and since his death she carried on the business superintending it herself.

Duval wrote her a letter, giving a history of the Jackmans, and asking her to aid him in securing for them a home in Philadelphia. Of Jarl he wrote, "My interest in the lad is founded partly on pity, and partly on sentiment and his real worthiness. I ask you, my dear sister, on my account, to take some trouble to serve these deserving people, feeling confident that your kindness will he rewarded when you come to know them as I do."

The most hearty affection existed between the brother and sister, and she caught the sympathy manifested in her brother's letter. She wrote a reply filled with the most gracious expressions of zeal toward those whom she termed her brother's pilgrims.

"There is at this moment," she wrote, "a comfortable house on the next street, which I have already secured at a moderate rent."

"I have long been anxious to follow your example and retire from business, but the trouble has been to find one whom I can trust with the management of my affairs. I hope to find in your miller the man I want, for I take it he should be familiar with the grain and feed business. They may come on at once."

The Jackmans were ready to start.

The Duvals had driven over in their carriage, which was to carry the pilgrims to the railway station.

The time to leave is up.

Duval is very quiet.

His wife is fussy and noisy.

Charlotte is crying and listening to Jarl, who talks big and looks brave.

Prudence is busy with the luggage.

And Nate, what of him?

Oh, he is as gentle and disconsolate as a child taking its last look at its dead mother, before the coffin lid is closed down on her forever.

He has been going in and out of the old mill all the morning, like a lost dog in search of its master. He draws the flood gate, when the great wheel turns groaning on its ponderous iron gudgeons and sets the mill in motion. Then he smiles at the rattle and roar of the toiling giant. He shuts off the rushing waters, when the thunder of the machinery ceases, and the old miller stares at the dead Titan. He wanders among the bins like a ghost visiting the ancient castle of its forefathers. The pigeons flock about his familiar form, and the rats grow bolder as they keep him company in his melancholy tramp. Then he started like a frightened animal and fled to the cottage, where he sat gazing into the fire on the hearth. Uneasy there, he took down his cane and wandered out the front gate.

Prudence watched him till he sank down beside a grave away off on the distant hill-side. She followed after, and came back leading the disconsolate mortal.

Ah, Prudence! thoughtless maiden, what have you done? When you planned your scheme of migration little you dreamed of the heartache it would bring your father. Pulling up stakes was to you, as to all young people, an easy and exciting adventure; to him, and to all old people, it is pulling up long rooted ties; it is tearing out heart-strings that were fastened and strengthened by the slow and wholesome growth of sixty long years. Migration to Nate Jackman was banishment; dwelling among other scenes, be they never so lovely, was exile. Old trees do not bear transplanting; old people do not bear migration.

Farewell to the cottage where he was born, to where he brought his blushing bride, and where his child was born! Farewell to the Old Mill where for half a century he had ground the sweet golden grain! And farewell to the grave of his wife! *Home*, sanctified by toil, beautified by love, and hallowed by death, Farewell!

The time is up; let the birds of passage take their flight.

Prudence would have given the world to stay at the old mill. That awful look on her father's face weighed on her heart like lead; that solemn look was an accusation against her soul.

It was too late to drive it away; the mill and cottage belonged to strangers now.

Duval sighed as he felt more impressively than ever before, the solemn, almost awful responsibility he had assumed in advising the miller to move away. The generous Jarl would have borne with years of disquiet if he could have stayed with his foster-father at the old home.

Too late! Too late! Let the coach drive on. The ties are broken, the cords snapped asunder, the heartstrings drawn out by the roots, and the bewildered old man, bent and broken in an hour he never should have seen, is lifted into the carriage and driven away. His pale, mournful face was pressed against the coach window, from where he gazed with glassy eyes at the Old Mill, until the brown hill, covered with the leafless trees of winter, shut out the sight forever.

PART SECOND.

FIDES PUNICA.

CHAPTER XII.

"If knowing is but sorrow's spy,
'Twere better not to know."

If they but knew how weak she was—she the beautiful woman who sang with the eloquence of an angel! Alas that beauty and frailty should so often dwell together in unity!

The scene was one of splendor and gayety. It was the reception by the Italian embassador in Washington. The elegant parlors were thronged with the beauty and talent, local and transient, of the gay American capital.

Among the honored guests present was Theodore Bannemead, the well-known millionaire of Philadelphia, and his handsome daughter, Miss Alice. She was then at the acme of popularity as the reigning belle of the Quaker City. The heiress of her father's immense wealth, and endowed with beauty, grace and culture of a superior order of merit, she was held to be a most attractive ornament in the fashionable world in which she moved. No assemblage was considered quite *bon ton* without her patronage. Her dress and style were the envy and despair of the women, as they were the rage and rapture of the men. More than one rival beauty desecrated, and more than one Adonis worshiped this Venus of fashion. She disdained her rivals and graciously received the homage of her devotees. She was queen of the beauties, and smiled on the tailor moths that singed their wings from buzzing too near her altar. The bedazzled victims submitted gracefully to the scorching, holding it better to have loved, though singed, than not to have loved at all. Miss Bannemead was a coquette, heartless and heroic, and arrayed cap-a-pie with love's glittering armor, though her weapons beguiled with their polish, or were artfully concealed.

As with all coquettes she expected that the conquering hero would come her way sooner or later, and when he did come she was prepared to disarm and hail him lord and master. But in the meantime, while the bridegroom tarried, she kept her lamp trimmed and burning, to singe the butterflies of fashion.

5*

Alas, vain girl! the time came all too soon when the last victim lay scorched under thy blaze of glory. The right one had come.

On the night of the Ambassador's entertainment, Miss Bannemead was present and radiant in her majestic beauty.

" We are to be favored wiz a zong by zee Signorina Rosetta Godardo, zee famous Italian cantatrice," said the Vicomte Bertrand, a decorated attache of the French Legation at Washington. "Will you permit me zee great honaire, Miss Bannemead, to bring you where you zee music can more enjoy?"

She took his arm and was conducted into the adjoining room, where a celebrated maestro was seated at the piano, evidently ready to begin the prelude. Standing by him was the woman who was to sing.

"What black eyes!" exclaimed Miss Bannemead, as her own met for an instant those of the strange lady. "And how beautiful! And how startling her beauty! Don't you think her beauty peculiar?" she asked the count.

"Yes, Miss; dark skin, zee raven hair, eyes so black! That the Italian for beauty, and zee picturesque."

"Decidedly. Does she remind you of any one you have met?" she asked, looking into the count's face to watch as well as hear his reply.

"Pardon me, Miss Bannemead if I offend, but in her I behold a strong resemblance to your ladyship."

"Do you think that quite a compliment?" she asked, with an affected feint at pouting.

"You zall pardon me; zee compliment is not in zee dark skin, but in zee eyes, zee hair, zee grand contour," replied the Frenchman, with a courtierly shrug of his shoulders.

The viscount was right; there were points of strong resemblance between Alice Bannemead and Rosetta Godardo. The difference was in size and complexion. Miss Bannemead was fair as white alabaster, her figure tall and queenlike; the Godardo was a dark brunette, and petit in form.

"Who is she?" asked Miss Bannemead.

The maestro interrupted with the prelude.

The song was the Aria from Rigoletto, "*Caro nome che il mio cor.*" She rendered it with a grace and spirit that evinced the finished artist, while her rich and mellow notes charmed the listeners, who manifested their approval by applause, perhaps too noisy and long continued. She declined to sing more, although the demand for encore was hearty and loud. The Italian minister introduced her to the guests.

When Miss Bannemead and the Italian woman met they grasped hands, and stood looking into each other's face as if fascinated.

Was it fascination, or was it distrust?

Is it possible that even then Fate was casting its shadows over the two women?—the impress of that occult and mysterious fiat which binds two beings in the thrall of one common involuntary destiny?

Madam, have you never felt an unaccountable fascination for a person whom you have met for the first time? You may not like, nay, you may even dislike, but some occult force allures you toward that person in spite of your judgment or your will. One void of emotion will scout the idea, but the impression with some is strong, scout who may. Like love for an unworthy person, it is unaccountable.

Or, if you disdain the obscure in metaphysics, you may believe that the two women shared a mutual interest because of their mutual resemblance.

" Perdono me, Miss Bannemead, but in thy eyes I behold mine," said the Italian woman, in a friendly voice.

" And I am struck with your resemblance to me, Signorina," replied the American.

" So tells me my—my—spechio; I the name forgot," said the cantatrice, holding her fan before her face to indicate her meaning.

" Your mirror," familiarly suggested a gentleman who stood near her.

" Ah! My mirrora; it is that. This my friend;

with me across the sea he came. Signor Michele Tancredi," said Rosetta Godardo, introducing that gentleman to Miss Bannemead.

A beautiful man, is a phrase neither required nor warranted by usage or good taste, and yet to say that Michele Tancredi was a handsome man, falls short of conveying a full appreciation of his elegant and noble appearance. Perfect in form and feature, complete in embellishments, and polished in manners, he was calculated to create a sensation wherever he went. Rich, young and noble, his pathway was already strewn with hearts and sighs, and other ponderable and imponderable trophies of female disaster. Many a dusky beauty in the land of olives had been led a willing captive by his charms; hence it was no discredit to Miss Bannemead's discernment when she too paid tribute to the brilliant Signor.

The admiration seemed mutual, judging from the marked politeness shown her by the Signor; the two devoted themselves to each other almost exclusively during the remaining part of the evening.

To Miss Alice the hours flew away with the soft speed of soaring doves, and to the enraptured Italian each melting moment precipitated golden opinions of the winsome American beauty.

"I begin to feel myself native and to the mansion born," exclaimed the literary bungler and love's exquisite, in a tone of ecstacy. "I shall be no more the Italian; the American to be I am resolved."

"Pray, Signor, when did you arrive at this sudden resolve?" asked Miss Bannemead, encouragingly.

"Since when here I came, and met with you," he answered, in a soft musical voice.

"Ah, indeed. You flatter me; but I shall not credit your declaration until I hear of your naturalization, and that takes five long years."

"The citizen to be—you shall see! I am delighted with this countree, and with you."

"And what of the Signorina? Will she, too, become an American?"

"Oh, the Godardo? I not can tell. That is not for me to tell, for I know not. What to do she, is nought to me; what to do I, is nought to her."

"Why, you brought her here, so she told me; and surely you must have some concern for each other's actions."

"Not; Signorina Godardo is the cantatrice, the artista, and to her art belongs. She came here to engage in her profession for livelihood, but I have no control over her actions."

"Did you not bring her over the sea?"

"No; she came to fulfill her engagement, and belongs to the maestro—the management. In the same ship sailed I; that is all."

"But you accompanied her to this city."

"The minister is my friend, and he honor me with politeness to attend the reception of the cantatrice, his illustrious country woman—her introduction to the American public."

The Bannemead carriage was announced, when the father and daughter were driven away. Tancredi politely saw them off, and he stood gazing after them until the coach was lost in the gloom of the distant street.

"Michele," said some one in a low voice near him.

He turned and saw the Godardo watching him.

"Order our carriage," said the woman.

They were driven to their hotel, where they retired to their rooms. The woman was sulky, and the man sullen. A storm in Italian was brewing between the two companions. Let us contemplate the sighs and tears as they might appear to Italian eyes and ears.

"Thy devotion is not so constant on this side the ocean, Signor," said the woman, as she fretfully pulled at her gloves in removal.

"Devotion! My presence in this strange country, where I have neither business nor pleasure except to be with and serve you, attests my devotion," replied the man, in a wounded tone, as he quietly removed hat and cloak.

"Was it serving me to neglect me all through the

tedious evening, and bestow your gallantries on Miss Bannemead?"

"I was considerate of your interests. It would have been in bad taste for me to monopolize you, when I saw you in demand. You were brought here, not to meet me, but the American public. Surely you will not complain of any lack of attention shown you!"

"It is not long since you were furious if you did not have me all to yourself; but now—"

"But now! How it would read in the papers, the cantatrice was monopolized all evening by an Italian nobleman! These Americans are so different from Europeans; they are so prudent, so hospitable, so circumspect, that I believed I was showing you a kindness by leaving you free in their society."

"Yes; you left me to their grating *ings* and *ouses* all evening."

"You must learn their language."

"But not their manners. Do you think Miss Bannemead beautiful?"

"She looks like you."

"Only she is larger, you would say. You have often piqued me on my littleness; does her size please you better?"

"Miss Bannemead is a queen; you are a fairy— my own fairy."

"Men admire fairies, but they never love them.

They laugh at fairies, but pay their homage to queens."

" Yes, to fairy queens. You are my fairy and my queen, and to you I pay my homage."

The little lady, evidently well pleased at the flattery—the flattery spoken so low and soft and musical, came and stood beside him and peered into his attractive face.

"We start for New York to-morrow," she said, satisfied to change the subject. " On Monday evening comes my debut, and on the following Saturday you sail for home. I want to have you with me all the time till you go away."

She sat on a low stool at his feet, and leaned caressingly on his knees, as a tired child clings to its friend.

" Rosetta, I shall not return with you to New York. I will meet you there on Monday and be present at your debut."

The child unclasped its hands from the support, and sprang to its feet enraged.

" Not going back with me to New York! May I ask why ?"

" You may ask."

" Nay, I know why; you remain to visit the Bannemead."

"Wrong; she returned to Philadelphia on the night express."

"Tell me, then, why you wish to remain?"

"You have heard me speak of a friend who resides in Philadelphia. I remain over to visit him, and shall visit him to-morrow."

"And me—why may I not accompany you?"

"It is not necessary. I would be absent from you all the time while there, leaving you to mope at a strange hotel. You must return to New York to attend your rehearsals; for you know the maestro only brought you here to advertise you, and you must return with him in the morning."

"I know! I know!" exclaimed the woman, walking to the mirror and viewing herself therein. "Miss Bannemead lives in Philadelphia."

"She does; what of that?"

"You go there to visit her," she exclaimed, turning fiercely upon him her marvelous black eyes gleaming with jealousy. She went to the window and stood looking out at the ragged clouds wind-tossed in the cold moonlight. How different from the warm fleecy clouds floating in the soft skies of Italy!

"Michele," she said, after a long silence. "You wished to return home by this week's steamer; I persuaded you to stay for my debut."

"Yes; well, why do you speak of it now?"

"You may start home this week, and I'll return with you."

"I shall not leave America for some time; I am thinking of remaining here permanently."

"That is sudden!" she exclaimed, in a low voice, but with suppressed astonishment. She came again and stood before him.

"Did the Bannemead so soon induce you to renounce your country for hers? And is it for that siren you so readily fall in love with this barbarous people! Oh, for shame!"

"How absurd! What puts such wild fancies in your head?"

"Come here!" she said, taking him by the hand, and half-leading, half-dragging him to the window. "Michele, look out at that sky. See the clouds torn and drifting before the cruel winds! How cold and black and broken they look as they sweep in anger out on the desolate sea! They are flying away from these cold shores to our own sunny clime, where they will melt into fleeces as soft and warm as my love for thee. Let us leave with the clouds these cold skies, and follow them to our own glad, bright Italia!"

"Rosetta, what is the matter with thee to-night?"

"Oh, I cannot tell! I wish I never had come to America. I wish I was back in dear Italy. I feel so lonely here. Everything and everybody is so cold

and strange.   Thou art not so tender ; everybody
seems to draw thee away from me.   If I thought
thou art to be won by that Bannemead I would kill
her !"

The disconsolate woman threw herself on the
floor, where her sobs told how violent and dangerous
she might become, if driven hard.   Tancredi saw the
menacing danger, and assuaged the stricken woman.

CHAPTER XIII.

"Heaven has no rage like love to hatred turned,
Nor hell a fury like a woman scorned."

ROSETTA GODARDO was, as has already been indicated, a professional soprana singer in Italian opera. Though quite young she was already famous in the capitals of Europe. A celebrated maestro had engaged her to appear before the American public, which she was expected to take by storm. The time was fixed for her debut in New York.

Michele Tancredi and Rosetta Godardo were natives of Naples, Italy. His infatuation for the fair songstress had induced him to come to America. Indeed, she would not come without him. He was himself a most accomplished amateur musician, and he possessed a voice of rare richness and power. Among musicians he was reckoned a genius, and was held to be an authority in matters relating to music and the lyric stage. He was intensely Italian in taste and style, doubtless because he was an Italian and descended from ancestors noted for their musical talent and their partialty to the Italian school. As he had neither the inclination nor the necessity to go on the stage, he contented himself with employing his musical culture in swelling his already formidable array of embellishments.

It was through his fondness of music, and his familiarity with musicians, that he first became acquainted with and then enamored of Rosetta. At a charity concert given in his native city he sang with her a duet, which created a sensation even in that land of song. It was said by those who heard them that their blended voices was as the singing of angels. Fabulous was the sum offered him to appear with her in opera, an offer which he declined. He secured for Rosetta a no less flattering offer, which she accepted. From that time on he was her teacher, patron, lover and companion.

The passion for each other was mutual. Her love for him was of that intense, fiery character, peculiar to southern blood. She would sit entranced under the sound of his magnificent voice, and was never so happy as when singing with him. Great and glorious might have been their career had he been poor, obscure, or even ambitious. But alas for art, alas for morals, and alas for the woman, he was rich, noble, and void of ambition.

As with impulsive and emotional women, love to Rosetta was more than the mating instinct, more than ambition; it was a grand, absorbing passion, which led reason captive, and thrust aside prudence and all thought of the future. She was not exacting, but she was jealous; she was not imprudent, but she braved all for him, and exclusively surrendered herself to the luxury of lingering in the smiles of the man she adored.

Never a woman loved man more madly than Rosetta Godardo loved Michele Tancredi. It was not the cantious, secret love of intrigue, but open, transparent and defiant. So well was her passion known that he was constantly consulted concerning her professional engagements, and as much anxiety was felt for his condition and whereabouts as for hers. More than once she had disappointed the public because Tancredi had disappointed her. If he was with her she sang, if he was absent he was hurried on, and if his arrival was not timely, there was no singing by her. The public held her to be erratic and unreliable, it was because she was true and steadfast to one individual, and only one in all the world.

The knowledge of all this made him hesitate before sending her back to New York without him, and against her will. He therefore yielded, and consented that she might stop over with him in Philadelphia, while he made his proposed visit to his friend.

The truth is he was invited and had promised to

pay a visit to the Bannemeads. He was sorely annoyed to find that he could not call on his new acquaintance without a jealous mistress at his heels. For the first time he began to chafe at her importunate surveillance, and to sigh for that freedom so often vainly coveted by the *roue* tangled in the toils of his own indiscretions. From that time on his longing and study was to shake off the thralldom, which, at first so delightful, was now become so galling and embarrassing.

The two companions went to Philadelphia. By strategy, he succeeded in escaping from the clutches of the Signorina, and in making his call on Miss Bannemead.

That lady was at home, but if she expected him, she was artful enough to effectually conceal it. The tact and coolness which had made her so successful as the coquette, placed her at once at a familiar ease in the presence of the Signor. She received him as she might an old acquaintance. The inward truth, which she so well concealed, was that she felt highly gratified at the distinguished acquaintance and his promptness in paying court to her.

In the dreamy atmosphere of the new charmer the glad hours flew by unheeded by the Italian. His attention was profound, his deference broad, and his devotion sublime; his behaviour filled space in all directions. He would have wooed, but the lady, true to her ruling passion, was not ready to be won. It was present joy enough to feel sure of conquest, for ambition had made the calculation and settled that it should be a conquest.

A servant hastily entered the room, but before he could speak, a woman glided past him and stood glaring at them in imminent wrath. It was the Godardo.

A wordy encounter took place between her and her renegade lover. As it was carried on in the Italian tongue, Miss Bannemead was spared the patent mortification of knowing that she was the provoking cause of the quarrel. But she knew it all the same.

The cantatrice marched away with her recalcitrant lover to the hotel, where the conflict must have continued, for the result was her throwing up the engagement with the opera agent. She refused to even talk of going on the stage.

Tancredi, driven to the wall, now blazed forth and demanded immediate and unconditional separation. His tenderness for her was turned to fear and hate. But it was all the same to the maddened woman. The more he repelled, the closer she clung, until, worn out with entreaty and threatening, he took her with him to New York, where they settled down like two hostile armies after a drawn battle.

So far the woman had the better of it, for, while

he refused to return with her to Italy, she as persistently refused to be separated from him.

At the end of a week's seige, this was the position in which Trancredi found himself.

He was in a new country and in love with a new woman. But the woman of his old love was not shaken off, nor was the prospect for getting rid of her flattering.   Rosetta persisted in refusing to fulfill her operatic engagement, and it was cancelled, leaving her entirely on his hands. She would not return home without him, she would not stay if he went, she would not be separated from him. Concerning this point she swore in her fierce way that she might die, but compromise, never.

What was he to do?   He had tried entreaty, exhausted strategy, bankrupted threats; she outwitted and outbraved them all.

Should he fly from her?   This was practicable, but there were many reasons why he should not. She was a woman, a stranger in the land, and well nigh penniless. She had ventured abroad on his promise of protection.   *Roue* though he was, he still retained a business sense of honor, and felt the binding force of his commercial obligations to her.

She was a woman, violent and perverse it was true, but she loved him—how much none knew better than he. Intriguer though he was, his heart retained the memory of its bygone tenderness when she alone filled its chorded chambers.

She was a woman, scorned and at bay, and the observant voluptuary knew well what was in her heart;—she had murder there for him, mischief for herself. She was a blind Samson who could, and, if driven to despair, would, pull love's temple down in one promiscuous ruin about his head.

At the then present time Tancredi dreaded scandal, and leaving Rosetta Godardo by flight meant scandal. He had transferred his affection to the charming Bannemead, and scandal would utterly destroy his aspirations in that quarter. His love for her, or his manifestation of the same, was the cause of his present dilemma, and whatever he might suffer, or what other risks he might run, were as nothing compared to the importance of keeping his intrigue with the cantatrice from the public. Miss Bannemead must not know of the liaison, come what might. If he harshly dissolved his relations with the Godardo, the public, and through it the Philadelphia belle, would discover the whole story. If he sought refuge in flight it would cost him his new love adventure. He was too deeply infatuated with Alice Bannemead to turn away from her forever. He would stay and conquer destiny. He would conciliate Rosetta, and trust to time and chance to favor his ambition.

Accordingly he seemingly succumbed to the entreaties of the earnest woman, and began treating her with his wonted consideration. He established her in a cottage in a suburb of New York, and himself lodged at a hotel.

CHAPTER XIV.

"Thy love is lust, thy friendship all a cheat,
Thy smiles hypocrisy and thy words deceit."

Was Rosetta Godardo insane?

Emotionally her mind was jangling and out of tune, because of jealousy. Is a mind in such a state sane?

She had never held a check on her passions, she never tried to control her emotions. She allowed her fancy and feelings to run away with reason, and she knew of nothing, had nothing, to curb them into restraint. Jealousy absorbed her being when love was driven out. Is jealousy a form of insanity?

In a degree it is, for jealousy is unreason, unreasoning, and unreasonable. It is ever attempting to coerce unwilling love—love that will not be coerced; and jealousy never acts from a rational motive. These are traits of insanity.

Hatred or love, scorn or respect, contempt or esteem, may be felt, one or the other, and one at a time, and by one sane person for another person ; but it is only the jealous or insane who can feel all and practice all at the same time toward one and the same individual.

A jealous woman should not be despised, but pitied; not abused, but petted. She is a woman emotionally insane. Her disease demands treatment. If she is neglected, worse may follow—she may become mentally deranged.

The Italian prima donna was a monomaniac, but her paramour guessed it not. To him she was a perverse and ungrateful woman. His mistake was worse than insanity—it was criminal.

He detailed two of his servants to wait on her, and spared no expense to make her abode comfortable. One day, a servant brought word that she was acting strangely, and begged him to visit her. He went.

She welcomed him with all her old tenderness, and began at once to talk of Italian scenes, of orange groves and sunny skies, and song, and home life, as though they were back in their old land she loved so well. It was evident that she was delirious. She was dressed out in one of her stage costumes and talked of the opera in which she believed she was to appear. Her eyes had in them a strange glitter, and her cheeks were dusky with the fires of fever.

"I want you to hear me sing," she said to him in her native tongue. "Oh, I'll surprise you! I'm sure you'll be proud of me to-night! And don't forget the

flowers; mine must be the prettiest and the sweetest.
But I must sing for you.   No, they call me; that is
my cue!   Stand there!"

"You'll hear it at night,
When the moon shineth bright,
You'll hear it at dawn,
In the gray twilight;
Though none knew its minstrel,
Or how it came there.
Listen! Listen!
'Tis the harp in the air!

"It telleth of joys that are faded and gone,
It tells of a knight,
Of a Moorish maid,
Of a broken plight
And a heart betrayed.
There! There!
List, pilgrim, list!   'Tis the harp in the air!"

No words can fittingly describe the wild pathos,
the air of tender desolateness, the wailing despair of
the poor creature as she poured forth the song to her
false lover.   It was the fitting requiem of a broken
heart.   The proud man bowed his head and wept like
a child at the contemplation of the fair ruins—the
damnable work of his treachery.

The sight of the stricken woman wrung his heart
with remorse, and he resolved then and there to make
every reparation within his power.   He dispatched
for medical aid, and resorted to every approved means

to serve her and restore her to health and reason. He
visited her daily, and was in every way concerned for
her welfare. After many anxious days, the fever
abated, and the weighted brain once again lighted up
with intelligence. He rejoiced at her hopeful
improvement, and at that critical time would gladly
have quitted with her the New World forever.

But as the patient slowly progressed toward convalescence his remorse began to wane, until at length
it was felt only as a hateful dream. By the time convalescence was fully established his inclination to
repair the wrong done her was gone, and he began to
sigh for that gay world wherein he had been so brilliant a reveller. When remorse was dead truant
ambition arose from its grave, and visions of the bewitching Bannemead floated before his imagination.

Soon after the physician had pronounced Rosetta
out of danger, he found himself in Philadelphia. Of
course his visit there was on account of his friend and
fellow countryman who lived in that city; but how
natural it was to think of Miss Bannemead while in
such mesmeric proximity to her dwelling, and how
excusable for him to reason out his duty to call upon
her. Common etiquette required no less, he thought;
indeed his abrupt and unceremonious departure from
beneath her roof made it in a sense obligatory on him

to visit her and make honorable amends for his discourteous conduct.

He was admitted to the lady's presence.

A less assured or less experienced inamorata would have felt and probably shown embarrassment on entering the presence of his lady love under such unpleasant circumstances. Even this veteran, who had managed many affairs of the heart victoriously, was distrustful of his courage, and inwardly trembled with anxiety at his possible reception. He never met with so decided a rebuff as at the hands of the spirited American lady. While it is true her scorn and haughtiness did not ruffle a single feather of the chevalier, yet he was annoyed and chagrined. And yet he rather enjoyed the exhibition of American pluck; it was a new sensation to him. Seldom was opposition shown him, for he ever swam the tide of smooth, easy conquest. Here was a beauty who disputed his supremacy, but her hauteur only irritated his vanity, and aroused his determination to conquer the arrogant woman.

"I am surprised, Signor," she said with disdainful voice and flushed cheeks, "painfully surprised that you should attempt to renew an acquaintance so scandalously interrupted when last you honored me with a visit. I flattered myself with the belief that you would spare me the mortification of recalling that dis-

6*

graceful scene.　Your presence is exceedingly unpleasant to me."

" Perdono mea, Miss Bannemead ; but your servant tell me you are at home.　Did he mistake, or did you ? The mistake is not by me.　He tell me you are at home and bring me here."

The lady blushed at being reminded of her awkward, if not inconsisted behavior, for being at home meant tacit and voluntary permission given the Signor to visit her.　She had given him audience at her own option, she could not dispute that fact, and could only bite her lips at being detected in so palpable a blunder. She was compelled to blame herself, even if she could not pardon him.

" Since you are here, Signor, I shall indulge you so far as to hear your explanation of the extraordinary scene which took place in this room at your late visit," she embarrassingly replied.

" What shall I explain ?"

" Explain away the wrong you did me, if you can."

" Good heavens ? Miss Bannemead ; hear I what ! Wronged you !　How?　Speak !　See the apology at thy feet !" exclaimed the Italian, kneeling before her, with his hand over his heart, and contrition limned over his handsome features.

" Do you pretend ignorance of the offense to

which I refer?" she asked, unmoved by his tragic repentance.

"Ignorant! Yes, Madame, ignorant! How could I knowingly offend where I worship?"

"Then, Sir, make no attempt to explain, since you are unconscious of having committed an offense. Rise, Sir; you mock me!"

She was now thoroughly angry. She turned from him in disdain, and stood by the window gazing abstractedly out on the street.

"Oh, now to see, I begin! You speak of the intrusion—the child—the Godardo—into this house, when last I had the honor of calling on you? Is it that?"

"Your memory begins to serve you," she replied, contemptuously, without turning from the window.

"And that the offense is?"

"Is not that sufficient cause for offense?"

"Perdono mea, no. It misunderstood by you, and your resentment comes by that. It makes me much satisfaction when you permit me explain the mistake; which I can do—which I will do; for am I not right to make myself heard where so evil I am judged?"

"I shall not prevent you from explaining," she coldly answered, still looking out the window.

"Signorina came here to make complaint of the

command,—*of the insult*, which she receive from the manager ordering her to go instantly to New York. She not like that. She not used to be ordered about like the slave. She very angree; and she come to me. She know where I was—I tell her that. What she tell me make me very angree, too, for the poor girl. We both furious, and we abuse the tyrant, the maestro, in your presence. That why she came so sudden; that why we depart so unceremonious."

She had turned away from the window while he was delivering his explanation, and looked at him with a quizzical expression made up of scorn and admiration—scorn at his falsity, admiration at his ingenuity and audacity. Mephistopheles was no longer a myth.

Did she believe him? And did she accept his statement as true? To the credit of her head she believed not a word; to the discredit of her moral sense she accepted his statement as the true and satisfactory explanation.

And, after all, what was he or his quarrels to her?

His baseness and brazenness deserved punishment, and the punishment that would mortify him most, would be to encourage him — raise his hopes to the clouds and then dash them on the rocks. This proud, presuming man must have a fall, and such a fall as would knock all egotism out of him.

On her velvet specimen tablet was just room

enough for one more moth, and this gilded butterfly must be pinioned there.

"Your explanation is entirely satisfactory, and I absolve you from all blame," she said, extending her hand and smiling forgiveness on the enraptured nobleman.

He gracefully kissed the hand and received his absolution with joy.

"And the Signorina, she did not appear in opera, as announced ; may I ask why?"

"She not used to the tyrant, the maestro. His treatment she not can stand. She go cancel the engagement."

"I hear she is ill ; is it true?"

"I know not. She back to Italy gone. She sing never in this countree."

"And you? You did not return with her to Italy?"

"Why should I? This is my countree. Here I stay, for here my queen I find."

The *tête-à-tête* on this occasion was not interrupted. Their talk was common-place, on safe subjects — the weather, the crops, kindred topics, and therefore harmless. The Signor was inclined to be amorously demonstrative, but the lady suppressed his ardor, and led him gently back to and along the more prosy path so well beaten by people of small talk. Their maudlin vocal essences are not attempted here ; such colloquies

are more difficult to reproduce than Newton's calculus,
or Keplar's Laws; besides their narration would destroy
the harmony of this book, which is Love without
Labor.

The long tedious convalescence of Rosetta was to
Tancredi the golden opportunity, which he cultivated
industriously and successfully. One day found him
in the sick chamber of his mistress, the next at the
feet of the Bannemead.

His passion for the latter increased on acquaintance, and presently became so all absorbing that he
made a formal declaration of his love, and begged her
hand in marriage. This prayer remained unanswered
for some time.

Theodore Bannemead had made the necessary inquiries into Tancredi's antecedents and had found
them highly satisfactory. But still the daughter pro-
crastinated the answer from day to day. One day she
would be cold or exacting, sullen or stormy, the next
she would be affable, even tender, and drive her lover
mad with her smiles. She was an enigma to him, but
none the less adorable. Her very whims and moods
were charming, and even her imperious tyrannies
tightened and strengthened the chain that enslaved him.

Her initial plan contemplated the elation of his
hopes heavenward, followed by the sudden dash
toward the other extreme; but she hesitated to

carry out that plan, now that the crisis had come. Jilting lovers, after luring them on to a proposal, had become such a habit with her, that she almost ached to see how wretched and crestfallen this noble lover would be by the declination of his proposal.

The time was ripe for springing the trap ; the Italian's downfall must be immediate or never. But she hesitated, and the woman who hesitates is in love.

Her feelings and designs in relation to Tancredi were modified since the day she resolved to entice him, none knew how better than she, but she was not clear about the part where the ruin came in. His distinguished appearance, seductive manners, noble birth, exalted station, and, last and greatest of all, his devotion to her, had jointly combined to weave about her a web, which for strength would have astonished her had she attempted to hurl him on the metaphorical rocks suggested by her vengeance.

He had danced attendance at her court, had been her gallant at fashionable assemblages, had been patient, delicate, zealous, and in every way exemplary. She could not help admiring him. Her father was pronounced in his liking for the man, the fashionable world held them betrothed lovers, other moths had forsaken her shrine and blazed at other altars, her friends held it a splendid match. In brief, pride, convenience, and ambition sanctioned the union of her destiny with that of the Italian. She concluded to procrastinate no longer; she made up her mind to accept the hand of Michele Tancredi.

Arrived at this conclusion, she discovered that she liked him better than she did any one else; as much as a woman ought to like any man.

It was an afternoon in the middle of March. The Signor was seated in the company of Miss Bannemead at her home on Walnut Street.

"This horrid weather!" exclaimed Tancredi, eyeing with dismay the single speck of mud on his immaculate boots. "At Naples, there is no frost, no mud. There the trees are in bloom, and the people are resting in the shade of the olives."

"Don't you wish you were in Naples at this moment?" asked Miss Bannemead, laughing at his annoyance.

"Shall I say it? Yes, with you."

He took her hand and pressed it to his lips

"Oh, I would prefer Venice to Naples. I have heard so much of the gondoliers and their romantic songs I could float all day in the bright sunlight, or under the cool shadows of the marble palaces, and drink in the songs of the boatmen. And O! what moonlight must be in the City of the Sea!"

"But Naples! You should see my Naples! Ah,

my darling, the sun shines brighter there, the moonlight falls softer there! And the boatmen's songs on the bay! How shall I make you hear their music? But one way there is—to take you there. O, give me my bright, glorious Naples—and you! It shall be—when? Don't make me longer the miserable! Name the happy day."

"For your departure to Naples?"

"Yes; accompanied by my queen, my wife."

"What! To remain there always!"

"To remain where you will, so I am with you. Wherever you are most happy, there also shall be my happiness."

"And you won't insist on keeping me in Italy one day longer than is agreeable to me?"

"Certainly not, my darling."

"That is kind of you, for I love my own dear Philadelphia as fondly as you love your Naples. My home must ever be here."

"And here shall be my home, if it best pleases you."

"You agree then that I shall be allowed to dwell in this city as long as I wish."

"To that I agree."

"Then, there's my hand. It is yours—in Philadelphia."

"It is mine all over the world! By it I lead you

to visit my Italy, my Naples, and, if it pleases you. Venice too."

"O yes, I shall be delighted.　We'll make the grand tour, of course."

"Shall it be—when?　The April that is to come?"

"That is too soon.　April is a tearful month."

"April .too sudden and too sad?　Then May? Sure that a sweet month."

"I like June better."

"Oh!　You like June better?　So do I.　Shall it be June?　Shall we be married in June?"

"Yes; there, I have said it; does it suit you?"

"Does heaven suit me?　Does it suit me—the angel, the best angel there?"

The lovers joined hands and put their heads together to perfect the details of the grand event.

The next day found him in the presence of Rosetta Godardo.

"How well the roses are coming back to thy cheeks, pretty one!" he said in Italian.

"I rejoice to hear thee say so.　But art thou in right earnest, and look I so well?　Berta, bring me my mirror; I must see if thou mocks't me," replied Rosetta, pleased at his notice and encouragement.

She turned the small glass about, viewing herself

therein with such a woe-begone expression that the maid out of pity took the mirror from her hand.

"My prettiness is coming back slowly, very slowly, and I fear me some of it will tarry on the way."

"Foolish Rosetta? It will return with more bloom than ever."

"Believest thou so? I wish it for thy sake. Michele, dos't ever hear of the Bannemead?"

"No, my little one; she is in thy thoughts; why is she there?"

"I feel that she must be handsomer than ever, since it was she who stole my beauty."

"What a superstitious child it is! What put such absurd fancies into thy head?"

"Dos't think I grow stronger every day?"

"Nay, I am sure. Thou wilt soon be strong enough to ride out with me."

"O, what joy! Strong enough to ride out, and with thee! What joy."

"Yes, my little beauty, with me."

"Then it will not be long until we shall sail for our own dear, warm, bright Italia. Oh, what joy!"

CHAPTER XV.

"For never, I swear by my mistress whom I revere most of all, and have chosen for my assistant, Hecate, who dwells in the inmost recesses of my house, shall any one of them wring my heart with grief with impunity."—EURIPIDES.

TANCREDI led two lives; one for the Godardo, the other for Bannemead. Both lives were successful, reckoned from the standpoint of his motive. His motive was Satanic. His object was to deceive both women, and he succeeded.

He was more completely successful in deluding the Godardo, at least his treachery wounded her deepest. His double dealing with her was the more flagrant and heinous, because she was more entitled to good treatment. His treatment of her should have been the best; he gave her the worst. He should have been true to her, although he was false to all the world besides. She lived in and on his faith—it was Punic Faith.

Godardo's love for him was superlative, yet he elected her to be cheated, and robbed and broken. The love the other woman bore him scarcely deserved the name; her attachment was recent, and the result of pride and ambition, yet he laid at her feet the offering of a noble name, he surrendered to her his heart and hand.

Godardo continued to languish for months, and it was the glad summer time before she was strong enough to ride out in the open air. As convalescence became more fully established she took deeper interest in her lover's behavior, and grew more exacting of his time and attention. His more and more infrequent and hurried visits were noticed and commented on by her, but the wrecked woman was powerless to actively molest him.

He trembled as he watched her grow strong, and as the flush of returning health crept over her cheeks, the ashen hue of dread grew on his brown face. He realized fully what would be the reckoning should his perfidy become known to her. His hope had been, as were his efforts, to prevent her from learning of his visits to his affianced. So far he had been successful. If he could only keep her ignorant for a brief time he would be married, with the sea between him and her wrath. Even in this he almost succeeded.

He had now been married a week, and yet was no further on his voyage than New York. The sudden and unexpected death of his wife's aunt on the day after the wedding, had delayed the trip abroad, and the time for departure was postponed two weeks.

One more week of suspense and dread, at the end of which, if Rosetta could be kept at home, he would be on shipboard moving away from her anger. The ashy hue of dread deepened on his dusky face.

His trusty servant, Berta, Rosetta's maid, had been instructed to keep a close surveillance over the sick woman, and prevent her from seeing the newspapers, which were filled with accounts of the marriage in high life.

How she evaded them none knew, but she did discover that the marriage had been consummated, and then, oh, then!

Ocean storms and desert simoons have been so graphically delineated with pen and pencil that one almost feels the earth tremble under the fury of the maddened elements. What pen can describe the storm that swept over this forsaken woman, what pencil portray the simoon that plowed across the desert of her life? As she loved, blindly, furiously, so did she rage, now that love was dead. The poet who wrote

> "Heaven has no rage like love to hatred turned,
> Nor hell a fury like a woman scorned,"

must have felt the wrath of a jilted woman.

The well-disciplined Berta gave Tancredi timely warning of the raging storm, and he kept under shelter. Rosetta sent for him, but he came not; when she started out to hunt him down, wearing a stage dagger, his gift, in her emaciated bosom.

Failing to find him in New York she visited Philadelphia. Gone to New York, the domestics told her, and back to that city hied the human sleuthhound. She visited the hotels during the day, and wandered among the theatres at night, seeking her prey. The pretty woman with eyes like a wild beast's attracted notice wherever she went, but none learned her name or her errand. One evening a woman fainted in Niblo's Garden Theatre, and she was carried into the adjoining hotel. It was the Godardo.

On the next day a party of ladies and gentlemen were assembled in the same hotel to say *bon voyage* to Signor Tancredi and his wife, who were to sail for Europe that day. In the midst of the salutations and farewells a veiled woman entered the room and stood unnoticed among the guests, until she raised a glittering dagger and struck the bridegroom a vicious blow. The ladies screamed, the gentlemen caught the assassin's arm and tore away her veil, revealing to the astonished group the haggard face of the Italian cantatrice.

Madame Tancredi saw and recognized that terrible face, and fainted away. The Godardo was thrust from the room. The Signor would not wait to have his arm dressed, but ordered his servants to bear his unconscious wife to the carriage in waiting; when they were rapidly driven to the pier, where they embarked on the steamer.

He instructed the officers of the ship to prevent the ingress of a women whose personal appearance he described. A lookout was kept for her, but she came not.

As the falling darkness gathered over the American hills the good ship turned her prow toward the open sea, and the Italian breathed free once more.

But the trouble with the other woman, who was now his wife began, and it lasted for some time. The Tancredi had a rough voyage; it stormed without and stormed within. The fainting fit of Madam went off in hysterical sobs and tears. The guilt-stricken husband kept out of her way, and each passed the first night of the voyage in solitary and nauseous meditation. On the following day the sea-sick and heart-sick man skulked in convenient localities, where his wife found him to eject on him the spleen of an injured woman.

"You led me to believe," she said to her husband, "that you had given up that singing woman."

"So I believed; but it is not so easy to throw—Oh dear! this dreadful sea!—Not so easy to throw off a tiger when it fastens on you," he replied in a voice as flabby as dough, and with the air of a martyr.

" What authority, what power does she hold over you? She must have some claim on you. She never would follow and attempt to kill a man unless she had suffered some wrong at his hands."

The husband was silent.

" Are you under obligations to her? Do you owe her money? Does she have any claim against you?"

" None whatever."

" Why then does she hunt you like a wild beast? Do you merit her anger—the anger that would kill? Why don't you answer me? I must, I will know all or the next ship takes me back to my father's protection."

" My dear wife, I am too sick to talk—to tell you all. Trust me till I am better. Your feelings are too much for so trifling a cause."

" Is it a trifling affair when I see my husband assaulted by a fierce woman—a woman he brought to America? And is it a trifling affair when your wife sees in it cause sufficient to renounce you forever unless it is satisfactorily explained away?"

" Why, she is only a singer! She has no claim on me—at least no claim that would weigh in my country. She demands no money, nor do I owe her any. Her ambition is disappointed, but that is her fault, not mine; she cancelled her engagement as prima donna against my protest, and now she seeks to recover her place, and, I suppose, struck me for refusing to aid her. I never promised to marry her, and she never expected I would, for I am noble, while sne is the artist and of obscure birth. Marriage with her would have been impossible, even if I had never met with you. I think she is crazy. You will likely never hear of her again."

"You told me that she had gone to Italy."

"So I then believed. Her appearance and actions yesterday were as unexpected to me as to you."

"My impression is that you once loved this woman, if you do not now."

"How much better and stronger I love you witness my giving her up for you," exclaimed Tancredi, in that low, musical voice so peculiar to him, and so effectual when pleading his cause. He kissed his wife's hand as tenderly as the unsettled state of his digestive organs would permit.

She was not thoroughly convinced of the honesty of his statement, but she restrained her misgivings for the time being, and a tolerable reconciliation followed between herself and husband.

She had ever been accustomed to a life of ease, leisure and frivolity, and yet neither her temperament or her position in society warranted a life of indolence. A haughty and independent self-reliant person, such as she was, cannot be, and never is, lazy. Her natural pride—and she was very proud—dreaded scandal and misery; she therefore naturally inclined toward objects and pursuits that were bright and joyous, and in harmony with her fashionable life. She now turned away from the hateful scene witnessed the day before, and looked to the bright east where the sun was to rise on her long wished for glory. Her long cherished wish to marry into a noble and illustrious family was now gratified, and she was about to enter the charmed circle of European society, and realize its famed pomp and grandeur.

Her husband was distinguished by birth, wealth and personal attractions; his conduct, so far as she knew, had ever been characterized by gentleness and honor; his behavior towards her had been respectful and loving, without that gush—that vapid billing and cooing too common among her married acquaintances, a practice she utterly despised. It was evident he loved her and was proud of her beauty.

The pacific side of the question preponderated, and she gradually yielded to the fascinations of ambition. The newly-married pair landed on the shores of the Old World with smiles on their lips and peace in their hearts.

The first move made by the cautious Italian on disembarking, was to institute such precautionary

measures as would prevent Rosetta Godardo from following him to Europe.

He now looked forward to a delightful honeymoon
among the gay capitals of the continent, where he numbered so many friends.   His attractive wife would
certainly create a sensation in society, and meet with
deserved ovations, but the carnival must not be endangered by a jealous mistress with a knife and vengeance
in her bosom.   To keep her out of the way he wrote
full instructions to his trusty servant, Berta, the companion and custodian of Rosetta.   Berta was directed
to retain the cottage, induce the Signorina to stay
there, and draw on his banker for funds necessary to
maintain them in comfort.

That tragic affair off his mind, the homesick man
turned to Italy, from whence he had been exiled for
so many months.   He started with his wife for
Naples.

CHAPTER XVI.

"Like ships that sailed for balmy isles,
　　But never came to shore;
A ship that sailed o'er sunny seas,
　　Was never heard of more."

WHEN Rosetta Godardo was taken from the parlor of the hotel at the time she attempted to assassinate Tancredi, he had the presence of mind to dispatch instructions to Berta.　By the time he was on board the vessel, that faithful guardian had taken her mistress in charge, and was on her way back to the cottage.

The reaction following her violence brought on alarming prostration, and she was as passive as a child. Her system, not yet fully recovered from the recent illness, now gave way, and she suffered a dangerous relapse.　The fever fires were relighted, and the mind once more wandered in the mazes of delirium.　The poor creature lay all powerless to follow her lover, too delirious to even bestow on him a single malediction.

Berta was not the malevolent, cold-blooded crone that her office would seem to indicate.　Prudish people will, doubtless, be swift to condemn her, and with a degree of justice, but prudish people should know exactly how much, and on what grounds to condemn her, lest they lose their reward—the reward of having done a worthy act from a worthy motive. A vicious right is no more impossible with people of strong prejudices, than is a virtuous wrong. That Berta may have justice awarded her—justice, neither more nor less, it is necessary to be more explicit, and establish her compound relation to Godardo and Tancredi.

She was about fifty years of age, had been all her life a servant of the Tancredi family, and the favorite maid of the late Signora, Michele's mother. She had been so long and so intimately attached to the family that she looked on it as her own. Its good was hers, and the commands of the master her higher law.

By the master's orders she had entered the service of Rosetta, and, as a high duty she never dreamed of shirking, she remained at her post and obeyed all instructions. She had been in the Signorina's service ever since the intrigue began, now over four years. During that time she had witnessed her master's attachment for Rosetta, and she refused to believe else than that he still loved her as ever, although he was married to another. She knew that in Italy the marriage *de convenance* was common among the male members of the nobility, and she supposed that her master had taken the right accorded him by usage.

She had learned to love Rosetta for her own self, but there was nothing in that love incompatible with fealty to her master. Indeed, he had always encouraged such affection by rewarding her for her zealous and respectful attentions. Why should she not love and continue to love Rosetta? Had not Tancredi, even in his late trouble, manifested the most tender solicitude for Rosetta's welfare?

The relationship between the two women was really more like that of easy and familiar companionship than that of mistress and maid. Berta was old enough to be Rosetta's mother, and, indeed, manifested much of the concern for her that a mother would for her daughter. When the child was wayward, she scolded it; when it was grieved, she consoled it; and when it was ill, she nursed it. Rosetta, on her part, with her warm confiding nature, clung to her one female companion with childlike trust and devotion.

Berta's conception of her duties in the premises was thus predicated on a complex basis—a basis too hard for thin-skinned morals to rest on with comfort. Her appreciation of duty, and her estimation of morals, was no better or worse than the cause and people she served.

She held first and foremost her fealty to her master, who, she believed, could not be guilty of a dishonorable action. Even if he had deserted Rosetta, still he had rendered her *quid pro quo*. But he had not deserted her; his attentions were but temporarily deflected from her and bestowed, as it were, on his own family; and she felt confident that sooner or later he would wander back to the only woman he had ever loved.   At all events, he had not discarded her, as proven by his appropriation of funds to keep her in comfort.   Her duty was plain; she must guard and console her charge until further orders.

Berta had been too long schooled amid the convenient profligacies of European society to feel any compunctions at her position as the agent of a meretricious alliance.   The agent took her charge home from the hotel, put it in bed, summoned the physician, and took her place as nurse.   The vital spark, which but now glimmered low in its socket, almost gone out in darkness forever, again began to glow with the pale tint of returning convalescence, and the mind commenced feebly to reason.

"What did I, then, that thou should'st scold me so, kind Berta?"

"Thou did'st try to kill the master, child."

"But he deserved killing."

"Say not so!   Would that punish him?   Would that help thee?   Would killing him bring him back to thee?"

"But he has betrayed me."

"Nay, he loves thee yet; I'll be bound!"

"Think'st thou so?"

"Nay, I am sure."

"How shall I be sure?"

"Try him, trust him, wait on him."

"And how shall I try him, good Berta?"

"Win him back from the Bannemead; he loves her not as he loves thee."

"But I am ill and ugly! She it was who stole away my beauty with her evil eye. He will not look on me."

"Be not so despondent. Regain thy health, my child, and thy beauty will return, and so will he."

"Do'st really think so? Or talk'st thou thus to console me? Mock me not, kind Berta; I pray thee, mock me not!"

"Nay, I mock thee not! Wilt thou try my experiment?"

"And thy experiment is—'

"To win Michele back to thee."

"That I will try; but how?"

"And thou must promise to take no heed of him till he first notices thee."

"Nay, that is too hard; Berta, ask me not that."

"I know these men better than thou know'st them—court them, they fly; disdain them, they kneel at thy feet."

"But will he ever come; dost thou know that he will return to me?"

"As surely as the summer follows winter; as sure as the swallows homeward fly. If thou heed'st me I promise his return to thee."

"Then I promise to get well ; and to remain quiet ; but, oh, my Berta, that is hard, hard, hard !" sobbed the weak woman, as though even the promise of in- action was an effort that summoned all the fortitude of her disconsolate soul.

CHAPTER XVII.

"She walks in beauty like the night
Of cloudless climes and starry skies,
And all that's best of dark and bright
Meet in the aspect of her eyes."

THERE are people yet living in New York who will recollect very well the yellow cottage which stood on a slight elevation a little back from the old Harlem Road, in what was then called Yorkville, a suburb of the city. The building and grounds were for many years owned and occupied by an excentric Englishman who was a mate, or, what was his chief duty, a pilot, on one of the packets that plied between New York and Liverpool. His name was William Orange; his neighbors call him William, Prince of Orange, and his yellow cottage the Orange Box. He was laid at the bottom of the sea long ago, the roadway has been widened, graded and paved into the sweeping avenue, and the ochery dwelling has given place to the stately brown-stone front.

Rosetta occupied this cottage. Shade trees and trellised vines in front made a pleasant retreat and half concealed the building from view. A commodious garden was situated in the rear of the house.

Rosetta's nearest neighbor was a widow named Taplan, who, with her son, lived in the adjoining two story brick. The son, John Taplan, was a brawny young man of two and twenty, and a mate, or sea pilot, by occupation. He had been a favorite of William Orange, who had interested the boy in the art of navigation, and taught him so well that he was now mate on one of the packets with which his tutor had been so long connected. He was frugal, and his earnings not only kept himself and mother in comfort, but overran their wants and were satisfactorily filling the provident stocking—the flattering neuclus of prospective wealth. They owned the brick dwelling and enclosed grounds, which was prima facia evidence of well-doing people.

Many neighborly civilities had been exchanged between the inmates of the two dwellings. During the tedious illness of Rosetta, Mrs. Taplan had been ever willing and ready to render any help in her power. Of course she knew nothing of Rosetta's antecedents, nor was she curious to know. Her neighbor, since her advent into the neighborhood, had behaved with decorum, and that was all that Mrs. Taplan cared to know.

The topography about the two dwellings was such

that a full view could be had of the garden in the rear of the cottage by any one looking out of the back second story window of the brick. When Rosetta grew able to walk out she passed much of her time in lounging among the cozy shadows of the garden. It was while thus occupied that John Taplan first saw her from his bedroom window, while home on his brief monthly visit. He was struck with her grace and beauty; he thought that never before had he seen so neat a figure, and he stood gazing at her until the stars came out and she went in.

The next morning he learned from his mother all she could tell him of the beautiful neighbor, when he went whistling away and steered his ship across and back across the sea, thinking of the pretty woman of the garden, and strangely blending her with the Polar star. When next he came home he found his mother prostrate with a dangerous illness, which compelled him to give up his ocean trip.

When Rosetta learned of her neighbor's illness she gratefully remembered the kindnesses—the savory stews, spices, jellies and kindred dainties of invalid store, which the kind American housewife had prepared and brought to her bedside, when she herself was ill, and needed a friend. And now, when opportunity presented, she did not hesitate to repay in kind. Besides her sense of gratitude it was a real treat to sit with some human being outside her own household. She visited the sick Mrs. Taplan every day, often twice a day; and sat for hours fanning the bedridden neighbor, or soothing her with her sparkling prattle.

Rosetta Godardo was not a strong-minded woman; her thoughts were not usually deep thoughts, nor her speech eloquent. It took passion to rouse strong thinking, and attune her speech to the key of eloquence. There was nothing stirring in a sick chamber, nothing in an invalid to incite eloquence, but she could and did cheer and amuse Mrs. Taplan with her kind prattle and childlike ways. The face of the sufferer would light up with gladness when the lively little Italian came to her bedside.

One morning, when Rosetta made her accustomed visit, she found a strange man seated holding the sick woman by the hand. It was too late to retreat, and she was introduced to John Taplan.

The son's leave of absence extended through many weeks of vigil at his dying mother's side. Rosetta was shy for a time, but she gradually became accustomed to the presence of the brawny sailor, who seemed to have about him the depth and the perfume of the sea. She made her usual visits to Mrs. Taplan with her wonted punctuality. Thus it came that, in their common solicitude for the sufferer, the Italian maid and the ocean pilot were daily thrown into each other's company. A quiet but pleasant acquaintance sprang up between them. With John Taplan, sentiment began at gratitude, and, with a rapid crescendo, ran the gamut through respect, admiration, love, tenderness, devotion, up to the crowning key of adoration for the dark-eyed beauty.

Taplan possessed one prominent trait in his character budget that made him a remarkable person, that was his earnestness. It is literally true to say that there was nothing trivial in his sight. Everything at all worthy of consideration was of serious import to him. Everybody and all things that came within his notice was estimated with seriousness. Straws pointed leeward, and had significance as well as the needle that pointed to the pole. Life to him was never a travesty, but an awful reality—the *vitam impendere vero.* He possessed about as much appreciation of wit and humor as a Hottentot of Beethoven's symphonies, or the color blind of rainbow tints. He was good-hearted, patient, cool, ready to help, and fond of quiet society, but his conception of conviviality was rudimentary. He went through life with few smiles, looking at men and objects with earnest eyes in a sober face.

With woman, he himself confessed he was a failure. He was too morose for female friendship, too sedate for female gayeties, too cold for woman's flip pant love. Even as a boy, he could not get along with the girls. He never could enter into the mud pie industry with that spurious faith which is sometimes more gratifying than the genuine article. , "Make believe" was labor lost, and he withdrew from childish sports in disgust. The screams of the girls irritated him, and their hoydenish ways drove him furious. They called him "crank," "Grandpap," or the "Old Man," and treated him like a Dutch uncle, or as they fancied that mythical kinsman deserved to be treated.

When he grew up it was worse. He, who could handle a ship, could not manage a woman. On the darkest night, and amid the raging of the storm his boat would obey her helm, but when he attempted to direct a woman, she sheered away, perverse and adverse to all approved principles of navigation. John would tackle a ship when the waves ran mountain high, and he would bring her into port, but he would not tackle a female in the deadest calm that ever lulled the upholstery of a drawing-room—no, not to be made master of the craft.

His mother, of course, had understood him better; all bashful boy's mothers do; she trimmed her sails to keep him company. He liked his mother the better for that, and, up to the time when he met Rosetta, he liked his mother better than any woman he had ever met.

This little black-eyed woman—he soliloquized—this strange woman, who spoke his language so quaintly, and yet to musically, seemed wondrously like his mother in behavior and disposition.

Don't you see how he was already prejudiced in her favor? she seemed to sail on the same tack with him, or lay alongside as though they had been life's voyagers together. There was no mockery about her, no sneering in her manner, none of the malapert in her behavior. Even her beautiful face was sober and earnest.

And to the lonely girl, suffering with a heartache not assuaged, this strong, sedate man, seemed like a prop, a tower, a secure refuge, which she had dreamed of, and longed for, but knew not that such sanctuary could be until he came with his force and will. His very physical proportions—the broad shoulders, deep chest, and square face, lit up with earnest gray eyes, impressed her with a sense of power and safety; while his direct manner, and unaffected, almost blunt, speech, revealed to her the intensity and earnestness of his character. She began, unconsciously and involuntarily, to lean over on his tack, and to sail along in his company.

Of course it was not the beginning of a new love

with her.   It is to be regretted that it was not.   Even if she had reached no higher than respect for the sailor, and remained there, it would have been better than a ruby mine for both.

No; it was not the beginning of a new love attachment on her part.   Such women as Rosetta Godardo—there are such—love but once, and that with their lives.   She had loved that love.   There was no new germ for a new growth.   Such women are like plants that give out but a single fragrance, and die with the perfume.

Rosetta's love was ground into a broken urn; no contiguous vase could imbibe the subtle fragrance.

CHAPTER XVIII.

"Her precious pearl in sorrow's cup,
Unmelted at the bottom lay,
To shine again when all drunk up,
The bitterness should pass away."

"Don't you think my mother is much better, to-day?" asked John Taplan of Rosetta, one evening in the parlor, as she came from the sick chamber.

"Alas, no! she no better!" she quietly answered.

"But, the color has come back to her face; isn't that better?"

"It the burning that; it the fever."

"Tell me, did you ever see any one die?" he inquired, after a brief silence.

"Yes; my mother I saw; my little sister, too. I saw both die. My father and brother, they go sink in the bay. I never saw them—no one ever saw them come to shore. The boat it come back."

"You mean they were drowned?"

"My father and brother—yes, they drowned. No one see them. My mother and sister not; they die—the fever made them to die. I see *them* when they die."

"Have you no brother or sister left?"

"None, Sir, none; no one but me!"

"You are alone; as lonely as—as I am lonely!" said he, after another interval of silence.

"More lone; much more lone than you. You your home have, your mother, your ship, your friends, your country have. But me! Alas, I nothing have!"

As she spoke her arms fell listless at her side, and her head sunk on her breast. The sailor made a step forward as if to catch her in his arms, but bashfulness restrained him, and he tore open his collar, which felt like an iron girdle around his throat.

They stood thus for a few moments with the silence only broken by the hard breathing of the sailor.

"Your name is Rosaetta?" at length he asked.

"Nay, not so much; only Rosetta," she replied, looking up to him and smiling.

"May I call you Rosa? That name is easier for me; besides I like it better."

"Call me Rosa? Yes, if it likes you," she said, with a look of wonder and pleasure.

"Well, then, Rosa, will you let me be your friend?"

"You are good! Same like your mother! You my friend? How glad! How it sounds! Your friend! And will you have it so?"

" Do you ask if I mean it ?"

" Yes, the same it is."

" I more than mean it."

" It gladdens me that you will have it so! And you shall be my good friend, as is thy mother, and I will be your good friend," she cried, and joyously reached out her hand to him.

Ah, what an actress she was! but here her acting was true and real, for it was prompted by her heart.

The two new friends met daily beside the death couch, until the mother closed her eyes to mundane light. When John saw her lying before him, cold and silent, he gave one great sob, as if told for the first time what he knew before, that man loses his first and best friend when his mother dies.

He was alone in the world, without a single blood relative near or distant. One bright inspiration shone through the gloom, it was the sympathy of the one single being who came with words of condolence at his bereavement. She came over in the soft twilight and sat in the pensive gloom of the house of woe, talking like a child at the stricken man. She followed the body of her late friend to its final abode, and that was the last John saw of her for days.

But his ship was in port, it was almost ready for the return voyage, and John reported for duty.

It was the evening before he was to sail. He had

been ruminating and meditating all day, trying to make out the answer to the half-formed and obscure enigma that confused and bothered his mind. He knew not himself why it was or what it was, but there it was—an ill-defined disquiet he never felt before. John Taplan was perplexed, but what at he did not know. His own expression was that he didn't know where to go, nor what to do after he got there. This much he did know, that the enigma related in some vague way to the beautiful neighbor, but why, he could not tell. He knew that without her there would be no vague enigma to puzzle his brains. Without her he would summarily dispose of his house and effects and turn his whole attention to the glorious sea. But with her in the case he hesitated about making a radical change, and he compromised by bidding the domestic in his employ keep the house in order until his return.

That much of the enigma was cleared up; but the most perplexing part remained—Rosetta, what of her?

He had not seen her since his mother's funeral, which already seemed an age ago. He must see her before he went away—he must see her that evening. He entered her gate, her door; he found himself, in surprise to himself, in Rosetta's presence.

She took no trouble to conceal her pleasure at his visit, and extended her hand in welcome.

"I start away to-morrow and came to thank you for your kindness to my poor mother, and to say good-by."

"So?   But you will come back, and we will be the neighbors?"

"That is for you to say, Rosa."

"For me to say?   Then I say come back and be my neighbor," she replied in a hearty, unaffected manner.

"No; I don't mean that; or I mean that and something more—a great deal more. Will you be more than a neighbor to me, Rosa?"

"That more is the friend? Is it that?" she inquired, looking down and tapping the floor with her foot.

"Will you be my wife?"

"That is sudden!" she almost whispered, as she glared around the room with a startled look, as though dreading a lurking foe.

"Will you be my wife?" again asked Taplan, reaching out his strong hands to her.

"Signor is good!   Sir, you are kind, very kind! I the honor deserve not!"

"That is for me to judge, Rosa.   You and I are alike in many ways, and most like in being alone in the world. I have no one to care for me, if it is not you; none to call me friend, if it is not you; I have no one to love, if it is not you. I can give you a home and my love, and we can give each other happiness. Think of all that!"

" What if I the better like alone to be? What if it best pleases me to be by no one loved?"

" Then it shall best please me also. Is this your answer?"

" When come you home again?"

" In about forty days."

"Then I will answer you. Ask me not now. A good voyage to you, and safe return, *my friend*. Till then, good-by."

The next day the young mate went away to sea.

Berta wrote one of her fortnightly letters about this time. Here is a translated extract:

" I wrote you of our neighbors, the American family, and of the death of the mother, who left a son, a young sailor. He has just gone to sea, the first trip since his mother's death.

" Do you believe it? he is in love with our Rosetta! He proposed to her last evening. And what said she? I hear you ask. She told him to wait a month for her reply! To wait till his ship comes back. What do you say to that? All this she has told me ; what she will do I know not. She wants my advice ; what shall it be ? She loves him not as she once loved you."

When John Taplan left Rosetta Godardo a new era seemed to burst on her life. The two conventional angels that are appointed to hover in the circumambient presence of mortals, had a fierce combat, which ended in the Demon of Evil being driven howling away, and its place occupied by the guardian angel of Good. The benignant spirit overshadowed the woman with peace and content.

As she sat alone in the gathering shadows of night, after bidding her lover adieu, the drama of her life, past and prospective, passed like a thrilling panorama before her. She fancied she sat among the olives where as a child she played ; she saw her father's cottage, and she beheld his boat on the bay ; she again looked on her mother bending over the spinning wheel under the shade of the chestnut tree.

Then came the maiden with her beauty, her innocence and her song, when, lo ! a dark shadow crept over her form, and enveloped her in its foul gloom ! It is the blight of the execrable, the false Tancredi ! Scalding tears filled her eyes and blotted out the hateful vision.

But, behold ! While she yet weeps, the hideous

shadow fades, and the form of John Taplan stands among the sunlit olives. He holds out his hands to her; he points to a smiling valley, aureate with waving grain, and musical with birds and bees.

The guardian angel looked on approvingly and smiled applause.

It was not love that lured her toward Taplan, or she could not have seen so clearly and reasoned so correctly what she had been and what she might yet become. Love would have blinded her. It was pride, self-respect, the instinct of virtue, that inclined her toward him. She looked to him as to the knight, noble, brave and strong, under whose shield she might find shelter, and in whose affection she might find refuge from shame and sorrow. She looked to him as an ark to bear her over the waves of passion and despair.

The guardian angel whispered approval.

His was the first honorable love ever made to her; his was the only offer of marriage she had ever heard.

How different it all was from her experience with Tancredi! How striking the contrast between the two men! The nobleman had treated her as he would a slave; the sailor paid her the homage due a queen. Under the sway of her old love passion ran riot, and judgment sat appalled on its tottering seat. She had indeed ruled on a gilded throne, but the hair-suspended sword had fallen, and her false lover had walked over her prostrate body to new conqnest. The stout sailor had reseated her on the throne, and had removed the menacing sword. She was no longer scorned and rejected, but was the queen, in royal robes, and in her right mind.

Peace, content and secnrity settled down on the Italian maid like a benediction. Her sleep was no longer disturbed by the spectre of unrest; her dreams were of her childhood.

Rosetta resolved that she would become the wife of John Taplan. As was characteristic of her, the resolve was not weak with a cold hesitancy. She gloried in the prospect before her, and, as the tedious days went ronnd, she longed for his return, impatient to tell him how glad she was to become his wife. She felt every joy that a pure woman feels when about to enter into happy wedlock with the man she loves. Under this contented frame of mind, and its stimulating effect on her system, her vigor and beauty returned with astonishing rapidity. With these happy changes came back her girlish tastes and ambition. She took again to song, hunted up her neglected music, and the cottage rang with her melodious voice. She especially loved to sing songs of the sea.

Berta stared with wide eyes at the change in her young ward.

"What has come over thee, my pretty one? Thou art as gay as the lark!"

"Say'st thou so, good Berta? And why may I not be gay? One cannot always be sad!"

"Heigh-ho! Thou art ever thinking of the young American sailor! Ah me! thou wilt soon desert thy old friend Berta!"

"Nay, thou shalt ever remain and be glad with me."

"No, girl; when thou go'st with the sailor I shall return to my master."

"Hush, Berta! Let us not speak of evil! It makes me sad again."

"Is it evil to say I shall return to my master when thou art married?"

"Alas, yes, dear Berta, so it sounds to me."

"But it is natural that I should go to my best friend when I part with thee."

"He may spurn thee, as he did me. He will spurn thee when thou art in his way."

"*Dio vi benedica!* Think'st thou so evil of him?"

"*Caro mio*, have I not good cause?"

"Ask me not to decide that. He loves thee? Mark my words, he will return to thee again. All the fiends will not keep him from thee."

"May the arch fiend sieze me if I give him welcome!"

"Puh! how you talk! We shall see!"

"We *shall* see!" echoed Rosetta mockingly, and
she broke off the dialogue by going to the piano and
singing,

> "Like an eagle caged I pine,
>   On this dull unchanging shore;
> Oh! give me the flashing brine,
>   The spray and the tempest roar."

Berta watched her with the expression of a patient,
waiting demon on her cunning face.

It was pleasant to contemplate Rosetta in her new
rôle. She got a new dress, together with several
articles of personal adornment, the first since coming
to America. She placed many inexpensive decorations
in and about the cottage, and did many things to beau-
tify herself and her home, adornments which none but
a woman's head could have contrived or a woman's
hand executed. Her acts and industry were not all
for John Taplan; they were largely for the woman
redeemed from passion and disgrace.

Well, why stop to moralize? Why not proceed
with the story?

Ah, friend, is it not going too fast when you gallop
rough shod over the hoping heart of a weak and
crushed woman? And is it not really proceeding with

the story when you linger to learn her anxious, almost terrible, resolve, to redeem her life from pollution? The potentiality of a fallen woman's will is a bri.tle texture when strongest; why may we not tarry long enough to strengthen it with our sympathy?

And, Madam, you who are most clamorous for the rapid turning of Ixion's wheel, may it not be that you are too prone to pass by in disdain an erring sister, when, perchance, encouragement from you would redeem? Here is a young creature possessed of every quality that gives grace and charm to womanhood; she has been tempted as only a beautiful girl can be tempted, and is even yet surrounded by the most vicious and perilous circumstances. From the depths of her danger and degradation she reaches out toward the light, and hails with joy the prospect of standing redeemed in that noblest of all stations—the true wife of a true man. For God's sake, don't trample her back into the mire! Let her rise again. There are hellish temptations awaiting her; help her overcome them all.

CHAPTER XIX.

"Oh, how this tyrant, doubt, torments my breast!"

On the morning of the day when her lover's ship was expected to reach port she was early astir, and in a carriage hired for the occasion drove down to the pier to meet and welcome him home.

The ship was not in, but a vessel supposed to be the packet had been signaled off Sandy Hook, and it would be noon before she could reach her pier. The time was long, but Rosetta waited.

The packet was at her mooring at last, and the crew not on duty, was disembarking. Among the members was the young mate, whom she hailed as he drew near. John was astonished and confused at being accosted by a beautiful woman in the presence of his ship-mates, but when he saw who it was, and learned why she was there, he came as near smiling as his temperament would permit. He was more than pleased.

His companions, curious to learn who was this charming female who so familiarly addressed their comrade—the woman-hater,—and why he stood so high in her favor, lingered near, waiting for him to rejoin them. Their presence and behavior attracted her attention.

"These are your friends?" she asked, nodding toward the group of sailors. "You shall bring them here and make me the introduction."

"This is my neighhor, and my mother's friend," said Taplan, presenting his comrades to her.

She gave her hand in uneffected greeting to every one, and by her modest and graceful manner made her way to the good opinion of all. One of the officers lived in the direction of Yorkville, and she insisted on his riding with them, when they started off together.

In the evening John went over according to appointment, and sat and talked with Rosetta, or rather, listened to her, for he was a good listener, to whom most people liked to talk. Taplan was better informed than most persons in his vocation; his silence was not because of ignorance. He sat enchanted under the spell of the musical speech and charming ways of the Italian girl, feeling it almost sacriligious to interrupt the harmony with his big round voice. Besides he was in suspense.

"I came for the answer," he at length abruptly exclaimed, after the evening had well advanced.

"The answer? Meeting you at the pier was the answer."

"And the answer is—"

"I your wife will gladly be," she replied, placing both her hands in his.

The young sailor folded her in his arms, and kissed her most daintily.

How did he acquire the art? He never had any training; it was the first embrace he ever bestowed on a woman, his mother excepted, and yet he kissed his affianced with the grace and delicacy of a Chesterfield! If kissing goes by favor, it comes by heredity.

The four days he stayed on shore were gala days to John Taplan, and their memory lived long as a bright oasis in his life. He passed his time until late in the evening by her side, and at night dreamed of none but her. He was quiet, almost solemn, in her presence; but he was earnestly happy. Rosetta whiled away the time with her unaffected, childlike manner, and made him wish the day would never end.

They talked most of the future; and soared away to gossamer castles built by that volatile architect, Hope. O Youth! O Beauty! Why may not thy ethereal days roll round forever.

The wedding day was fixed to come off in the glad spring time—in the following May, which, to the

8*

young pilot, was a remote future, but still the millennium worth the waiting for.

"Before you go away, I must tell you this which most troubles me, my only trouble," she said to him on the evening before he was to sail.

"What can trouble you, Rosa?"

"Oh, my friend, it is the hard, hard story! I tell it all to you some day. It is the wicked story; it pains my heart when I think. You know not what you have made for me. For all the good you make for me, the good God will bless you! But one more good you must make me, then I the happy woman will be."

"Name it, Rosa," he said, taking her hand, and encouraging her with his firm grasp.

"The person—the one who here me bring, makes this home for me. I like it not; I will not have it so. I can no longer his bounty accept. It is your wife that is to be who speaks this trouble."

"I am not sure I understand you,—some friend provides for your maintenance in this cottage, is that your meaning?"

"Yes."

"And you can no longer accept aid from him, now that you are my promised wife? Do you mean that?"

"Yes, yes; it is that. How kind you under-stand."

"Then you are right, quite right; my future wife must look to me entirely for support. But, tell me, Rosa, who this friend—this person is? Tell me all about it."

"Oh, no, no, no! my good, kind friend, ask me not that! Some other time! oh, please, some other time! It is the hard, wicked story, that makes me wild, that makes me crazy when it I think. Some other time, do, please me! Before we married, I tell you all. Let us be happy to-night. The great sorrow is past; let us not feel wicked any more."

While pleading, she knelt at his feet and clasped his knees in the agony of her supplication.

"As it suits you," Taplan said coldly, as he looked down in her upturned face and saw the wild gleaming of her dark eyes.

Neither spoke for some time. The sailor wore a troubled look on his face, which the observant woman saw with consternation. She clung to his knees as she had once clung to Tancredi. and looked up into Taplan's face so beseechingly, so piteously, and so alarmed.

He placed his great hands on her shoulders as if to repulse, and said, earnestly, almost fiercely, "Tell me, Rosa, is it a crime?"

"God pity me, yes; but not my crime!" exclaimed the dismayed woman, bowing her head in his lap, and sobbing as if grief were breaking her heart.

He raised her up, lifted her as lovingly as the angel of mercy lifts up the fallen.

"Rosa, that is all I wish to know, all I have the right to know. You are innocent, tell me the rest or not, as it best pleases you."

The distressed creature nestled close to his bosom, and laid her head next his heart, like a troubled child clinging to its dearest friend. She felt secure there; evil and distress could not reach her in that asylum. She looked up in his face and smiled through her tears.

That woman was pure in the sight of her lover; she stood redeemed in the eyes of a merciful power.

Was it the Magdalene to whom the resurrection first appeared?

Rosetta Godardo met there the Resurrection of a New Life.

On the next day John Tappan hunted up the agent of the cottage and to him prepaid the rent for the ensuing quarter. He left positive orders with Rosetta to accept no pecuniary help from any one but himself. On that day she saw him off on his voyage.

Two more translated extracts from the Italian letters are here given. The first is Tancredi's reply to Berta's letter already given.

"It is impossible for her to love him or any one as she did me. She loved me too well, better a thousand times than a woman should love any man. But, poor girl, she couldn't help that; it is her nature! Her too ardent love for me was the cause of all the trouble; but for that, she might be happy this day.

"I am glad her beauty has returned, as you state; but still I trust she will marry the sailor—I think you say he is a sailor.

"It is uncertain when we shall return to America. It all depends on Madam, who is so capricious as to be no two days alike.

"Has Rosetta's voice come back with her beauty? Tell her that I would like to hear her sing one of the old songs we used to sing together. Tell her, also, that Signora Lucia, with whom she quarrelled at Madrid, is become the rage of Europe, and is now the queen of the lyric stage. Lucia and Rosetta were rivals, but our Rosetta would have distanced her were it not for her foolish resolve to quit the stage.

"If she asks my advice, tell her I say to marry the American sailor."

Berta wrote in reply:

"Our Rosetta has accepted the sailor. They are to be married next May. I don't think she loves him, and yet she cares a great deal for him. She acts more like a woman moved by gratitude than love. The sailor (he is a sailor) will give her an honest name, a home and protection ; for all of which she feels grateful.

"She was furious when she heard of Lucia's success. 'I'll triumph over her yet !' she muttered, with gleaming eyes. What she meant I know not. When I had finished reading to her your letter, she sighed, and went to the mirror, where she adjusted a scarlet ribbon in her hair. You always told her how well scarlet became her.

" She is now in the parlor singing ' The Harp in the Air.' Why does she always sing that song when troubled about you ? She sings better than ever before. The sailor is gone to sea, but she is not impatient at his absence as she used to be when you were away."

John Taplan was seated in the officer's cabin of the outward bound packet talking to a comrade.

"Taplan, do you recollect the Italian nobleman and the singing woman who came over with us in this ship from Europe to America more than a year ago ? The woman, don't you remember, who charmed every body on board with her singing ? Don't you recollect ?"

"No."

"Oh, of course not! Why ask such a question of a woman hater? You never go into the grand saloon, especially if a lady is there."

"Why do you ask if I recollect the Italian and the singing woman?"

"Oh, do you know, that the woman you introduced me to, looks like that opera singer."

"What! Rosa? Impossible! Why do you think that?"

"Because, as I said, your sweetheart resembles the Italian lady, because your friend is an Italian, and, you say, sings like an angel."

"You astonish me! And yet I can see no wrong, even if Rosa should turn out to be the woman you speak of."

"Wrong? Certainly not! But everybody seemed to think that she was the Italian's wife. Is your sweetheart a widow?"

"Damnation! What are you driving at? I never asked her such a question; I never thought of such a question. She may be a widow for all I know or care, and still I maintain there is nothing wrong. Why, in the name of the furies, do you talk so? She is to be my wife; what do you mean?"

"I mean nothing bad; I know nothing bad, nor do I think anything wrong; only it is a matter for remark that the woman who crossed in this packet should bear so close a resemblance to your wife, that is to be. That is all, old fellow. That is all. No offense, I hope."

" We'll let the matter drop."

" As you choose. I have nothing more to say on the subject ; it's none of my business."

" No ; it's none of your business."

Although Taplan controlled his tongue he did not his thoughts. The subject was continually uppermost in his mind. It troubled him deeply, as does all mystery connected with one's sweetheart. And yet, he reasoned, that, when the mystery came to be cleared up, as it would be some day, it would then be no longer a mystery, but probably a very simple and innocent affair. He would trust Rosetta, as he said he would, until she herself voluntarily explained the mystery, as she promised she would, and as she would in due time.

He recalled her words on the subject, and analyzed them.

" It is the only thing that troubles me," she had said. She meant it troubled her, as it should the prudent woman and affianced wife, to accept pecuniary aid of another. That was highly commendable ; but who was the person alluded to ? Doubtless some relative who reluctantly gave her that support provided for her by contract.

Was this *person*, could he be the Italian nobleman of whom his mate had spoken? Or was she his widow, and provided for in his will?

"It is the hard, wicked story that makes me wild when I think of it," she had also said. Then it must be a story intimately connected with her life—a hard, wicked story. But she had said that it was a crime; but not her crime. That is to say, others had done the wrong, had wronged her, and were perhaps even now wronging her. Certainly no reasonable man who pretended to love a woman could have any misgivings after so direct and emphatic a statement as Rosetta had made to him. He would think no more of the case; such thoughts implied doubt, and he would not wrong Rosa by doubting her word. He would wait for her story.

But it is to be feared that he did not succeed in dismissing the distracting subject from his mind.

CHAPTER XX.

"Still panting o'er a crowd to reign,
　　More joy it gives to woman's breast,
　　To make ten frigid coxcombs vain,
　　Than one true, manly lover blest."

THE Tancredi made a very brief stay in Naples. The fastidious Madam found only stupid natives, two-thirds of whom were lazy or ill-bred, the other third guides or beggars. She saw no society that came up to her standard of excellence. Even the strangers came and went like wanderers, seeking only pleasure or health. This was Naples as she viewed it, and after a sail on the bay, and a ride in a rough diligence, she shook the dust from her feet and turned back to Rome.

There it was even worse. To her eyes the populace was made up of mendicants, banditti, and a sprinkling of artists, antiquarians and church dignitaries. The industries of the city were divided into begging, seeking curiosities, rambling among ruins, or holding conclaves. She soon tired of Rome, and started with her obliging husband to Venice.

That place suited her better, mainly, no doubt,

because she was committed favorably beforehand. She had pined for the City of the Sea, and now that she was there she was bound to affect delight, even though she did not feel that way. She was entitled to some praise for her consistency in this, for at heart she was disappointed. To her Venice was a city washed by the sea, and yet filthy and odorous of fish. The gondolas and gondoliers, at least, from their proximity to water, might have kept themselves clean; but the former were not only rank with dirt but were infested with vermin that held Venetian carnivals among their napless cushions, and the boatmen looked like coal-heavers of the Thames. One of the gondoliers, whom she said was tipsy, paddled her about with a broken oar. She saw no gondolier of romance, unless dirt, rags and insolence are picturesque and romantic.

Their stay in Venice was protracted to a fortnight, apparently for no other reason than that Signor Tancredi wanted to get away to the cool air of the Alps.

Thus far Madam Alice was disappointed. She had not met with nobility, had not tasted the sweets of distinguished society, and she began to suspect that her husband's marriage was looked upon as a mesalliance by his kindred, and that polite Italy, on that account, was bent on excluding his wife from the privilege of her husband's class and station.

He protested that society in cities was out of

season in that latitude, and that fashionable Italy was taking its accustomed airing on the lakes and among the passes of the cool mountains. This statement only partially re-assured her. She was fast becoming a suspicious, exacting and capricious wife, bent on leading her husband a Gilpin gallop over the domestic course.

He submitted to her whims and tyrannies with a tameness surprising in so spirited a man. He yielded to her every wish, regardless of how unreasonable or unjust it might be, for no other reason than that he really and truly loved her better than any woman he had ever met. Her proud beauty and haughty spirit held him spellbound. Her course, probably, was the very best she could have taken to secure his affection and constancy. Had she been the yielding, tender and humble wife, she would most likely have met with coldness and neglect instead of love and homage. She took the rôle of the arrogant monarch and maintained her sovereignty with an iron hand and gratifying success. Signor Tancredi possessed the very wife he required, and she got the husband she deserved. Objectively and subjectively the Tancredi-Bannemead alliance was a success.

How often it occurs that the Sabyrite, who made every one bend to his will while a bachelor, is metamorphosed into the meekest and most amiable of husbands! The contemplation of such a man's career is an argument against future punishment. A reformed rake makes a good husband, is the proverbial outgrowth of this rather common experience. The saying, however, has the ear-marks of a woman, with whom "meekness" and "goodness" in a husband are convertible terms. This kind of a good husband engenders small respect in the wife, if she happens to be high-minded. Tancredi came very near being classed as a "good" husband.

They passed the remainder of the summer in the north of Lombardy, at the town of Isola, situated on the mountain river Lira, among the Rhaetian Alps. This place, although somewhat out of the route of continental travel, is an exceedingly picturesque and delightful locality, much frequented by the Italians and the visitors at lake Como. The idle life of the lake dwellers was often varied by visits among the Rhaetian and Leopontine ranges, which stood like huge, gray-hooded monks frowning at each other across the Splügen Pass.

A distinguished coterie of the Signor's friends were already quartered at the Splügen hotel, the principal hostelry in Isola, when he and his wife arrived. Among the number was his sister, Signora Adelaide Cyrello and her husband, the latter an official high in favor at the Italian court.

Signora Adelaide was very like her brother in appearance, and was a most intelligent and estimable woman. She had been taught the English language, but did not speak it as fluently as her brother, not having had his opportunities for practising the speech. Her willingness to learn, and her sweet, musical voice, so like her brother's, compensated for her slips of grammar and faulty pronunciation. She thought well of her brother, but not always well of his doings, among which latter was his marriage with the American. In a letter, in answer to his, bearing to her the announcement of his marriage, she had freely expressed her adverse opinion of that transaction, which she felt must be irregular, if not disgraceful. She shared in the general opinion then prevailing in Europe that Americans were semi-barbarian democrats, among whom the social scale was kept level by lowering rank down to the vulgar strata. As a member of an ancient and noble house she could not realize how her brother could affiliate with Americans, without relinquishing his social status at home. However, she was not so bound by prejudice that she was unwilling to hear his side of the story. Besides, he was her brother, her only brother, and the head of the Tancredi house.

Up to the time of the arrival of her brother and his wife, Signora Cyrello was in a state of uncertainty in regard to the question of etiquette proper on the occasion of the reception.

Signora Adelaide and Madam Tancredi met for the first time in the salon of the Splügen hotel. When the former was brought face to face with her brother's wife, she drew back in surprise, and, bestowing a frown on Michele, swept from the room towering with indignation.

The guests were, of course, painfully embarrassed at this episode, but the American maintained her self-poise with the equanimity of one receiving an ovation instead of contumely. Before the awkward silence was broken, Tancredi came in leading his sister, whom he had followed in the wake of her exit.

"My dear wife," said he, "my sister made a painful mistake; she mistook you for another person. She hastens to repair the wrong, and crave your pardon."

"Tell your sister that it is a matter of indifference to me what or whom she mistook me for. If her opinion, made up by a glance, is unfavorable, I beg her not to alter it."

"Oh, say not that! you, who deserve so well!"

"I was not trained to accept politeness as a beggar does alms, nor will I."

"But, my dear wife, you will not permit my sister to explain; that much is due her."

"And how much is due me, pray ? Insolence and insult ?"

"Nay, believe me; that was a mistake; a mistake that you yourself might have made."

This conversation was carried on in a low voice, and aside from the company.

"If Madam will but bear my unfortunate blunder for one little minute, I think she will not so unkindly judge me," interrupted Signora Adelaide in her sweet voice.

"I bear with your blunder because I choose, and not to please any person."

"I not quite understand ; you forgive me ?"

"You have not asked that."

"But I will. I do ask you to pardon my mistake. I was mistaken ; I was wrong ; I am sorry. I mistook you for another woman. My brother my mistake inform me, and now I see my painful mistake."

"My sister mistook you for the Godardo," whispered Tancredi, in his wife's ear, prompted by the necessity for a full and immediate explanation.

"I forgive you with all my heart," she eagerly exclaimed, extending her hand in a hearty manner.

The candor with which she forgave impressed her sister-in-law very favorably ; she was led to believe that Madam Alice was possessed of a generous and amiable disposition. The husband saw in his wife's behavior delicate malignity.

In a *tête a tête* between the two women, a full explanation was had of how the error came to be made. The Italian woman would have avoided further discussion of the unpleasant subject after she had said enough to vindicate herself in the eyes of her sister-in-law, but the latter was irrepressible until her curiosity in that direction was satisfied.

The Signora spoke of her brother's liaison with forbearance and palliation. She had seen the cantatrice only twice, once on the stage, and on another occasion in a carriage.

"When I met you," she said, "I was confident that you were the cantatrice. I felt very bitter toward my brother for what I believed to be his base deception, and for bringing shame and disgrace on his family. I left the room, sick at heart, angered and mortified. He followed and gave me his word of honor that I was deceived, and that you are worthy of my esteem. And you do resemble the singing woman as I remember her. But you cannot know my joy at finding it is you and not her."

Madam Tancredi was also full of joy—was overjoyed. What at?

First, the implied rebuke to her husband ; second, the compliment paid to herself.

The Godardo, though an Italian, would not have been received into the proud Tancredi family, while she, the American, was welcomed to full membership. She took much comfort out of her success.

Sometimes, in choosing the lesser evil, we forget that it is still an evil. It is probable that the revulsion of feeling in Signora Adelaide's case blinded her to the fact, that although the American was not a professional singer, she was still plebeian.

Madam Alice at one bound established herself in the good graces of the distinguished company at Isola. It was a real enjoyment to see this beautiful woman, almost without effort, breathe in the *savoir vivre* as she did the Alpine air. Her inborn grace, and her intuitive ambition of elegance, attracted all to her side, and before two weeks had gone by she was as completely the reigning queen of that circle as she ever was in her native city.

The company had talked much of her before her expected arrival. They had promised themselves much amusement at the backwoods bizarrie of the western barbarian, as they had named her. They were astonished to find, instead of the uncouth barbarian, the lady of fashion, grace and refinement, and a woman who outranked them all in beauty.

With the gentlemen especially she was first favorite; indeed was so popular that her distinguished husband was scarcely permitted to **pay her the most common conjugal courtesies.** Even in their more secluded moments he experienced small share of that wedded bliss of which the young so fondly dream, so many sigh for, and but few realize. He began to suspect that he had found one woman who did not worship him, and that woman his wife; the person of all others who should pay him tribute. The conqueror of hearts was daily acquiring new and unpleasant experiences in his relations with the proud American beauty.

His egotism waned, but, strange to **say, his love** for his wife increased in like proportion. **He caught himself** thinking, saying and doing things **which he** formerly held beneath the dignity of a Tancredi. **Did she slight him,** he fawned the **more;** was she indifferent, he became more **adject, and even** her insolence humbled the proud man in the dust. **He was un-happy, his observant friends saw it,** and lowered their estimation of **the once** audacious Lothario.

The almost daily excursions **by the guests** were usually shared by Madam Alice, nor was she concerned about her husband's consent **to go** and come as she willed. **A bevy of** gallants **were** always ready to attend her every step or accompany her on her rambles among the mountains, or assist in her adventures, some of which startled the **discreet Adelaide.** The latter would sometimes remonstrate in a sweet, sisterly way; but such appeals generally ended in a kiss, and in Madam having her own way. The two women became greatly attached. Madam Tancredi was sagacious enough to discern the true nobility of Adelaide, and that on her more than any one else she was dependent for her exalted place in society; while the Signora saw beneath the frivolity of the American a pure and good heart, ruled, it was true, by a brain a little bit turned by her sudden success in securing an exalted position in society. Besides she was the adored wife of her brother, and the promise of a better life for him.

Madam Alice had come to Europe to have a "good time," as expressed in her western vernacular, and she was bent on having it in her own way. Her marriage was for a peculiar object—the real bridegroom was European Aristocracy, to which her husband was a little closer than the priest who officiated at the marriage altar. She therefore paid her principal homage to the real object of the union—society, forgot the priest, and ignored the husband. She was filled with ambition, and, as two bodies cannot occupy the same space, she had no room for conjugal love. The old passion for conquest relit the fires on her altar, and she longed for the incense of singed moths.

It is scarcely necessary to protest that this is not a

homily on coquettes or against coquettry. Let that muliebrous pastime continue; it is woman's dearest sport, where she draws her keenest weapon, and the victims her proudest trophies. Men will come and go, but coquettry goes forever.

Keep it up, ye gallant dames! You will never lack for pupils or victims. The Fool's school must not and will not languish! But beware of two contingencies, and one of which is bound to overtake you at last—you will singe the wrong moth, or your lamp will go out for want of oil. No homily is needed against an evil that carries with it its own punishment.

Madam Tancredi singed the wrong moth.

Among the guests of the Splügen hotel was one Baron Sebastian von Waldland, a German nobleman from one of the Rhinish provinces, *unt der beste Freund von Herr Tancredi*. The two men had become acquainted in Paris, and the Signor had spent two months of the previous summer at the Baron's home. They fell into each other's ways, and the friendship was so strong that Waldland had come all the way from Germany to Isola to congratulate Tancredi on his marriage.

The Baron was short in stature, rather overweight, had a rosy complexion, blue eyes and flaxen hair, and was as jolly and good natured a fellow as could be found anywhere. Madam Alice thought he was the queerest looking and queerest acting man she ever met. He reminded her of pictures of Santa Claus, and she called him Kriss Kingle. She was moved to laugh in his face, but the gravity of his rank kept down her risibilities, and she compromised by smiling on him.

Baron Sebastian was not young, he was not even passibly handsome, he had an affected style, acquired by long association with stylish people, he did not talk well, or dress in good taste, but he was good-natured, and always beaming with kindness and politeness, at least as he understood what kindness and politeness should be. Above everything else was his devotion to Madam Tancredi. Her service was his, her pleasure his charge, her words his commands. Her smiles captivated him.

What happens when a homely man lays earnest siege to a lovely woman's heart?

It generally comes to pass that his suit is more favorably received than that of a more pretentious suitor.

If a lover is devoted to his mistress, without being too servile and obtrusive, it is small consequence what his exterior may be, or whether or not he is rich, noble, or stylishly dressed. Indeed, as the lovers of the latter class presume on their personal attractions, rather than on their devotedness, the chances are very much in favor of the plain suitor. Ben Jonson preferred a cripple for a sweetheart; probably because she had small temptation to share her charms with others. A homely man, being little in demand, is not likely to divide his attentions among many charmers. It is the plain, unpretentious dove that perches on the leafy bough and coos in love's lament, while the valiant eagle soars high and far, and looks down on a hundred admirers. Baron Sebastian was a social dove.

On one occasion a hastily made up party was making ready for a run down to lake Como, and a dance; the diligences were at the door, some were already off, and others only waited on the life and queen of the circle—Madam Tancredi. She was brought in from one of her rambles.

Make haste, and get ready. It was time to be off. Was she not going along?

The time was too short; the notification so sudden; why had they not told her sooner?

She knew it almost as soon as any one. Signora Adelaide was one of the leaders who had got the impromptu affair up, and she was even now well on her way with her husband to lake Como. The Signora fully expected Madam to be one of the party.

But the Signor, Madam's husband, was out on the mountains, and would not be home till dark.

There was the Baron; why not press him into her service! He would willingly superintend the transportation of her valise.

Yes, she would go, and away they went to Cemo, distant ten miles.

Signora Adelaide was a little displeased because her sister-in-law come on without her husband, and she expressed her regret thereat.

"What possible harm, my dear Adelaide, is there in my presence here without the Signor?"

"The harm is only in appearance, dear."

"Who will judge it wrong, even in appearance? Are we not friends, coming and going *carte blanche?* The very informality of our associations ought to prevent such hypercriticism."

"Well, sister, we will not call it wrong."

"And, besides, have I not the purest and most discreet of sisters for my chaperon? Both of us have that zealous protector, Signor Cyrello. Then there's my lackey, Kriss Kingle."

"I wish the Baron had not come with you."

"What! Not jealous of the Baron! Why, he's the most inoffensive creature in the world! He prefers wine to women, and would prefer capon before talking love, even to me."

"And yet he does not pine all his time eating and drinking, for see, he comes! and I'll wager he seeks you for the waltz."

"Done! Baron, we were speaking of you. Tell us, do you prefer wine to our society?"

"Ah! you honor me, ladies, by making so much notice for me! My friends will row on the lake, and sent me to ask you two ladies to join us. Will you go?"

"Don't you prefer a waltz to a sail on the lake? Hear the superb music!" said Madam Alice.

"Ach Gott! The diligence make me tired all over! The boat is better as the dance."

Signora Adelaide declined the Baron's invitation, but urged Madam Alice to accept. The latter went with the Baron.

The German had posted a band of musicians—a harpist, violinist, and a performer on the guitar, with a quartette of singers, on one of the islets near. The soft, sweet strains of the music came floating over the drowsy waters like mystic melodies from isles enchanted.

The night was Italian. The moon hung like a burnished shield of silver in that gorgeous ether seen in no other sky. The dreamy lake lay like a steel mirror in the mellow light, while islands and castles cast grotesque shadows on the polished surface.

Far away in the northwest the solemn mountains lifted up their spectre peaks against the azure; on the southern shore the broken hills stretched along like giants asleep, and from their gloomy dells an occasional convent bell rang out on the still night.

Madam Tancredi, beware of where thou art drifting!

She heeds not! She is entranced! She dreams on the drowsy waters; she hears you not small voice! Call louder !

Float on, lotus-lulled woman, nor dream that thou art drifting from husband, and peace and good name!

At midnight, Tancredi, haggard and excited, entered the place of revelry.

"Where is my wife?" he asked his sister, as soon as he could catch her private ear.

"She is here. How troubled you look, Michele What is the matter?"

"But, take me to my wife; I must and will see her immediately."

"Now, I think me, she is out on the lake; it is time for her return. Sit down while I order refreshments; you look tired and hungry."

"On the lake? Who is with her?

"A party of friends; the Baron is one."

"Damnation !"

"Michele! My brother! Now I see; now I

understand all !   Do not speak it ; let me not name it !
Let me appeal to thee, thus, and as thy better angel,
implore thee to banish the fiend from thy thoughts."

While speaking, she drew her arm around his
neck.

"But her conduct, my sister."

"She is sometimes imprudent, never false. She is
too proud to be else than true."

" Believ'st thou so, my sister ?" asked the miserable
husband, pleased to meet with doubt and opposition to
his suspicions.

"I am sure it is as I say ; I cannot be deceived in
her. And now, let thy sister advise thee ; show not
thyself to the company to-night, but retire at once.
Seem not to suspect thy wife, ·for if she detects thee
in that, thy happiness will be marred forever.   'Tis
thy sister that pleads with thee, thy sister, who is as
jealous of thy good name as thou cans't be. Go ; and
remember that thy wife is here by my request, and
that with my knowledge and consent she is now enjoying a harmless sail on the lake. Good-night !"

The next morning, to the astonishment of the
guests, the Signor put in an appearance at breakfast.
He showed by his demeanor that he was acting on his
sister's advice.

But, in spite of re-assuring remonstrances from
Signora Adelaide, in spite of his own reasoning and

his sense of honor, the green-eyed monster took up its
residence as his skeleton-in-closet.   It grinned at him
with fanged jaws, and by times beat at the door as if
about to burst forth and scandalize the world with its
hideousness.   He succeeded in suppressing every
revolt, and keeping it locked up in the dark.

Early in autumn Signor Tancredi and wife crossed
the Splügen Pass, traveled through Switzerland to the
Rhine, and down that stream to Holland, and on to
Paris, where they arrived in October.

CHAPTER XXI.

"Lie in the lap of Sin and not mean harm !
It is hypocrisy against the devil."

Among the persons whom Tancredi first met in Paris was the stolid and irrepressible German, Baron Sebastian von Waldland. If that nobleman had been endowed with the minimum *sal Atticum* he would have instantly seen that the Signor, his late friend, was anything but pleased to meet him. But either he did not, or pretended not to feel the cold shoulder.

"I was looking for you everywhere, and I think you was make lost, my friend," he said, as he shook the Signor by the unwilling hand.

"I thought you were in Madrid by this time," replied the Italian, coldly.

"I changed my mind."

Tancredi attempted to pass on, but the obtuse fellow would not be shaken.

"I am glad you come ;" said he, standing in the way of the impatient Signor. "I wouldn't rent rooms till I got your opinion. Will you look at them to-day, and shall we go to them now ?"

"Not to-day. I am but just arrived myself, and not settled down. It is impossible for me to look at them now."

"Well, then, to-morrow. Shall I expect you to-morrow?"

On the morrow forenoon the two men inspected the rooms referred to, situated on the Rue Lafitte, and as they were pronounced fit to shelter a prince, the Baron closed the bargain with the petit hostess, who carried enough keys at her girdle to open all the cells in the Bastile itself.

In the afternoon, Tancredi rented an establishment for himself and wife on the South Boulevart St. Germain, as far removed from his evil genius as was consistent with living in fashionable Paris.

But go where he would, he met the Baron. He did not wish to quarrel with the fellow, for that would require explanations which his sense of dignity could not tolerate. The dullard would not take the broad hints offered him. If he would only commit some overt act which would serve as an ostensible excuse for cutting his acquaintance; but no, each day found him more and more complaisant.

He had, notwithstanding his stupidity, a cunning force about him which inveigled the Signor into dining with him.

"My rooms must be christened, you know," he

said, and, in spite of himself, Tancredi found himself seated at the Baron's board, with the spirits of a monumental urn at a funeral repast.

It was next to impossible to evade the suave but pig-headed Sebastian. His stolidity was proof against excuse or argument. Indeed, with him, argumentation was an organic blank, as is the musical faculty in a mule. He never argued, scarcely knew the meaning of the term. All the indignant Signor could do was to grin and bear with him, and in a measure return his civilities. Before ten days had elapsed, the Baron had resumed his familiar footing in the Tancredi family, which had been abruptly broken off in the valley of the Lira.

Madam Alice had not the slightest suspicion of her husband's jealousy of the Baron, or that his friendship for that person had cooled. She was really gratified at the renewal of the acquaintance with the droll fellow, and said so. She was a stranger in Paris, and trusted that he might serve in driving away the *ennui* which already threatened her. Her husband's friends were not to appear in Paris until after Christmas, and until they did come, it would be convenient and agreeable to have near her one of the old Alpine companions to talk over the exploits of the past summer. Besides, the Baron had the *entree* of good society, and was therefore capable of rendering her good service.

She had not a spark of feeling for him that could be construed into love. She had no more thought of flirting with him, than she had of eloping with Signor Cyrello, her brother-in-law. A feeling equally well defined alike by honor and pride would have kept her clear of indiscretion, even if she had been tempted to flirt with the Baron; but she was not even tempted.

And yet she liked the German nobleman in a way. That way carried with it its own interpretation to her conscience, but it would have been remarkable if her husband and the Baron did not misinterpret her behavior.

Her husband saw in her actions the occult but significant encouragement of the Baron's almost open passion for her. Jealousy lent him her spectacles.

The German was attracted by her smiles. Her apathy for her husband confirmed him in the belief that she was partial to his suit. His hope was carried along by stages, until he finally believed that by devotion and patience he was sure of his coveted prize. Devotion and patience constituted his stock in trade, and he settled down in earnest to the siege.

It has already been shown how Madam Tancredi viewed the affair, or rather how she did not view it, for as an affair it had no existence in her mind.

She was so accustomed to flattering attentions from the men that she had come to hold their homage as her due, and hence she received the devotions of the Baron as her right to a claim established by custom and usage. She respected his title, was flattered by his keen interest in her welfare, and grateful for his generosity; but she never dreamed of him as a lover, and least of all as her lover. He was to her an unassuming, harmless, good-natured fellow, too platonic for romance, and too epicurean for so ethereal a passion as love. Yet she did flatter herself that, next to eating and drinking, he liked her better than he did any one else, just as many other men of her acquaintance admired her. Thus she came to monopolize his attentions, and finally to elect him a kind of knight errant, for which service she paid him in smiles and gracious words.

Had a friend said to her, " Beware of the Baron!" she would have laughed, and mockingly replied, beware my hairdresser, the butler, the *valet de* **chambre**, or beware any man who serves me. Baron Sebastian is my factotum, not my lover.

Thus this single and simple affair, which should have been plainly intelligible to every unbiased mind, was warped and colored by the three minds, weighted with vanity, jealousy, and lust.

It is not a question of which passion is the more blameworthy, since each one put out the eyes of reason and led the victim into folly. Mischief is the inevitable sequence when a coquettish wife, a jealous husband and a voluptuary are thrown together. The story of the eating of forbidden fruit may be a fable, but it contains the triune elements which make it possible.

It was about this time that Tancredi received Berta's letter.

The Signor began to feel, with Othello, that his occupation was gone, when he learned how readily Rosetta turned from him to another. He was no longer in demand among females; even Rosetta had forgotten him. The coldness of his wife surprised and pained him, but he was dumbfounded at the behavior of the cantatrice. If he had ever felt secure of any woman's love, it was that of Rosetta's; and, behold, it was gone! He could believe anything after that, even the inconstancy of his wife. He was prepared for any new humiliation.

If Rosetta had played him false, what could he expect of his wife? The latter had never loved him with the tithe of the passion felt by the former, and therefore it would require less temptation to deflect her from the straight line of honor and duty. He distrusted his wife more and more after hearing of Rosetta's desertion, and saw every day what were to him flagrant proofs of her inconstancy.

Apart from the fact that the Baron was playing

with fire over a powder magazine, it was amusing to watch his actions in the rôle of a Lothario. He exhibited three sides to view, the philosophic, the tragic and the humorous. He started a problem in race physiology. What effect has race on a lover?

The North American savage courts his dusky squaw by prowess and strategy. He is fleet of foot and long-winded.

The Englishman is mated by primordial stipulation—his matrimonial fate is provided for by decree. Leisure, beef and conservatism take the place of passion and adventure.

The Frenchman wins his way to woman's smiles by blandishment—he bows and gyrates, he is agile, witty and polite.

The American courts, as he does everything, in a sweat. He is restless and lean, daring and ambitious.

The German Baron was lusty and healthy, stolid and conceited. He had ever paid his court to woman as to an inferior being—a being educated to receive his caresses as his right and her duty, not to be questioned.

But now he was paying his court to a woman graduated in a different school. Her love was to be won, not commanded; he therefore changed his tactics. His change of methods included a change in the man also. He began to sweat and lose flesh. He grew restless, lost his appetite, drank less wine, slept less soundly—he went to work on the American plan.

He became more lavish and exquisite in dress and jewelry, had his towy hair dyed a smoky black, drank cocktails, and even went so far as to come out a radical Whig, and violently assailed the administration of Jackson. The Baron sank his nationality, sacrificed his class prerogative, and assumed a character which, although ridiculous, would have been creditable had his motives been patriotic and his love honorable.

Of course Madam Tancredi's head was turned with the beautiful, the voluptuous Paris, where pleasure is reduced to a science, and practised as the first of all fine arts. She was about to enter into its exquisite mysteries, and drink of its famed enchantments. She was wealthy in her own right, was young, beautiful and accomplished, and wedded into a noble and influential family. No society was too patrician for her. Her conceit began at the *faubourg du beau monde*, and stopped in the centre of *le grand cercle de Tuilleries*.

Her first step was to secure an establishment in a fashionable quarter, and in keeping with her rank and station. She summarily vetoed the selection made by her husband, and prevailed on him to secure a mansion on the handsome Boulevart des Italians, which was not then filled with shops as now.

The external wonders of the city, its boulevards,

public buildings, picture galleries and theatres, occupied her time, and afforded her passable amusement until after Christmas, when the Cyrellos joined them.

Madam Alice gave a ball in honor of the arrival of her sister-in-law. It was a fair success, most a success as the initial of a round of merry-making in which Madam played a conspicuous part, and all through which, to the very close, she maintained her reputation for beauty, grace and grandeur, with as much ease as when she ruled queen of the more sober assemblages of the American republic.

But she had her worry. With her, ambition was not quite satiated. She could not forget that her position in European society was due to the influential family into which she had married. Every acquaintance she had made, and every pleasure enjoyed by her, were owing to the patronage of her husband and his family. She keenly felt the abasement. In spite of her independence she was dependent. This proud, self-willed American, imbued from her cradle up with the doctrine of equal rights—that seductive slogan of republics—could no more brook social kings than political kings. She felt herself the equal of any Tancredi that ever wore a coronet.

This subjection, so galling to her pride, was one reason why she treated her husband so disdainfully. She could not shake off the Italian guiding reins, but she took the bit in her teeth and run away with the proprieties. She was exacting, tyrannical, imprudent and headstrong. She selected the Paris residence, and she claimed proprietorship over Baron Sebastian.

At a soirée given by Madam Milon, a friend and schoolmate of Signora Adelaide, she met, for the first time since her marriage, the Vicompte Bertrand, the attache of the French Legation at Washington, and spoken of in a former chapter of this book.

Here was one acquaintance she did not owe to her husband or his family. He was her own friend, and, compared with those about her, an old familiar friend. She had met him in the long ago, during the romantic days of maidenhood, in America, at home.

Those who, on distant shores, have met persons from home, from the same loved home, will appreciate Madam's feelings at meeting the Count under such circumstances as surrounded her. The heart almost leaps out to meet our acquaintances on such occasions. Long and bitter feuds have been forgotten and for-given by an accidental meeting among Alpine solitudes, and the coldness of a formal acquaintance has melted into the warmest friendship by a toilsome companion-ship among the snows of Jung Frau, or the glaciers of Mont Blanc.

The stately atmosphere surrounding Madam was quickened by the warm presence of her friend, Count

Bertrand. The sight of him awakened memories of home and country. He was at her side in a moment, pouring into her willing ear congratulations at her marriage, and his pleasure at meeting her in his native land.

"Welcome to Paris, my dear Madam, welcome! If you will permit one to greet you, who is himself but just arrived after an absence of three years."

"Thank you, Count Bertrand. But are you just come from America? And what news do you bring from there? Pray sit down beside me and tell me, for I am starving to hear from home."

"But just arrived, Madam, and the news I bring is, your countrymen are preparing for the *coup d'etat ;*—what do you call him?"

"Change of administration?"

"Yes; the inauguration of President Van Buren. What a mistake your General Jacksong make! What opportunities! What a destiny he throw away! He like the Grand Emperor in everything but that. Bonaparte not act the infant, the imbecile, like that! The Grand Bank! The Grand Armee! Your infant Jacksong he fling zem all away! The imbecile!"

"You don't understand. My countrymen are all sovereigns, and jealous of other rulers, even of Jackson, the man of whom they are proud. The people are wary of bestowing patronage and power in the hands of their officials, and they are right. Were the people of the United States to give their President the Bank, it would be giving him vast patronage and power, which would be the source of danger in the hands of the unscrupulous. All honor to Jackson for refusing it! We might as well give our President a crown as a National Bank."

"Ah! Bien Dieu! That the mistake, the grand mistake of America! The ignorant, the demagogue, the irresponsible to rule; that the grand mistake! It can't last forever."

"No government lasts that long, not even France, that has experimented with all forms of government from imperialism to anarchism, and back again, and yet contented herself with none. But tell me something outside of politics, for it is plain that you and I will not agree on that topic. Tell me of American society, what it says and does."

"It misses the charming Miss Bannemead."

"Ah, I see you have not forgotten how to flatter! I should think that after three years sojourn among plain dealing republicans you would have learned what candor means. You are the true Parisian still!"

"Shall I tell you, candid, what I learned in America?"

"Yes, pray."

"I learned that you are the most charming woman

in the world.   You deserve Paris, and Paris deserves you."

"There you go, again!   Worse, and more of it! You don't believe the half you say."

"Not believe!   Ah, it is you who doubts!   You will never know how I worship you!"

"I shall put your devotion to a severe test, nay, to many severe trials, ere I leave Paris, my friend.   But before the ordeal of battle, I give you one more chance to renounce your hasty declaration."

"Learn then that I am your slave.   See, my ship's burning!"

"There, that will do, Count Bertrand.   I will not allow you to compromise your freedom in so forlorn a cause.   Repentance will follow your rashness, and you will desert me at last.   Beware!"

"Put me to the test, Madam;   I am ready to obey your every command."

"Well, I am here to enjoy Paris; you can help me.   Can I count on your knightship?"

"I pledge my glove to lift lance in no cause but thine."

This conversation was only the badinage of temperament, seasoned with the hyperbole of polite license, and as harmless as the sparks struck from flint and steel.   At least it was harmless while it remained the confidential by-play of two wits, as were Madam and the Count. But unfortunately such *jeu de mots* are too often followed by conduct correspondingly free and easy, when it is no longer simple pleasantry between two friends.

The flirtations carried on between Madam Alice and Count Bertrand were not concealed, nor was there attempt at concealment, since they were only meant as innocent pastime of two dashing people. But society, and especially the observant and suspicious husband, was not so charitable as to view their conduct as they meant it should be viewed.

The Baron, too, saw and formed his opinion. He took pains to impress the Count with his competitive presence, and the two men tacitly agreed to hold each other as enemies. The Baron was inclined to show his teeth, but the gay Count treated him with the disdain he would a menial, which only exasperated the German that much the more.

Madam Alice looked on and smiled at the rivalry. To her it had no serious aspect, and was only a stirring compliment to her. Not many ladies could boast of having two noblemen at dagger's point on their account. It required the most skillful finessing to maintain her supremacy with both lovers. Partiality shown either would offend the other, and possibly precipitate a discreditable scene. The Baron was the more stubborn and troublesome, while the less importunate Frenchman was disposed to yield rather than endure the presence of his despicable rival.

Let not the behavior of these two gentlemen be misunderstood. It was not flagrant, it was scarcely indiscreet, and is equalled every day by society men, who are not supposed to infringe on the rules of decorum. Their conduct was reprehensible, chiefly because of its exclusiveness toward a married woman with a jealous husband.

The truth is, Madam Alice, although not always circumspect, was sagacious, and firm as a rock; it was no effort for her to permit passion's wave to rise so far, but no farther. While her speech and manner had in them the banter of invitation, yet there was a proud haughtiness in her demeanor that restrained her admirers, and kept them within the bounds of respectful moderation.

The Baron, too, was cautious, and yet his sneaking, underhand ways, indicated the degree of his infatuation and determination. The attentions of the vivacious Frenchman were open, and, in a way, manly. His *bonhomie* gave him license; she laughed at his compliments, and treated his vows as the empty gallantries of a privileged courtier.

CHAPTER XXII.

"High minds of native pride and force,
Most deeply feel thy pang's, remorse."

FIFTY years ago!   If any one lives who knew
Paris that long ago, they will surely recollect the *cafe
restaurant, Cadran Bleu,* at that time, and for many
years the most famous establishment of its kind in
that city, and, for that matter, in the world.   It was
situated fronting on the Boulevard du Temple.   On
the first floor front, was a cozy alcove, formed by a
partition built to conceal an unused stairway.   This
retreat, named *trou dans le mur,* contained a small
table and two chairs, and was the favorite lounging
place for the idler who was fortunate to find it vacant.
In addition to its seclusion it afforded its occupant
opportunity for seeing all that went on in the main
saloon without himself being seen.

It was two days after the court ball, given by the
King, Louis Phillipe, that Vicompte Bertrand was seated
in this alcove, leisurely sipping wine and smoking a
cigar.   He gazed abstractedly out the front window
at the throng on the street, while his thoughts ran on
the king's ball and the people he had met there.

Among them, and now uppermost in his thoughts, was Madam Tancredi, who rivaled the proudest beauties of the brilliant French court. Her dress, worn on the occasion, was a marvel of gorgeous beauty, and never was her loveliness more bewitching or her wit more sparkling than when she stood among the illustrious throng that filled the salons of the Tuilleries. The praise of *Le Belle Americaine* was on every tongue; the Citizen King himself honored her with flattering notice.

The gratified husband forgot his heart-burnings as he watched his proud wife. Her triumph, to his mind, was the deserved tribute paid the most admirable woman in the world. As she swept past him leaning on the arm of a prince, his heart swelled with joy and pride. She filled the measure of his ideal woman, for whom no sacrifice was too great if repaid by her smiles.

But her smiles that evening were not for him. He was consoled, however, when he saw that she had no smiles for her usual satellites, the Count and the Baron.

The persevering Baron, by rare fortune, or by his impudence, did manage to secure her for a brief waltz. With this exception, the two rivals were baffled at every turn by more distinguished suitors, and they expressed their common chagrin by scowling at each other.

All this was running through the Count's mind as he lounged in the hole-in-the-wall at the Cadran Bleu. He had not met Madam Tancredi since the ball; and he regretted the rash vow he had made to never see her again. He sighed, and poured out another glass of wine.

He now became conscious of the presence of a loud-talking party of gentlemen in the main saloon, where they sat around a table drinking. A remark made by one of them, struck his ear as a familiar voice, and on looking through the small opening in the wall he saw that the speaker was Baron Sebastian von Waldland.

"And you, too, Baron, are one of the favored friends of the beautiful American; how lucky!"

"I have that distinguished honor," replied the Baron, with affected modesty.

"You even danced with her at the Tuilleries Ball! Lucky fellow! Where did you make her acquaintance?"

"In Lombardy. I passed the summer with her and her husband."

"What sort of a person is he? The Signor looks distinguished, and, I am told, is an Italian nobleman."

"Oh, he's so, so! He is an Italian nobleman; but

what of that? I don't think his wife cares much for him," answered Sebastian in a contemptuous tone.

"Indeed! Why, he appears very fond of, and devoted to her. How's that?"

"Oh, very watchful and jealous, you mean," exclaimed Waldland.

"Jealous? Of whom should he be jealous, pray?"

"That is a leading question; do you think it would be just the square thing to give that person away?" asked the Baron, with a wink, and a leer around the table.

"O, Lord! Not jealous of you, Sebastian!" exclaimed one of the party.

They all laughed at the contemplation of Tancredi's endangered honor, and the vanity of the Baron in the invidious inuendo which made him out the intriguer.

The laugh was interpreted aright, for he attempted to look savage.

"Why, didn't you know that the Baron is a lady-killer?" asked one of the gentlemen, who appeared to be but slightly impressed with the ridiculous bravado of his companion.

"No! you don't tell me! I have heard him spoken of as one who has killed his man, but never as a lady-killer," replied another, with the evident intent of ridiculing the statement made by the Baron.

"Well, I suppose we may look for a duel one of these mornings before breakfast. What say you, Sebastian; is there a prospect for a fight between you and the Italian?"

"Amuse yourselves, gentlemen," replied the Baron, goaded into showing his mettle. "Your talk may have a more serious meaning than you intend."

"What! has it gone so far as that?"

"It has gone so far that the Signor, who was my best friend, is now my worst foe. What can be his grudge if it is not his wife's partiality for me, and mine for her?"

"Do you really think that she is partial to you, or that the Signor's coldness for you is caused by the suspicion that you are her lover?"

"What else? But what care I? Is she not worth risking a life for? For her I would fight a duel any day. Say, you who have seen her, is she not worth fighting for?"

"Her beauty and grace are unquestionable; but will fighting win her? For my part I do not think so. She is not the style of women that get mixed up in our too common liaisons," said a pale youth, who spoke for the first time.

"Ah, Clarence; child. You are always looking at women as you do at your paintings—beauty and virtue, one and inseparable. All beautiful women are

not Madonnas, my friend," said the Baron in a patronizing manner.

"And you are always placing a base construction
on the acts of every woman who may be polite to you.
A chaste woman might as well sleep under a Upas as
look kindly on you. Now, I believe that this beautiful American has been polite to you and nothing
more," retorted the young artist, with a rising flush of
anger on his pale face.

"I'll wager you a thousand francs and the supper
that before next May, Madam Tancredi will be with
me in Madrid," exclaimed the Baron, rising to his
feet.

"I accept the wager," defiantly cried the artist,
throwing down his purse on the table.

Count Bertrand sprang from the alcove with the
agility of a cat and dashed a glass of wine in the surprised Baron's face.

"Scoundrel! You shall answer for this! You
know where to find me," exclaimed Bertrand, and was
gone before the party could fully realize what was
done.

As the Count anticipated, he was that evening
waited on by a friend of the Baron with a challenge
to fight.

"I name the Grand Cascade, Bois de Boulogne,

10*

the place; sunrise to-morrow, the time; the rapier, the weapon," was the answer.

It is not necessary to accompany the duellos to the sanguinary field. By staying away the battle can be waged to suit the more or less martial disposition of the individual reader, and fancy can have full play in the field drama, accordingly as it shall endow the rival swordsmen with skill, bravery, or good fortune. Of course it is probable that all will sympathize with the gallant Frenchman, who has undertaken the perilous task of punishing the traducer of a lovely woman's character; but history must be inexorable if worthy of credence, even if patriots bleed in vain, traitors trail freedom in the dust, or woman's tarnished honor goes unredressed. The Count was disabled by receiving an ugly but not mortal thrust in his sword arm. The Baron immediately fled.

Too many persons knew of the affair, besides it was too fond a sensation, to remain a secret from the gossipy Parisians, and before twenty-four hours the duel was the talk of the town.

Tancredi and wife were seated at breakfast when he first learned of the affair by reading the account in a newspaper.

"So, Madam, your penchant for surrounding yourself with profligate adventurers is beginning to bear fruit! Read that!"

The alarmed woman seized the paper and read what is given here as a translation.

" Two gentlemen, well known in the fashionable circles of Paris, have just terminated a sanguinary conflict with rapiers in the Bois du Boulogne. Vicompte Bertrand Tridensat is the victim, having been transfixed by the weapon of his rival, Baron Sebastian von Waldland, and it is thought cannot recover. The Baron has fled from France. It is the more pity, since the quarrel grew out of the jealous rivalry between the two noblemen for the favors of the woman called the Belle Americaine, who so recently flashed like a comet on society. It is said that she tried the experiment of dividing her charms among three men—her husband, and the two lovers. The result is the duel, which proves what has been proven so often before, that such an amorous feat is impossible. She was foolish, but the greater fools they. She may, now that she is likely to have leisure, profit by looking up the precepts of Monsieur Franklin, her illustrious countryman."

As she finished reading, the paper fell from her hands, and she turned in consternation to meet her husband's anger. He was gone! She rang for her maid, who assisted her to her room.

Servants were sent in search of the Signor, and

others dispatched to summon Signora Adelaide. The husband could not be found; the sister-in-law hurried to the Boulevart des Italiens, where she was immediately shown into the presence of Madam Tancredi.

"You have heard! I see by your face you have heard!" exclaimed Madam Alice, hastening forward to meet the Signora.

"Alas! yes, my sister I have heard!"

"But the cruel newspapers—the heartless account they give—have you seen them? And do you think me the guilty thing they make me?"

"No, sister; no. I shall believe that much I know; that much and nothing more."

"Oh! tell me what you do believe—what you have seen in my conduct deserving of blame. Tell me—help me to conclude, for I cannot think for myself. As God is my judge I never meant to do wrong."

"Ah, my sister, we sometimes do wrong when we mean it not. Your wrong is that, nothing more, nothing worse. That is what I think of your conduct."

"Thank you for that! Oh, I thank you for that, my kindest and best of sisters," cried the distressed woman, putting her arms around her sister's neck.

The two women talked the matter over until they came to understand, trust and love each other, as they never had before. The American was contrite and humble, the Italian forbearing and tender. Madam begged the Signora to intercede with Signor Tancredi on her behalf.

" Had I heeded your sisterly admonitions, my best of friends, had I patterned after your discreet example, I would not now be suffering from shame and remorse. I must set about repairing my errors at once, and I wish to begin by asking my husband to forgive and restore me to his confidence."

Tancredi could not be found. It was two days before he returned to his house.

On leaving his wife reading the account of the duel, he went straightway to the *prefecture* **de police**, where he learned that the department had no official knowledge of the combat or the whereabouts of the combatants. He next visited the lodgings of the principals, but their servants knew nothing, or affected to know nothing, of their masters' movements. He made a trip to the spot where the duel was said to have taken place. From a keeper of the Bois he learned that a person supposed to be one of the duelists was seen on the morning of the fight hurriedly crossing the bridge that leads to the Versailles highway. He followed to that city to learn that the fugitive had fled toward Tours. Arrived there he lost all trace of the Baron, for the description suited that person ; when he returned to Paris. He revisited the lodgings of

Count Bertrand, where he found that nobleman, and to whose presence he was admitted.

He learned from the Count the full particulars of the cause which led to the encounter, and, of course, how Madam Tancredi became implicated in the scandal.

Throughout the interview the Signor acted in the most dignified and honorable manner. It is true he did not, he could not, condone the scandal by extending his hand in fellowship to the poor Count who craved it, but he thanked him for his intentions, which he thought were possibly honorable.

"You should have remembered that I am the only custodian of my wife's honor. You should also have foreseen that any attempt on your part to vindicate my wife's reputation would result in misunderstanding and misrepresentation by the public, even as it is misunderstood and misrepresented. Your act places me in a delicate and mortifying position, and you must see and agree that henceforth our hitherto friendly relations must terminate."

The information obtained at the interview with Count Bertrand modified and mollified his indignation toward his wife. He now saw that, although she had been indiscreet, she was innocent of any direct complicity in the disgraceful affair. He blamed her for encouraging the presence of such a debauchee as the

Baron had proved himself to be, but he cleared her of any flagrant wrong-doing. His entrance into her presence was, therefore, marked by the most praiseworthy tenderness and forbearance on his part. She clung to him imploring his forgiveness, and manifesting more hearty consideration for him than ever before. She saw and appreciated the delicate though spirited indignation that prompted him to terminate the friendship between her and the Count ; while he, on the other hand, was re-assured by her humble penitence.

The storm that shook the domestic sky, lulled into quietude, and vanishing clouds let in more and more beautiful sunlight than ever shone on them before. They began to entertain for each other, if not love, respect, a passion more reliable, more reasonable and more enduring.

It was agreed, for reasons that are apparent, that they should leave Paris forthwith. Tancredi was joined by his sister in favor of Naples, but Madam was so tired of society, so broken by the scandal, and so homesick, that a compromise was made on Philadelphia. Inside a week, Signor Tancredi and wife were on their way to America.

CHAPTER XXIII.

"And you, my friend! how shall I thank you?
What shall I do to show my grateful heart?"

THESE few more last words connected with the subject of the duel, may seem chronologically out of place; but some reparation seems due the gallant Count Bertrand, who risked his life to vindicate a lady's good name, and who, after receiving a wound in her cause, was summarily excluded from the society and friendship of the family he had so disinterestedly served, and whose gratitude he deserved. If reparation is to be made, it must be made here.

Besides, the historian has recently come into possession of additional and later testimony in the case,— testimony which is sufficiently important to open up the case, repair the injustice done the Count, and vindicate the honor of the family of Tancredi.

The two very brief letters referred to as new testimony, came into our possession lately, through the kindness of a renowned tenor singer, who spent some time in Paris, where he became acquainted with and warmly attached to Count Bertrand.

It will be seen that the author of the first letter

was the son of Madam Tancredi. It will also be seen that he, happily, knew absolutely nothing of his mother's reputation as a coquette, but only knew that Count Bertrand had once performed for her a gallant deed, in that he attempted to punish the traducer of her character.

And that was all he should have known of that transaction. Had he, unfortunately, known all, it is probable that his filial piety would have suffered a severe strain, and it is almost certain that shame would have prevented him from doing justice to the brave Count.

Oblivion, after all, is kind, if not just. It does seem sad and cruel to see noble deeds—the heroism and romance of the past, prostrated and broken by that insatiable iconoclast, Oblivion! But there is in it all, a beautiful compensating mercy in the burial of the ugliness and wickedness which marred the symmetry of the lost creation.

Young Castlerank has been engaged for the past three years in sowing wild oats. He fled from home and country the other night to escape an appalling harvest.

What a much larger crop he would have sown had he known of his father's youthful labors in the same field! Pretty girls and wild oats are not modern products, nor their cultivation modern industries.

Old men charge young men with being the wick-
edest of all times. The accusation is a libel on youth
and the present age. Morals are older, immorals
fresher; morality lingers with the aged, and is the last
glimmering spark of virtue that goes out with the
dying heart, while immorality runs riot in young
blood and gambols with the lambs. That is a great
difference, and why they are so easily distinguished
from each other.

Oblivion covers up the dens and ravages of the old
foxes; the ancient reynards forget what cunning
cubs they were among their neighbors pullets. They
were right in giving up their youthful follies, even
in memory, but wrong in expecting the young to give
them up. If blood will tell, and it will, then fathers
should expect their boys to sow wild oats.

But, the letters.

Philadelphia, Sept. 30, 18—.

To Count Bertrand Tridensat.

My Dear old Friend.

I hasten to write you a note on the heels of
my letter of yesterday.

I meet with surprises every hour. At this rate
I shall be compelled to write you every day, or lose
my identity altogether. Sometimes, even now, I
pinch myself to see if it is myself.

Learn what I have fresh discovered!

I incidentally mentioned your name and title to Madam, who is now my mother, no longer ago than last night. She was greatly moved when I informed her that you and I are as bosom friends.

What, think you, she did?

No less than take me to her boudoir, where, after having locked the door, she proceeded to narrate the account of a duel which was fought on her account, and in which a certain gentleman of my acquaintance was severely wounded.

So, *mon vieux*, you had your wise secret from me all the time we have known each other! What a sly old comrade it was not to disclose its romance to me! But you see how cleverly a woman has exposed you! And I bless you more for good than ever! Protector of my mother's good name, I thank you everything.

Adieu,

C. TANCREDI.

PARIS, Nov. 4th, 18—.

CARL TANCREDI.

Mon cher Garçon:

What do you think happened? The little *fille de boutique*, Fanchon, came tripping into my room just as I sat down to enjoy your letters, and I think is now my enemy, because I would not allow her to read them. She affects to believe that you have another sweetheart in America; but I understood her ruse. We compromised by allowing her to furnish the *papier a lettre* for my reply. Her message to you is the perfume on the paper,—jessamine, it is not, and exquisite ?

Say nothing of thanks, my dear boy, for what you are kind enough to consider a deed of valor on my part. You know very little about it. It was not considered valorous at the time, I painfully remember, now nearly a quarter of a century ago; at least one of the persons most interested did not applaud my action in the matter. But times are changed, and opinions also.

I proceed to tell you something never told before; and which no one but I can tell.

Baron Sebastian von Waldland fled to Madrid, I think to escape the vengeance of your father, the Signor. Six months after the duel I heard of his whereabouts and followed him there, determined to renew the combat; for, you see, it was an accident that disabled me, and not his skill,—my foot rolled on a loose stick.

When I reached Madrid he was dead—stabbed by a stiletto in the hands of an outraged husband. I stood on his grave.

In haste, yours, as ever,

B. Tridensat.

CHAPTER XXIV.

"Thy words convince me; all my doubts vanish."

When Rosetta Godardo returned to her fireside, after having seen her lover off on his voyage, she sat down alone and meditated over her new environments. Joy was the dominant emotion in her breast—joy at having been rescued from the toils which Tancredi had woven about her. But a short time since her every thought was how to win him back; now her joy was at her escape from his thralldom.

And yet, there was a lurking disquiet in her mind; a disquiet which was akin to dread and remorse. She strove to banish the feeling, but it asserted itself more and more strongly, until it became the cruel absorbing thought.

This disquiet was because she had not told John Taplan fully and candidly all there was to tell of her history before she consented to become his wife. She had presumed on his clemency in advance of the claim on which his forgiveness was predicated. Next to the doubtful honesty of withholding the statement due him, and which he must know sooner or later, was the painful thought that explanations and statements would not now come with the same spontaneous grace, nor be received by him with the same respect, as they would had she made a clean breast of it at the start.

John Taplan was her accepted lover; and what a lover! How delicate, how considerate of her feelings, how concerned for her welfare! And what a trust he had confided in her! "You are innocent: that is all I have the right to know, all I wish to know," were his very words. Was her candor equal to this trust? Was her innocence equal to his confidence? And his considerate kindness in providing for her welfare during his absence! "My future wife must look to me alone for support," he had said. She was no longer dependent on the bounty of a false lover—the wages of shame! She was provided for by the purest and noblest of men! How should she, how could she repay him for his generosity? How, indeed!

By making him a true, devoted wife; by helping him. Helping him! How could she help him, as she understood help! Her mother had helped her father by spinning while he was absent on the bay of Naples. She could not spin, but she could sing.

Happy thought! She would return to the stage! While John was looking out on the dark ocean for a pathway for his ship, she would sing into fame and fortune, all for him. He should leave the wild and perilous sea, and stay with her forever.

She fell asleep in her chair and dreamed that she stood before the footlights and received the plaudits of a house packed with people enraptured at her singing. Flowers covered the stage and rolled at her feet. She looked for John Taplan in the vast audience, when she was startled by Tancredi, who came on the stage and placed a glittering necklace of diamonds around her throat. She shrieked at his touch, and awoke to find that the mischievous Berta had stolen into the room and touched her throat with a ball of the first snow of the young winter.

"Mio Dio! How you frighten one! naughty Berta! It was you, then, who spoiled my beautiful dream!"

"Of what wert thou dreaming, pretty one?"

"Of the stage, and singing thereon. O Berta, the crowds of people that clapped their hands and filled the stage with flowers! It was at my singing."

"Yes, I am sure of that! When sang'st thou that thou wert not smothered with flowers and applause?"

"Never, indeed, kind Berta! Why, oh, why did I ever quit the glorious stage?"

"Better ask thyself, why not return to the stage. Thou sing'st better than ever before; triumph awaits thee if thou wilt return to thy profession."

"Believ'st thou so, sweet Berta? I am almost persuaded thou art right, and that I should go back where I ever triumphed. But I have no one to aid me in this cold country."

"Send for Michele; he will fly to thy aid."

"God's curses on you for saying that!" exclaimed Rosetta, in a tumultuous burst of fury, as she sprang from her seat and confronted the frightened maid.

"The Madonna preserve me! What have I done that thou should'st speak so fiercely, and look so terrible?"

"Done! I'll tell you what you have done. You have roused up a fiend. If I thought that you are scheming to re-instate your master in the unholy alliance which once disgraced me, I would take this dagger and hew your false heart into pieces so small that Eternal Wrath would not find it when he came to reckon with your treacherous soul!"

Berta sank on a seat, thoroughly cowed and frightened.

"Send for Michele! Let me speak it once for all, and heed you well what I now say, that, rather than accept favor from Tancredi, I would breathe in the foul vapors to destroy speech, attaint my blood with leprosy to blot out beauty, and work my fingers down to the bone earning my daily bread. I would creep into a reeking charnel house and make famine food of carrion corpse rather than accept one penny of his prostituted bounty!"

She paused in her rage, while she caught the terrified Berta firmly by the shoulder, as if she would drag her from her seat.

"And if ever I descend to pander to his baseness again, may the Great God, in his deep wrath, drive me forth a maniac wanderer over the earth, to die at last among strangers and fill an unknown pauper's grave!"

Berta put her hands to her ears and shrieked in terror, while the Godardo, exhausted by the violence of her raving, fell prostrate on the floor. Lying there, panting and writhing for a few awful moments, she at length reached out her hands toward the horror stricken Berta, who tremblingly seized them and raised the poor girl from the floor.

"The Great Father have mercy on us and pardon our sins! But what has come over thee, my poor child?"

"Hush, Berta!" she said in a hoarse whisper, while tears filled her eyes, and she sobbed aloud. "Why wilt thou persist in talking of that wicked man! Thou know'st that it drives me mad, mad, mad! Let us banish him from our thoughts, for ever."

Rosetta turned to the window and looked out on the night. The ground was covered with snow, or as

it seemed to her, with a mantle of peace and purity.
She thought of the young sailor, watching far out at
sea—the cold sea, that suffered no mantle of snow to
cover its restless and unpitying bosom. God's emblem
of peace and purity was falling all around John Taplan, but the wrathful winds swept it into the absorbing
sea.

John Taplan's distraction all banished when he
landed at the pier and met Rosetta with her hearty
welcome. The impetuous woman at once introduced
the subject uppermost in her thoughts, and the first
thing done when they reached the cottage, was to tell
John the full and true story of her life. She told the
whole of it without evasion, prevarication or reserva-
tion ;—told it so thoroughly and plainly that her lover
understood it better than she did herself, or, which
more clearly expresses the situation, saw better than
she what part of her life to condemn, how much to
regret, and how far pity and charity might excuse or
pardon her in it all. To his mental vision she was
more sinned against than sinning.

Perhaps he saw aright. It is well to keep in mind
how his love for her may have blinded him to her
frailties ; but who has the heart to condemn his clemency—condemn him for taking the side on which
Mercy stands ?

Society is not prepared to acquit John Taplan of

blame for espousing a fallen woman; it certainly is not ready to applaud his action. Prudery, if it says nothing more bitter, will say that he was a fool.

Why a fool?

*　　　*　　　*　　　*　　　*

Bah! Who can tolerate such nauseating inconsistency?

Where the inconsistency?

The inconsistency of giving welcome hands to fast men and tramping fast women back into the mire.

A chaste, respectable woman can marry without question or comment a Don Juan whose intrigues are notorious. Reverse the conditions, and what a howl goes up from Christian throats!

If the popular rule now applied to females were applied to males with the same unrelenting and merciless stringency, the Malthus theory would no longer be a stumbling block to political economists.

The most prudent marriage between two persons of approved chastity may turn out calamitous. Fidelity after marriage is of more importance than chastity before marriage, important as is the latter. And now, if the marriage contract meditated between Taplau and the Godardo turns out bad, this history will see to it that the blame shall not be laid on the former misfortune of the woman.

Rosetta made one serious blunder at this time—she

concealed from her lover her determination to return
to the operatic stage. Her motive for this secresy
was emotional, and therefore pardonable in a woman.
Her motive was to give him an agreeable surprise.
Her heart leaped with joy in anticipation of her triumph and his astonishment. Some time on his return
from his cruise, he would find her famous, with the
New World at her feet. He would hear her name
sounded on praising lips, he would see her name in
great flaming red posters, he would read flattering
accounts of her in the newspapers. And the wealth
she would bring! She would empty the gold, the
wages of her triumph, into his lap, and say, it is
thine, as I am thine!

The little woman chuckled with delight at the
prospective glory which awaited her scheme, the
sweetest part of which would be the sly way she
would bring it about, and the sudden glare with which
it would burst on her lover. It would dazzle him!

She never once thought that he might aid her, or,
possibly object to her going on the stage. John was
a sailor, with meagre knowledge of music or the theatrical profession. Besides he had no time away from
his ship. Why bother him with a scheme he could
not aid?

As soon as he was gone on his voyage she set about
the prosecution of her enterprise. She sought an

interview with the maestro who had brought her to America. He was absent on a tour with his opera troupe, but was expected to return to New York at a fixed date.

This was the first professional disappointment of her life; the sanguine woman had not counted on impediment or delay. In her professional career she had never known what effort was in securing an engagement; the proposals had ever come unsolicited, and the trouble had been to get her on the stage. The difficulty now was to get the stage for the willing actress. Besides she had always depended on Tancredi to manage her theatrical business, who had always attended to all details without inconvenience or annoyance to her.

She sighed as she felt how lonely and helpless she was.

Alas, for that sigh, and alas for its cause. Mrs. Browning says :

> ".. This passionate sigh .., .
> May reach and stir the plumes
> Of God's calm angel standing in the sun."

But her sigh was not for Tancredi nor his patronage. But it was a sigh for what she missed through him. It was the sigh of danger.

Taplan had come again and gone before she heard

from the maestro. He made an appointment which she kept.

"I wish to return to the stage, and came to you for advice and assistance."

"Do you forget that you once did me the injustice of disappointing me, to my great loss? I am not willing to repeat that experience."

"But I was ill; I lost my voice, my health, my beauty. Now they are all restored, and I am ready to make amends to you for the past."

"It is impossible. Besides the season is too far advanced to organize a new combination. I tell you it is impossible!"

"You dishearten me. What am I to do? Surely the public will be glad to hear me sing, even in concerted pieces."

"The public knows nothing of you. You have no reputation in this country, and you would not draw anything like paying houses. You desire to return to the stage, and on that point you seek my advice?"

"That is my desire."

"Well, heed this advice: Don't sell your talents cheaply, and make no effort to build a reputation in concerts. If you had a reputation, you could afford to sing concerted pieces; but no singer ever made a great reputation except in opera. Prepare yourself for a grand debut, such as was once prepared for you in this city. Ah, Signora, you missed the opportunity of your life when you threw up that engagement. Prepare yourself for appearance in grand opera, where, if you make a hit, it will be a grand success. If you would soar high—and I have all confidence in your ability—you must take wing from the mountain top, and not from the molehill. Opera is the mountain, concert the molehill."

"When can I appear in opera?"

"Not before next season."

"And will you engage me for next season?"

"That depends. I shall be glad to do so, provided you furnish me with acceptable security for the faithful performance of your engagement. 1 cannot afford to make a contract with you on other terms."

"But I have no friend in this country who will become my security."

"Then our interview is at an end. I wish you a good day."

Rosetta left the presence of the pompous musical autocrat with such a chill at her heart as she never had before. The revulsion against her profession was so strong that she almost hated her art—that art which she had always held higher than money, more sacred than barter. She learned that she and her gifts were only valuable to the maestro as the representatives of so much money. She possessed an ocean of melody *en resorvoir*, ready to be poured out in a deluge of song, but she had no means to regrlate the flow to suit the demands of the market. Her wealth, all told, was a thousand dollars, a few jewels, and an excellent wardrobe, the earnings of three years work on the operatic stage in Europe.

Who could she get to stand sponsor for her faithful performance of the contract? John Taplan? He was her only friend, and first in her thoughts. Should she ask him? If so she must reveal her cherished scheme of secrecy, and by that destroy its romance. Besides, was he rich enough to go on her bond? She had neglected to ask the amount of bail required. On inquiry she found that it would be twenty thousand dollars.

The amount appalled her.

When John came home she learned by indirect inquiries that the brick house and grounds would probably sell for five thousand dollars.

Her heart beat low at the low figures—one-fourth the sum required. John Taplan, as bondsman, was out of the question, and it was therefore unnecessary to tell him of her scheme. Foolish woman !

This was in the month of February. What should be her next move ?

Rosetta had more business pluck in her than she dreamed of.

In her present drifting life, some aim or aspiration was absolutely necessary to prevent her from falling into utter despondency. Action, busy, thrilling, absorbing action, was as indispensable to her temperament as phosphorus to her brain, fibrin to her muscles, or oxygen to her blood. Her passion for the stage was constitutional and irrepressible, and it became an all absorbing necessity, a necessity that would brook no hindrance, or stop at any obstacle.

She was honest in her desire to return to the stage.

She was justifiable in having honest desire, woman though she was.

But she was a woman.

She had the same right as a man to be ambitious. But she was a woman. If she were a man would she have fared better?

A man, possessing a voice equal in power, compass, sweetness and culture to that of Rosetta Godardo would have encountered no difficulty in finding a market for his rare gifts, and the price commanded by him would rate in accordance with the degree of his merit.

In the case of a woman it is different. When she applies for a public place her personal charms are considered and included in the estimate placed on her worth; and her art, whatever that art may be, will bring more or less as her personal attractions are great or small. Art has a commercial as well as a literal

11*

meaning, and there is male art and female art. Male art has its value based on art alone; female art has its value based on art and beauty, and like the Circassian maiden, woman's price rises or falls with beauty of person.

Expose thy youth and thy beauty for sale with thy art, maid of song; perchance some Turk may bid high for the pair.

She did not think of this dernier resort then, but the time came, when, despondent with effort and failure, she was driven to surrender the collateral of female art to secure a price for her gifts.

She asked for and obtained another interview with the operatic manager. He was as exacting as ever.

"If you furnish me with security for the faithful performance of your engagement, you can come to me and I will hire you. If I find a patron willing to endorse you, I will send for you. In the meantime, it is useless for you to bother me. This is my ultimatum."

She went home and formed a resolution. She would appear in public in spite of the repulses of the flint-hearted maestro. She resolved to appear in concert in some music hall. She would show the mercenary tyrant that she could secure recognition without paying tribute to him.

She rented the hall, had posters put up on walls to

be covered by more glaring ones, and had the performance billed. She was compelled to pay for the hall, printing, for everything, in advance. On the opening night about a dozen indifferent-looking people straggled in, one at a time, wearing a scared look, as though they had lost their way and had come to the wrong place to find it. There were no "dead heads," but plenty of space for them—she had neglected to compliment the press. The prospect was so slim that the money was refunded, when the miserable-looking stragglers went elsewhere to find their lost way.

Rosetta went home and flung herself on the floor, where she cried like a child that does not know why it cries, only that it should cry on general principles, leaving others to find out the exact cause of its distress.

Berta was the philosopher on the occasion.

"Don't cry, my poor Rosa! don't cry! Why should'st thou cry? Sure the public lost more than we. See what we have learned! We have learned that there is art and the art. Thou hast art, the maestro has the art. Separate, they are valueless; together, they are priceless. Without thy art he is nobody, without his art thou art less than nobody."

"Yes, Berta, about five hundred dollars less than nobody, for that is what the lesson cost us."

"Puh! What is five hundred dollars to thee, I

ask ? Why, with the maestro, thou shalt make the loss up in one night! Despair no more; I shall speak to the maestro."

"What, thou! Thou speak with him? Foolish Berta, how you talk! He will not so much as look at thee, much less talk with thee. Besides, what can'st thou offer which I have not already offered?"

"Leave Berta alone for that! I am older than thou."

It was now late in March, and John Taplan was at home once more. The day on which he landed was wet and dismal. A misty rain fell all day long and filled the streets with slush. The buildings looked like glazed prisons. A dense fog hung over the city, and reached out on the bay like a spectre shroud, through which the packet loomed like a phantom-ship bursting from a phantom world. Rosetta was at the pier in a close carriage waiting for her lover, and watching the people disembark. There comes Taplan; but who is it that glides in his wake and crosses over to the baggage-room ?

"Great God! It is the traitor!" she gasped, as she crouched among the cushions.

John sprang inside and held her in his arms, as they were rapidly driven away.

"Take me away! Oh, hasten! Tell the driver to

fly!" she cried, clinging to him as if to escape some impending evil.

"You saw—him, Rosa?" was all he said; but there was consolation in his strong voice, there was assurance in his encircling arm.

The historian often, and doubtless the novelist also, lays down the pen in despair when he encounters scenes too beautiful for words, too pathetic for speech. At such times inspiration soars beyond language and beats its wings in impotent desperation. Trooping fancies swarm in the brain, dressed in forms of matchless beauty, but the very grandeur of conception paralyzes volition, and the pen falls in despair.

This pen has been idle for days; it is now taken up to write its own impotence, and to beg of the reader to imagine for himself the beauty, the tenderness and the sadness which marked the companionship of those two lovers during those four days in March.

Do you remember the last time you sat with your friend? Neither of you dreamed that the parting was to be final, and yet it was.

The weather continued stormy and capricious; it froze and thawed, rained and sleeted, shone and shadowed, by treacherous turns, compelling those who had homes and loved them, to stay there.

John Taplan remained in the cottage all day long during his stay on shore. At first, Rosetta was reserved and pensive, which aroused the anxiety of Taplan, and prompted him to affect a joviality unusual with him, in order that he might dispel her sadness and bring back her smiles.

Rosetta appreciated his kind strategy, and shook off the shadows, to his intense gratification. The bitterness of her late fiasco gradually passed from her mind, and hope once again fired her breast with promise. When the hour of parting came not a shadow lay between them.

O Maiden of Song! Would thou had'st clung to thy sailor lover, even as the Christian clings to the cross!

O sailor on the sea! Better thou had'st gone down with thy gallant bark, than come back to a port of despair.

CHAPTER XXV.

"That virgin in Œchalia, yoked to no bridal bed, till then unwedded, and who knew no husband, having taken from her home a wanderer impelled by the oar, her, like some Bacchenal of Pluto, with blood, with smoke, and murderous hymenials did Venus give nuptials."—EURIPIDES.

TANCREDI and wife took up their residence in Philadelphia, where they settled down to prosy domestic life. The shock which Madam Alice suffered from the Paris scandal, was likely to influence her whole future life. She razed the altar, demolished the lamp, and tried to forget that she had been a coquette. She shrank from society, refused to take her familiar place among her friends, and declined all invitations except a few of a very exclusive character. She remained at home intensely occupied in learning that noblest of all arts, the art of housekeeping. The gratified husband was rejoiced to see his honeymoon risen at last. Madam was certainly greatly altered in demeanor toward him, while he gave promise of becoming an exemplary husband.

But where the domestic Eden without a trailing serpent winding its slimy folds among the sequestered bowers?

The serpent that crept into the Tancredi bower was in the guise of a letter from Berta to her master. Imitating its primogenitor it appealed to the subtlest vanities of the human heart.

Here is the abstract poison :

"You should see our Rosetta! How handsome! More beautiful than ever before. And her singing! You should hear her sing! It thrills one! And she has got back all her old ambition for the stage. I knew her love for the sailor would not last; it was not exciting enough, and she turns from him to scenes of her former triumph as naturally as the duck to water. But she has no one to help her."

Berta here gave a graphic account of Rosetta's struggles and failures to get back into her profession.

"It is a pity to let her pine away with disappointment, just from the lack of a friend. Why may not my good, kind master, help her as he once helped her?"

Apparently this letter had feeble effect on Tancredi. He flung it aside.

He turned to his own life and felt that it ought to content him.

But will it as he would, his old life of gay adventure involuntarily and persistently thrust itself into his thoughts, and he caught himself revelling in the memories of his old free days—their sparkle and pleasant experiences. He reread the letter.

No, it must not, should not be. He loved his wife, and felt secure of her attachment to him; what more could be added to his happiness? An indiscretion might ruin him. If his wife were to discover any attempt at intriguing on his part, especially with the cantatrice, she would make short work of his present domestic tranquility. No; the Godardo must henceforth be a stranger to him. She had joined her destiny with that of the sailor; she was welcome, and had his best wishes for a bright career.

But he beguiled himself into believing that the subject had an aesthetic side which was proper and prudent for him to consider.

The woman, Rosetta Godardo, was an artist, endowed with talents almost if not quite reaching to the height of genius, and her musical culture was of a very high order of merit. If opportunity were afforded her she bid fair to rival the most renowned singers that ever thrilled the world. Was it right, viewed from its artistic side, that she should be kept in obscurity from the beggarly want of a patron? Was it right to rob the world of her great talents?

Viewing the subject in this light, he saw strong reasons in favor, and none against lending her assist-

ance. As a patron of music, and especially operatic
music, he granted that he was particularly fitted to
render her aid, and that, too, without the risk of being
charged with improper motives. Even if the woman
were an entire stranger to him, still he felt that it
would be right and proper to help her, because helping her would be giving legitimate aid to musical
culture in America.

These were reasons of a general character; but
there were special reasons why he, before any one else,
should assist her.   She had been his protege, encouraged and assisted by him in studying and adopting that
profession for which she was so eminently fitted. He
had shared in her triumphs in Europe, and, on his
promise of protection, she had come to America to
fulfill a flattering engagement as prima donna of an
opera company. He acknowledged that he had not
kept faith with her, but, on the contrary, had prevented her from fulfilling her engagement, and finally
had deserted her.   She was a penniless orphan, bereft
of home, country, profession and honor, all through
his bad faith.

Did he owe her restitution ?

He persuaded himself that he did.

He took the letter up and read it the third time.

He could assist her without resuming his former
familiarity with her.   He was now married, she would

be in May, and temptation and opportunity would be removed. His patronage could be managed so discreetly that his wife would not hear of it or be dissatisfied if she did. Even Rosetta Godardo need not know who was her benefactor. His patronage could be and would be secret, æsthetic, paternal, Platonic.

He threw the letter on the fire and its flames wreathed fantastic forms of burning ships.

Tancredi went to New York.

He held a conference with his friend, the maestro, which resulted in a message being sent to the cantatrice summoning her to the office of the musical director. She was offered the position as prima donna of an opera troupe which was being organized for the ensuing season. Tancredi kept out of the way.

The contract stipulated that she was not to marry for one year. She demurred at this provision and got three days to consider. During those three days ambition was ever present, urging its claims, while her lover was absent, and ambition won. She signed the articles of agreement.

She signed the contract with no wish or intent to wrong John Taplan. It never crossed her mind that he might possibly object, nor had she the slightest wish to cancel her marriage engagement. She only saw in the offer of the maestro the golden opportunity to regain a foothold in her loved profession, an offer

coupled, it was true, with a disagreeable proviso, and
which she accepted under protest on John's account.
She doubted not that her lover would gracefully submit to the years delay, when he came to know the issue
at stake. True, she would have preferred to consult
with him about the postponement of their marriage;
but that would have spoiled her plans; besides he was
absent. She decided without his advice or consent,
feeling confident that all would be well.

Her gratification at the glorious prospect before
her was so absorbing that she had never thought of
the possible cause why the manager had so suddenly
relented from his former hard terms. She now began
to think, and among other things she thought of that.
During her late efforts before him he had said that if
he found a friend willing to go her bail, he would send
for her. He had sent for her, had engaged her, and,
inferentially, had found the willing patron. How else
account for her engagement on such liberal terms?
Her curiosity was aroused to learn more of the inside
workings of the office of the musical director. Was
it likely that some lover of art, familiar with her gifts
and European fame, had volunteered to come forward
as her patron? Some person who acted from genuine
regard for opera in America? If such a person existed,
she longed to know him and demonstrate to him her
profound gratitude.

At her next meeting with the maestro she inquired concerning the cause which led to her good fortune.

"Because I know that you can sing and act," said the manager, with a laugh.

"You knew that long ago; you knew that when you refused to aid me a few weeks ago. There is another reason; what is it?"

"How will this knowledge benefit you, Signorina? Is it not enough to know of your good fortune, and accept and adorn it without question of how it was obtained? You have gained what you desired honorably; rest satisfied."

"But I want to know why you relented from your former hard terms. You say it was obtained for me; surely one has the right to show gratitude for a favor such as is shown me!"

"It is right to be grateful, yes; I accept your thanks, if that is what you wish."

"It was you, then; you are my friend and patron?"

"No, Signorina."

"Then some one else,—who?"

"The particular person desires to remain unknown. I represent him."

"Ah, then you did find a patron?"

"Yes."

"What was his motive?"

"A sense of duty to you."

"A sense of duty to me! Indeed, you make me more solicitous than ever to know who this patron may be. Will you tell me?"

"No; I cannot. The knowledge can do you no possible good. If I tell, I betray a trust. I will not tell."

"Allow me to be the judge of whether this knowledge will do me good or harm. Some one who acts from a sense of duty to me?"

"Yes, Signorina."

"There is but one who could feel or talk that way; I don't want to believe that it is he."

"Believe what you please."

"Sir, it now becomes my duty to demand the name of this person. The affair can go no further until I know."

"Well, of all the whimsical, vaccilating women I ever knew, you bear the palm!"

"You refuse to tell me?"

"I have not the authority to tell you."

"Then our engagement ends here, and I bid you good day!"

"Stay, Signorina! You act in bad faith—very bad faith, not only toward me, but your patron."

"I will have no secret patron. You will not tell me?"

"Give me a day; allow me time to consult with this generous man, that I may tell him how fickle and ungrateful you are. Perhaps he may authorize me to speak his name to you."

"Very well, I will wait," she replied, and went away.

After two days she returned.

"I came for the answer," she said. "Who is this patron?"

"Signor Michele Tancredi!"

"Grando Cielo! I feared it! I feared it! Gracious God, why dost thou follow me with the Shadow of Death!"

She sat quite still, with her great black eyes staring into vacancy, while the maestro was gesticulating, and explaining the situation—apologizing, flattering—praising Tancredi—his delicacy, his generosity, his great honor, his sense of obligation to her. Without so much as looking at him, she abruptly arose and departed like a person in a trance.

When Taplan returned, Rosetta was confined to her room with a headache. At first she refused to see him, but he persisted so earnestly in his entreaty that she reluctantly relented, and allowed him to visit her. When he entered the room she was crouched on the hearth rug shivering with a chill.

He was frightened at her haggard appearance.

Her symptoms indicated a return of her peculiar attacks of nervous fever, called by her, "crazy spells," and not ill-named. The bare mention of Tancredi's name was sufficient to arouse her rage, but never had she felt toward him the same loathing and malignancy as when she learned of his attempt to resume his office of patron and friend.

When she reached home, she locked herself in her room, refused to see any one, and quarreled with Berta, although the bolted door was between them. She charged the maid with duplicity and treachery. Of course she was in the humor to resent even the friendly intrusion of Taplan. She thought that he, at least, might have allowed her the seclusion she craved. She took no pains to conceal her displeasure at his presence.

"You have no kind word for me, Rosa!" he ventured to say, after he had stood sometime without any kind of recognition.

"Why did you come?" she said, petulantly.

"Why did I come? Because—because—why, Rosa, what a question for you to ask me! I came here because I have no other place to go—no other place I want to go."

"But, you know I wish to be alone."

"Rosa, what is the matter? Why do you treat me so? Are you ill? What have I done? God knows, my little darling, that I never had it in my heart to give you a moment's pain."

"Oh, don't ask me so many questions! I don't want to be bothered! I want to be let alone! Go away, do!"

The amazed sailor stood for a moment looking pleadingly at her, when, without a word, but with a deep sigh, he left the room, looking like a man that had just come from an interview with death.

Berta intercepted him and told him of Rosetta's determination to go on the stage.

"But, she must not," he earnestly exclaimed. "Tell her I forbid it."

"Me tell her! I would as soon face a hungry tiger as tell her that! No, no, John Taplan; tell her yourself."

John did not tell her then, but on the following evening, which was the evening before he was to sail, he obtained another interview with Rosetta, when he found her less irritable than on the day previous.

"Is it true, Rosa, that you think of going on the stage?"

"Yes."

"Then, I forbid it."

"Is it you who gives me this order?"

"Yes, Rosa; I don't want my wife to be an actress."

12

"But I am not your wife and I am an actress. I was wedded to my profession before I promised to wed you."

"But you must give it up for me."

"Must you give up your ship for me?"

"Yes, if necessary; but that is different; I am to make our living by my work."

"I can make more money on the stage in one night than you can in five months."

"For all that you must give it up for me."

"What if I will not."

"I hope you will, since I wish it."

"But your wish is unreasonable. Besides you have no right or authority to dictate to me in anything, and I will not obey you in this."

"Does that mean that our engagement is canceled?"

"As you choose, Sir."

"Ah, Rosa, you can't mean that!"

"I mean that I will go on the stage if I choose; if you think that sufficient provocation to break off our engagement, you are welcome."

"But I claim the right to say what your life shall be as my future wife."

"Since you are so domineering over what you call your future wife, know then that I will return to the stage, and you and all the fiends shall not prevent me."

As she spoke she stood up before him defiant, and looking not unlike a fury called up by her invocation.

A glow of pain, or anger, or both, instantly mounted to Taplan's face, and as suddenly faded, leaving his cheeks as blanched as a corpse.

He reached out his hands to her, but she affected not to see them.

"You will think better when I am gone. Good-by, my darling, good-by! and may Heaven keep you from harm!"

He was gone.

A great, stifling, despairing cry arose in the woman's throat when she saw her wounded lover vanish through the door, which he so gently closed after him. It was a cry for mercy, a cry for pardon, for his love, for his return. She fell on the floor, where she lay unconscious.

Returning consciousness brought with it not remorse, but anger; anger at her lover for his heartless desertion. She meant for him to stay; she had meant to oppose him that her yielding might please him all the more, for all along it was her intention to tease and yield at last. She had meant to call him back, and tell him how repentant she was; and, in her frenzy, she would have sworn that she did call him back, but that, instead of heeding her cry, he had purposely and basely deserted her. She began to believe that he intentionally sought a pretext to quarrel in order to get rid of her. She began to despise him for what she believed to be his baseness. Where, then, would she find a friend in all the cruel world, now that John Taplan had deserted her?

There was one who remained faithful through all. Michele Tancredi!

Proclaim it aloud, ye brazen fiends of evil! Speak it with such clamor that the gentler voice of the guardian angel will not be heard! Sieze the trumpet and drown the humble name of Taplan with the cry of Tancredi.

The circumambient contra spirits re-exchanged places about the presence of Rosetta Godardo. The shadow of evil fell like a pall over the form of the doomed woman; while the bright angel fled sorrowing away, to return, alas, nevermore.

On the following day she went to the maestro and sealed her fate.

On the next, Tancredi began a series of artistic, paternal, and Platonic visits to the Yellow Cottage.

The longest, or what to John Taplan seemed the longest voyage of his life, came to an end at last, when he once again landed in New York, and for the second time missed Rosetta's welcome at the pier. This betokened evil; but he sought her at the cottage where he was met by Berta and informed that the Godardo was absent, and would be absent for a long time, perhaps had gone away for good. The maid handed him a letter which he carried home, and read what follows:

JOHN TAPLAN.

Respected Sir: Since you have stated so plainly and decidedly what are your wishes regarding the conduct of the wife of your choice, and since, after deliberation, I find it impossible to accept the terms you demand, I therefore and hereby terminate our engagement. All intercourse between you and me must cease at once and forever. Spare yourself any attempt to write or visit me, for I positively shall refuse to notice you in any way whatever. I hope you will be happy, and forget,   ROSETTA GODARDO.

"She didn't write it! She couldn't write such a letter as that!" exclaimed John, pressing his great palms to his throbbing temples.

Taplan was not endowed with a demonstrative disposition. He showed outwardly little of what was going on within. He was abundantly supplied with that class of nerves called afferent, or carrying-in nerves, which reach out and gather in external impressions, but he was poorly supplied with efferent nerves —the reflex system, by which internal impressions are outwardly manifested. His tentative perceptions were all for himself, as was his digestion. The impressions he received, good and bad, were digested and assimilated within, while very little bubbled over in smiles and tears. No one ever saw him weep; no one ever heard him laugh. Such men bear adversity badly, probably because their pent up anguish expends its frenzy within, instead of escaping in outward tumult.

To watch the great, silent anguish of the strong man, you would wish to see the safety valves opened, that the overcharged feelings might be lighted by a gush of tears. He did not weep, but sat with a far-away look in his lustreless eyes.

Within three days he visited the cottage many times, only to hear the phrase, "Not at home."

He read and reread the cruel letter many times every day, but he could not believe but what the letter was a forgery.

"She can't write English, and she wouldn't write such English if she could," he kept saying to himself.

He believed that if he could only see her alone, just for a minute, he could explain away every obstacle in the way of reconciliation. He had heard that all lovers quarrel once, at least, and happily make up again; this, he thought, was a lover's quarrel, and would have the usual happy termination. If he could only see her!

He wrote her note after note, hoping in that way to attract her attention and arouse her interest. Occasionally, during their happy days, he had composed fugitive verses, which she had set to music and sung to him. He did not pretend to write poetry, only "verses to his mistress' eyebrows," an industry common enough with lovers at an early stage of the fever. He now composed and sent to her the following lines:

'O can you forget!
Or do you regret
How fondly we loved in the past?
On that sweet autumn day,
How the hours flew away!
Too bright and beautiful to last!

Though fortune ill-starred
Our voyage has marred,
And storms drive us wider apart;
From the hurricane's track
Our love will turn back,
And hope cast anchor in the heart.

There's a haven of Rest
'Mong the isles of the blest;
My darling, we'll make that our goal,
And in patience await
At the crystal barred gate
That swings for th' pilgrim's weary soul."

His letter and his verses were returned with the verbal reply that the separation was final—was forever.

John Taplan's ship went to sea without him.

What cared he for his ship now, since the bonniest bark that ever sailed had gone down with all on board? How could he ever again guide a ship through the waves, now that he himself was storm driven, without helm or compass, scudding over an unknown sea where the only lights were pirate signals portending danger and disaster?

Let the winds howl! Let the ships sail out on the boiling sea! A ship had sailed away from port that would never be signalled again. Let Neptune shake the ocean with his wrath, that other men might wail with him for lost ships! Let Erebus ope its sulphurous caverns and vomit a deluge of fiends to overrun the earth with crime and hate and havoc! There was no more right, or justice, or love, or heaven, but a world turned into a reeking lazar-house, teeming with demons damned.

John Taplan closed his heart against his fellow-sufferer, man; he shut his soul against hope.

The cup of Punic Faith was filled to overflowing; who shall drink the envenomed contents down to the last bitter dregs?

PART THIRD.

DIES IRAE.

———

CHAPTER XXVI.

> " Let us rise up and part ; she will not know ;
>   Let us go seaward as the great winds go
> Full of blown sand and foam ; what help is **here ?**
>   There is no help, for all these things are so,
> And all the world's as bitter as a **tear.**
> And how these things are ye strove to show,
>   She would not know."

THE occupants of the cottage saw that John Taplan meant mischief, and they kept Rosetta Godardo
out of the way, trusting that he would become reconciled with his fate, or go away to sea.

But his vigilance abated not, neither did he go to
sea. He haunted the cottage for weeks, and often in
the night did Berta peep out at a haggard figure
standing sentinel, like a wan ghost before some ancient
castle stained with blood-marks of a long-forgotten
crime.

Suddenly and unaccountably he quit his post, much to the relief of the inmates of the cottage, who felt anything but easy at the menacing proximity of the huge man with the bloodshot eyes.

He knocked at the door of a tavern near by, where he was hospitably admitted. He took to the flowing bowl and drowned his sorrow in rum. He would sit quietly for hours in the chimney-corner of the rum-shop, swallowing great draughts of grog and nodding by turns, when he would abruptly stagger to his feet, as if impelled by the recollection of some urgent duty which could no longer be delayed, and go reeling homeward, muttering to himself in an earnest, incoherent manner. When he reached the point in the road, opposite the cottage gate, he would halt and face the entrance, as though on the move to enter. Changing his mind, he would slowly turn with bowed head and enter his own house, where he would sleep off the potations of the day.

One evening as he went staggering along the road on his way home, a carriage passed him, and drew up at the cottage gate. Tancredi alighted and entered the dwelling. The drunken man came reeling along with head sunk on breast and hat slouched over his half closed eyes, apparently oblivious to all about him. He also entered that gate, shambled up to the door, which he opened, and strode past Berta into the hall, and onward to the familiar sitting-room. A moment later, a crash was heard, and Tancredi was seen flying through the front window, carrying sash and havoc with him. Before another minute, John was floundering down the path on his way home as stupidly unconcerned as if he had done nothing but drink and doze for a week.

The next day the domestic, who did little else than extricate Taplan from his drunken boots, was instructed to advertise the brick house for sale.

"I shall go to pieces in this calm," he said. "I must weigh anchor and steer for another port."

As a compliment to his metaphors the servant painted on a board, in picturesque letters, " For Sail," and hung it on the house front. The result was a sale within a week.

When his household was broken he drifted into the city and established himself among the sailors in the neighborhood of the Five Points, where he continued to keep himself saturated with rum, and where he shared his store with his impecunious comrades as long as his money lasted. At length mania potu gave notice that his health was bankrupt, and the bank gave notice that his credit was in like insolvent condition. In two years time John Taplan was become one of the most abject of the vagrant brood that infested that squalid locality.

There were two friends, and only two, who clung to him through his degradation ; one was an old shipmate, named Haley, and the other was Mr. Wallace, an officer connected with the western terminus of the packet company. These two friends remonstrated with the besotted wretch, who, with all his abasement, still maintained his character as a harmless and peaceable fellow. He wronged himself, and that was the sum total of his offense. They offered to intercede for him and get him restored to his old berth on the packet, if he would reform ; and he was always ready to promise. But, alas ! what is the promise of an unfortunate being brutalized by chronic alcoholism ?

John would promise anything they asked, and, on the strength of his vows, would borrow a dollar " to make it more bindin'," as he expressed it. With the money thus obtained he would lay in a supply of cheap rum to brace his nerves up to the work of reformation.

But the good work soon languished, and presently subsided altogether—the rum did not hold out long enough to thoroughly establish reform. His nerves gave out with the rum, and he fell back into his old habits and the customary jobs by which he gained a precarious livelihood. Thus did he become fixed in the ways of a vagrant, lost to all sense of shame, reckless of the present, indifferent of the future. And thus the disgraceful years rolled round with him.

When it became known, that Taplan had left Yorkville, Rosetta Godardo returned to the cottage, where her restored paramour, Tancredi, passed much of his time.

It seems like paying tribute to immorality to say that she was happy; and yet it is true, she was intensely, acutely happy. Of course, it was not that calm, equable and secure content which she experienced while betrothed to the sailor, but rather the happiness of moral intoxication. She was peculiarly adapted to lead a vicious life, provided the vice and the life lead were of her own choosing. Her attachment to Tancredi was so all absorbing, and her moral sense so abnormally dulled by his contact, that all other impressions were swept away or disregarded. Her passion for him returned with all its former abandon and intensity, and she had no place or time for shame, anxiety or remorse.

Fate, however, was against her appearing in opera in America. The wages of sin was the salary she drew, and which cancelled the engagement with the manager. A male heir was born to the house of Tancredi in Philadelphia in January, and in the following March a male child was born in the Yellow Cottage in Yorkville.

The Yorkville child was called Carlo Godardo. The Philadelphia boy was christened Charles Tancredi. Both children grew in strength and loveliness, and the father, Michele Tancredi, should have been proud of them both. He discreetly suppressed that half of the joy he felt for the child at the Yellow Cottage. He succeeded in concealing from his wife all knowledge of his pseudo family; more than a score of years passed before Madam Tancredi knew of such a being as Carlo Godardo.

It would be tedious, unprofitable and falsely delicate to moralize on the evil lives led by Tancredi and the Godardo. It would be still worse to apologize for the narration of the story of their shame. Besides, there should be no attempted vindication of the coherence, the candor, and the fidelity of history. History must vindicate itself, must evolve and determine its own moralization. This history deals with the concrete, not the abstract; with flesh and blood, not with dry bones. This story follows individuals, not ethical theories. It narrates the actions of persons, what they actually did, not what they should have done; it follows them into vice and crime, as well as into virtuous ways, to find who rises or falls on the seething tide of passion. This is its aim; let it not be loaded down with the dead weight of prudery.

Evil, however cunning and secret, has a myriad

spies and as many betrayers. The husband of the Tancredi stripe must learn to assume the stupidity of the opium eater, and wear a mask as cold as the Sphynx. To hoodwink an observant wife, especially a loving wife, the more need of an impenetrable mask.

Since Madam Tancredi had given up fashionable dissipation she had turned her whole attention to her husband and her household. But, strange to tell, her praiseworthy deportment, instead of establishing correspondingly commendable habits in her husband, only tended to encourage his vanity, and drive him back into his old roving adventures. So long as he was uncertain of his wife's affection so long was he circumspect in his behavior, and so long did he dance attendance on her whims and wishes; but now, when he felt secure of her devotion, and especially since she had become a mother, his loyalty began to wane and he gradually drifted back into his old Bohemian life, and bestowed his gallantries away from home.

Wives are much, very much, to blame for such husbands as was Tancredi, and most to blame for their maudlin idolatry.

You have in your mind's eye a certain gentleman of your acquaintance who is possessed of an angel wife, whose only fault is her too slavish and zealous love for her husband. She guards his buttons and small clothes, stands sentry over his slippers and coffee, and lines his home life with velvet—in brief, idolizes him; and yet—well, you know his reputation.

How would you manage him if you were his wife? for you could manage him, you know you could. How often your fingers ache just to put him through ' his paces once. It is evident that his wife cannot manage him; she is so slavishly devoted to him, is so jealous, so persistently hanging around him, and so easily cajoled by him, that she could not carry out a rational plan of management to save her.

Poor woman! she is in love with him, while you are not.

And that is the advantage you would have over her, and over him, if you were to try your hand at breaking him in.

The philosophy belonging to this subject must be supplied or not by the reader. But after all, it is as it is, loving, doting, self-sacrificing wives, will go on spoiling otherwise good husbands.

There is nothing will drive men of the Tancredi pattern (there are such husbands) away from home and duty so effectually as that obtrusive and over zealous adoration practiced by some wives; nothing will keep them steady in the line of duty so effectually as a little indifference, or even neglect. A little streak of green jealousy is a healthy shade in the domestic rainbow in such cases.

Madam Tancredi marked her husband's wavering devotion with painful solicitude. He was much from home, and the excuses he gave for his absence were often contradictory and always unsatisfactory. Her hope that the child would attract him to his family turned out to be a bitter disappointment.

She redoubled her efforts to make home attractive, and tried a hundred arts to lure him back to duty, but in vain; the pampered man grew more and more negligent of his marital obligations. He would remain away for days, where, she knew not; and when he did pass an hour at home he was uneasy, and manifested but little affection for wife or child.

More than two years had passed in sorrow away, and Madam Alice despaired of ever being a happy wife again. She began to seek consolation and recreation outside the pale of her husband's society. Her health was broken, and she was ordered by her physician to the seashore, where she spent the summer with her cousin, Mrs. Wallace, of New York. About the first of September she went home with her relative, intending to remain for a two weeks visit, before returning to Philadelphia.

This cousin was the wife of Mr. Wallace, already introduced as one of the friends of John Taplan. The latter was often employed by Mr. Wallace to go on errands, or perform odd jobs about the packet's office. Thus it happened that John Taplan was the very man hired to assist in delivering the luggage of the two ladies from the steamboat to the Wallace residence. Madam Tancredi made some remarks about his haggard appearance.

"There is quite a romance connected with the poor man, as I have often heard my husband tell," said Mrs. Wallace. "When he comes home this evening he shall relate it to you."

That evening Mr. Wallace told Madam Tancredi the story of John Taplan, the sea pilot, a story with which he was tolerably familiar.

He told her of Taplan's vocation, his worthiness, his promise of a good life, how he had fallen in love with an opera singer who proved false after promising to marry him; that an Italian nobleman, who had brought the singing woman to this country, and who had married an American lady, had cut Taplan out, and that the latter, broken by their treachery, had taken to drink and become the miserable sot she had seen.

"What is the matter, my dear Alice?" exclaimed Mrs. Wallace, in alarm. "You are as pale as a ghost!"

"It is the story! My nerves are not much improved, I find. Don't you see I am still very nervous? But the story—your story; it affects me greatly.   Don't be distressed; I shall be better soon. There, now; I'm over it, already, see!   Do you know the name of the singing woman?"

"I do not.   I know nothing more than I have told you; but Taplan knows, and I'll ask him to tell me the name."

"No, I beg of you not; please do not ask him—do not speak of the matter to him; I ask this as a personal favor.   Pardon me for not stating my reason at present for this urgent request.   Let me ask him, for I am interested in the story of his life, and may be of use to him.   Will you kindly send him to me, to-morrow?"

On the following day she had a long interview with John Taplan, who gave her names, dates and facts readily enough.   She made it worth his while to maintain a strict secrecy, a not difficult task, for to his naturally reticent disposition, was added the stupefaction induced by long continued dram drinking. He agreed to discover whether or not the woman, Godardo, still occupied the Yellow Cottage, and if Tancredi still visited her.

Taplan's greatly altered appearance served as a complete disguise while scouting about his former haunts in Yorkville.   He hung around the place for two days before he was rewarded with a discovery. He then saw Tancredi, in company with the Godardo, drive from the cottage in a carriage, and he saw them return. He learned from the inmates of the tavern that the gentleman regularly visited the cottage every Tuesday and Friday. The visit he witnessed was on Friday. He reported to Madam.

On the following Tuesday, piloted by Taplan, Madam Tancredi drove out the road to Yorkville, where she met and passed Michele Tancredi and Rosetta Godardo taking a drive in an open carriage. On her return she saw the pair enter the cottage.

Madam Tancredi drove back to the city and dismissed John Taplan, leaving a liberal reward on deposit with Mr. Wallace.

On the following day, leaving her son with Mrs. Wallace, she returned to Philadelphia, where she met her husband.

Her interview with him on that occasion was the most serious and painful transaction of her life. All respect, all love, all regard for the man she had vowed to honor and obey, was gone, while pride and anger took their place and sustained her through the reckoning with her betrayer.

"I wish to speak to you on a very serious matter," she quietly said, as soon as they were alone.

The Signor came and stood beside her, ready to hear what she might say.

"For a long time you have regularly made visits

to New York. You go there on Tuesdays and Fridays; may I ask what business calls you there so frequently and so regularly?"

"You may, certainly, my dear wife; I have many times told you, as I do now, that I go there on business connected with my Italian estates."

"Nothing else?"

"No; why do you ask?"

"To satisfy myself of your utter disregard for truth and honor!"

"Your speech is unintelligible to me."

"Listen, while I make it plain to you. I was in New York on last Friday."

"I believe you were, since you say so."

"I was also there on yesterday, Tuesday."

"I admit you were; and I also was there yesterday."

"What part of the city did you visit?"

"I don't remember all the places I did visit. I was at my agents on Beekman Street, at my bankers on Wall Street, at my hotel on Broadway."

"You visited one other place which you neglect to mention."

The husband was silent. He sat down.

The wife resumed:

"I was driven out the Harlem road on yesterday. I was in the neighborhood of a yellow cottage in

Yorkville. I was guided to that spot by a sailor called John Taplan, the discarded lover of Rosetta Godardo, who now occupies that cottage. I passed you as you rode out with her ; on your return, I saw you enter her dwelling in her company. You drove out with her on last Friday. You visit her every Tuesday and Friday, and have done so for the last three years. You prevented her from marrying an honest man to whom she was engaged, this John Taplan, who would have given her a home and an honest name but for your perfidy, and who, because of your infamy and her treachery, has become a drunken vagabond !"

She paused, and for a solemn minute nought was heard but her husband's rapid breathing.

" The blood of the sailor and the singing woman be on your head !"

While the injured wife went on with her terrible reckoning, the husband bent like a trembling reed before the storm, and when she concluded with her awful imprecation, he buried his face in his hands and sobbed like a frightened child.

" Listen to me !" continued Madam Tancredi, rising and standing over the culprit. " I wish to avoid scandal. I wish to shield my family from the disgrace of a public exposure of your deeds. I want to guard my son from his father's shame. He must remember you as one dead.

"By the laws of this land you are a criminal, and the prison your place. There is but one way by which you may escape the penalty of your crime, and that is flight. This one chance of escape I grant you. You must leave this roof, leave me within this hour, and you must quit this country at once and forever. Go! There is nothing more to be said. Go!"

"Let me first embrace my child."

"You shall never again behold his face. I have taken the precaution to place him safe beyond your reach. You shall never, never embrace my child, never!"

"Surely you cannot, will not, refuse me this one last poor request?"

"I refuse you everything but the freedom to fly from me and mine forever. I renounce you as a traitor and a felon, unfit to live, and unworthy the favor of a dog! Begone!"

The crushed man went staggering from her presence and the house.

CHAPTER XXVII.

"Oh offspring of the earth, whom Mars once sowed, having denuded of its teeth the savage jaw of the dragon, will ye not uplift your staffs, the support of your right hands, and make bloody the impious head of this man, who, not being a Cadman, rules over these youths the basest of Aliens ?"—EURIPIDES.

ROSETTA GODARDO loved her child, madly and tumultuously, as was characteristic of all she felt or did.

She had no emotion which did not run over into passion, and no passion which was not akin to madness. With her it was never simple like or dislike, it was adoration or malignant hate. Her nervous system was ever attuned to the very highest pitch of the living sentient diapason.

She was jealous even of the caresses Berta bestowed on little Carl, and furious if he manifested preference for his nurse. She mapped out his future career, which was to be great and glorious, and gave Tancredi no peace until he pledged to do for her boy what he would do for his own lawful child. The father was really fond of his son, Carl Godardo.

Tancredi, justly, was more worthy than his deeds,

and deserved better than his fate. It is not meant
that his wrong-doings were excusable, or that he was
in the smallest degree irresponsible, it is not even
meant that his punishment was too severe; but it is
meant that he did not fully appreciate the heinousness
of his acts, or rather that his motives were less wicked
than his acts, and that he did not know he was so bad
until he came to view himself and his past from the
standpoint of an exiled husband and father. He was
naturally endowed with a keen sense of honor, and
was brave and generous to a fault; but he was also
vain and sensual, the outgrowths of wealth, indolence
and flattery. He had been so long accustomed to a
luxurious and voluptuous life, that marriage to him was
a mere conventional canon, to be strictly enforced as to
the wife, but loosely applied as to the husband. So
long as he was discreet and did not shock public
decency, and so long as he kept his intrigues from his
wife's knowledge, he felt no upbraidings of conscience.
Ignorance in the wife was his key of safety and his
maxim of wedded bliss.

But his wife's detection of his secret amour,
followed by her fierce denunciation, aroused his moral
supineness, and brought him to contemplate the subject of marital obligation as he never had viewed it
before. He went from her presence guilt-stricken and
overwhelmed with remorse. Before he left the city

13

he made one more urgent appeal for clemency. Finding her inexorable he sullenly submitted to the inevitable and went to New York.

He now turned his attention to his quasi family in Yorkville.

The humiliating blow fell so suddenly and crushingly that he thought of little else than his shame and the means of escaping from it. He was anxious to depart at once from a country in which he had suffered so much misfortune.

Bitter as were his thoughts, and vengeful as were his feelings against the whole world, there was still one left, he fondly believed, who would give him shelter and welcome—the Godardo. She would love him the more, now that others spurned him. He would go to her.

The Godardo! Was she not the silver-tongued siren who seduced him from home, country, and honor? Was not his whole trouble before and since marriage caused by her? Why should he go to her?

The *pomum Adamii* stuck in his throat; it choked him; it would not go down, it would not come up. It was the woman who tempted him; it was she who lured him to his ruin; on her he turned all his wrath.

Lived there ever a fallen man, who, in the hour of his humiliation, did not screen himself behind " The woman thou gav'st me ?"

Mea culpa, mea maxima culpa, is nowhere found in the liturgy of heroes. A man may be proud, and strong, and brave, and great, on the field or in the forum, but when he falls in the snare of his own making he is weak, and cowardly and small.

Let some ambitious romancer, by way of change and a challenge to credulity, picture a godlike hero, sunken in crime and shaken by remorse, and let this unnatural author put words in that culprit's mouth—words never spoken before—the sublime words of self accusation : "I am what I am because I am, and not because of a woman !" When such a hero is found the gods will make room in the heavens for one more constellation to be filled by him.

Tancredi attributed all his misfortune to Rosetta Godardo, and, while he stood self-confessed with having played the fool, he determined that she should bear with him one half the punishment. She had wrecked his life, and her life must also be wrecked. He determined to avoid her forever.

He set about at once winding up his affairs in America, preparatory to secretly leaving for Italy. He sent a trusty messenger to summon Berta to his hotel, and to come unobserved.

The dutiful maid, ignorant of her master's disaster, escaped, ostensibly for a walk with Carl, and reported herself to Tancredi. The poor child, unconscious of its father's feelings, ran forward, as was its wont, with a cry of joy and attempted to climb on its father's knee. He shook it off with a frown and a curse—spurned it as he would a reptile, when the amazed little fellow, with bewildered steps, slunk back to Berta, who gathered him in her arms.

" Why, Master ! what ails thee, that thou should'st spurn from thee thy Carl ?"

" I am ruined, and the boy's mother is the cause. I wish the devil had them both ! Why did you bring him here ? I meant you should come alone. I don't want either of them to come near me."

" *Grando Cielo !* What has happened thee, my good Master, that thou should'st talk of ruin ?"

" My wife has discovered my visits to the cottage. She followed me there under the guidance of that cursed sailor, John Taplan. She gave me the choice between prison and exile. I chose the latter."

" And thou go'st to Italy ?"

" Immediately. I sent for you to accompany me thither."

" And Rosetta ?"

" Her ? I care not what becomes of her, so that I never see her or hear of her again. I am quit of her forever !"

" Alas, poor woman ! And Carl, what is to become of him ?"

" His mother's fate !"

" *Dio Mio !* Not that, good Master, oh say not that ! Speak not so cruelly of thy own flesh and blood. See us on our knees at thy feet ! For the holy Madonna's sake, drive him not away from thee ! He is thy image, my own darling boy—thy boy, and, whatever his mother, he is innocent. Oh, how can you, good Master !"

The woman and child knelt before the scowling man, who bit his lip, determined not to yield to sentiment, or listen to argument.

" We sail to-morrow morning," said he, disregarding her entreaty. " You must be ready to accompany me. I shall leave a sum sufficient to maintain the woman and her boy, but I never want you to speak of them after we leave these wretched shores."

Berta fell prostrate on the floor, and gave way to noisy grief. The child looked on in wide-eyed dismay at the tumult of its nurse, when it flung itself on her body and joined in her wailing. The Signor went to the window and turned his back on the distracting scene.

The woman hushed her own cries to soothe the child, whom she took on her lap and hugged to her breast, consoling him with the most endearing words.

"Master," said Berta, softly and sorrowfully, after

she had succeeded in assuaging the grief of the terrified boy.

"Well, Berta, you speak; what is it you would say?" exclaimed the Signor, without turning from the window.

"I will stay with Carl."

"As you will; but know well what it is you do; you desert forever the house which has ever been your home."

"God pity me! I will not desert thy child!"

Tancredi had steeled his bosom against pity, he had spurned all ties of blood, but when the simple Berta braved his displeasure by defiantly standing up for the innocent child—his own child—his heart was reached through the stubborn armor. He turned from the window to the grouping on the floor with more of shame than anger.

The Italians seem endowed with the intuition of art. The attitude of maid and child, with bodies bent forward and hands stretched out in mute supplication, presented a touching tableau, to which the Signor yielded, and he gathered the boy in his arms.

"Go, get thee back to the cottage, mad Berta; I must bring you all back to Italy. But not a word to Rosetta, not a word. Do not tell her I am here, or that you have seen me to-day. Not a word to her, if you regard me, and do you steal away with the boy

by daylight to-morrow morning, and come to me.
Remember, not a word to Rosetta; leave her to me."

Berta promised obedience, and, with Carl, went
home.

The next morning, Tancredi, Carl, and Berta
were taken on board the ship, from where they did
not stir till noon, when the anchor was weighed and
they were off to sea. Once again, as before, Michele
Tancredi was flying from Rosetta Godardo.

When Rosetta came down to breakfast on the
morning on which the ship sailed she missed Carl
and Berta, but thought little of the fact, believing
that they had gone out to take their morning walk.
But as the day wore away and the evening came on
without news of them she grew impatient, and when
the dark night fell on the uncertainty, she became
alarmed and distressed. She walked the floor the
whole night through, startled at every sound, hoping that each noise betokened the return of the
wanderers.

When morning dawned she started the one remaining servant out to make inquiries; he returned at
noon without having found the slightest trace of the
missing members. In the afternoon she went to the
mayor's office in the city, where she set on foot an
organized search for the lost maid and child.

She kept up her search by day and her vigils by

night, and as each day and night came and went without tidings of the lost, she became more and more
distressed and excited. The loss of sleep, abstinence
from food, and bereavement, began to make their
impress on her peculiar nervous system, and the wild
demoniac look again gleamed from her eyes, presaging
another attack of acute mania.

Her mind was so absorbed by the mysterious dis-
appearance and the vain search, that she thought of
little else, and did not even particularly mark the failure of Tancredi in making his usual bi-weekly visits.
Still, when a whole week passed without his appearance, his unprecedented absence struck her as remarkable, and she wondered at the circumstance. She
believed that he could aid her, besides she felt that it
was her duty to acquaint him of the loss. She started
immediately to Philadelphia.

When Madam Tancredi became convinced of her
husband's infidelity, she rapidly mapped out the
course proper to be pursued. She made confidents of
the Wallaces, and prevailed on them to keep her child
until after the brewing storm had blown over, and
Tancredi had departed for Europe. Kidnapping was
entertained as a contingency, and to remove such dire
possibility it was determined that Charles Tancredi
should remain concealed until all danger was past.

When more than a week had elapsed without news

of her banished husband, she concluded that he had sailed, that the danger was over, and she wrote her cousin to send Charles and his nurse home at once.

By one of those coincidences which seem like inexorable doom, and from which dire issues sometimes flow, Charles Tancredi and his nurse were on the same train and in the same car which carried Rosetta Godardo to Philadelphia.

The two children, Charles Tancredi and Carl Godardo, resembled each other; they were nearly of the same age, and both were dark skinned. Rosetta, whose keen eyes were ever on the watch, saw the handsome child on the seat next immediately in front of her, and was startled at his resemblance to her own lost child. She was not long in making the acquaintance of the spry young nurse, and quickly established the most friendly relations with the child.

The nurse was young and attractive looking, was giddy, fond of being noticed, and easily cajoled. It was easy for Rosetta to pump from her all she knew. Nothing is more astonishing than the acuteness of the average servant in detecting family secrets. This domestic could have furnished material for a long chapter of the secret history of Tancredi's domestic life, and her facts would have been fairly authentic. Rosetta gathered from her enough information to

13*

learn that Tancredi had separated from his wife, and that he had gone back to Italy.

The true state of affairs flashed through her irritable brain like a blaze of inspiration, and she could scarcely suppress a cry of anguish. Tancredi had quarrelled with his wife on her, Rosetta's, account, he had gone home to Italy never to return, he had deserted her and had taken away with him her own child, Carl, along with Berta. Tancredi, the Betrayer! Berta, the Child Stealer!

Her first impulse was to turn back and hunt the traitors down; her next thought was to slay this child now reposing in her lap—this, his own child—kill him, and be revenged!

The pleased child twined its dimpled arms about her neck and toyed with the necklace at her throat; it looked up in her face in smiles, as would her own darling, were he nestling on her bosom. Kill thee? Sweet one! No! Thou art not thy perfidious father!

She had been robbed of her child, why not rob Madam Tancredi of her child? Why not steal him, and square the account with Tancredi who had stolen her child? Why not carry this child away where it would learn to love her, and console her for her loss?

Revenge incited and opportunity pointed out the road.

The caution and cunning, sometimes so marked in the insane, guided her in the sudden project and muffled the storm raging in her breast.

She applied herself to the task of pleasing the child and cajoling the maid. The former took kindly to the woman with the musical voice and the glittering jewel at her throat, while the nurse willingly surrendered her charge to the clever fellow passenger, and gave her attention to the flirtation carried on between her and two young men seated in front of her.

" Why, only see how soundly Charles is sleeping !" she exclaimed, looking around to see the child resting quietly on the lap of the strange woman.

The seat occupied by Rosetta was near the rear door. The train stopped at a station as it neared Philadelphia.

The woman, holding the sleeping child in her arms, arose from her seat, while her gleaming eyes watched the occupied nurse in front of her.

She stepped into the aisle.

She glided to the doorway, and stood on the platform outside. The conductor assisted her to alight.

The bell rang, the wheels revolved, and the train moved off, leaving her standing on the station platform with the sleeping boy in her arms.

She turned toward the North and disappeared among the green lanes of the country.

CHAPTER XXVIII.

"O Vengeance, take me all,—I'm wholly thine."

As the train approached the West Philadelphia depot, the passengers began that fidgetty stir of preparation peculiar to American assemblages when nearing the end of the play, the lecture or the journey, and which suggests the uncomfortable feeling that they should have remained at home, and not come out to annoy better mannered people.

When the train stopped, and the flirting nurse looked around to resume her charge,—lo, the seat was empty!

In trepidation she searched for Charles through the cars in vain; the boy and the strange woman were not to be found. While running about, thoroughly frightened, she came across the conductor, who learned the cause of her distress. He told her that the strange woman had alighted with the boy at a station just outside of the city. This was terrible news to carry to Madam Tancredi, who was waiting close by in a carriage to receive the darling of her heart.

"O Madam, forgive me! But Charles is lost!"

exclaimed the terrified girl, alarmed anew at sight of her mistress.

"What is the matter, girl; and where is Charles?" asked Madam in eager alarm.

"Madam, there is some mistake, and, I trust, only a mistake," said the conductor, coming forward and making himself known. "I saw the woman with the child sleeping in her lap, and I supposed that she was its mother and this girl the nurse; so, when she got off at the station a few miles back from here with the child, I thought nothing strange, and I offered no objection, but assisted her to alight. I feel confident that she meant no harm to the child, and that she will be speedily found and your child restored to you."

"Please describe as near as you can her appearance," she requested of the conductor.

"She was small, quick-motioned, dark-skinned, very handsome, and she had the blackest eyes I ever saw."

The look of anguish deepened on Madam's face as she heard the conductor describe the person of Rosetta Godardo, the person of all others she detested, the person of all others into whose keeping she most dreaded to trust her child. She mastered her feelings so well, however, that of all the group of listeners she was the most self-possessed.

During the whole of the past week, her mind had

been tortured with the dread that her husband might attempt to get possession of Charles, his and her son. After his damnable treachery, she believed him capable of any villainy. And now the boy was missing—stolen by his mistress and accomplice. Tancredi was, then, still in New York, (so she believed) where he had laid his plot, and from where he had sent out his paramour and companion in guilt, to kidnap his son, Charles Tancredi.

What other hypothesis would account for the abduction? Who besides the father would have any interest in stealing the boy? What other person could possibly have a motive for the deed? There was but one person in all the world that could have any interest in the abduction, and that person was the boy's father, Michele Tancredi. He had, then, not sailed for Europe, but was lingering in New York that he might get possession of his son to carry him away to Italy.

The plan of action she hastily planned was based on this theory. She saw hopes of yet defeating his plot, and she lost no time in useless lament, but started detectives on the trail at once. She drove direct to the station where the Godardo had alighted.

Strange as it may appear, and unfortunate as it was, none of the residents at or about the country station had seen the woman or child, and hence no clue could be had of the direction taken by the fugitives. The detectives decided, (they always decide, and often as in this case, wrongly) that she had entered the city—the decision acted on by them. A sharp look-out was kept for her at the railway stations, and indus-trious search was made high and low throughout the city.

On the next morning after the kidnapping, news was brought that the child was found in a village up the Delaware, where he was held for identification. When the mother reached the place the child was already restored to its parents.

Madam Tancredi was confidently assured by the detectives that it would be impossible for the child-stealer to escape arrest. But when the evening of the second day came without the slightest additional clue, she became impatient, and despatched detectives to watch the movements of Tancredi in New York.

There it was learned, from his bankers and from other sources, that the Signor had actually sailed for Europe in company with a woman and child, the lat-ter answering the description of Charles Tancredi. Indeed, one of the officers of the bank had heard the woman call the boy Carl.

When this report was made to Madam Tancredi, she was convinced that her husband had succeeded in escaping with her child, and that he was already far out at sea beyond the possibility of rescue. Accordingly she called off the detectives and gave up what was now a useless search.

The reader is now in possession of two links which, have places somewhere in the chain of this story. One link is the maniac woman who died at the miller's cottage, leaving the child, Jarl; the other link is Rosetta Godardo, the maniac avenger, who fled into the wilderness with Charles Tancredi, the lawful heir of her betrayer, Signor Michele Tancredi.

Poor lost woman of the fiery blood and heart of passion! Life to thee was a pendulum swinging between joy and despair. The grave none too soon gave repose to thy turbulent spirit.

Forgive her! Magdalene was the last at the cross. Forgive her! Magdalene was the first at the resurrection. Forgive her, for,

> " Though justice be thy plea, consider this,
> That in the course of justice none of us
> Should see salvation."

Madam Tancredi had found her child, but found him lost to her, and months must elapse before he could be restored. The proud woman was severely broken by the long continued disquiet, which reached its climax on the abduction of the darling of her heart, and for weeks she lay prostrated with grief and illness.

When her health was improved, she wrote and mailed
to Naples the following letter :

MICHELE TANCREDI.

Signor : You have robbed a mother of her child.
It was the only thing she had to love in all this whole
world, and she is deprived of it by you. By this time
you should feel sufficiently avenged. Surely you cannot, will not, be so lost to pity as to prolong a mother's
agony. What sacrifice will you name as the price of
his restoration to his distracted mother ?

ALICE TANCREDI.

After a tedious and harrowing wait, she got the
following reply :

MADAM ALICE TANCREDI.

The boy is with me. Nothing will induce me to
restore him to his mother, but your forgiveness and
our reconciliation.   M. TANCREDI.

Strong as was her love for her child her indignation toward her husband was stronger still. She could
not bring herself to condone his crime, even to satisfy
the cravings of maternal instinct. The martyrdom of
a childless life would be, if not less endurable, at least
more honorable than the reconciliation given in
exchange for what was every mother's right—the right
to possess and care for her own child.

In character and temperament Alice Tancredi was heroic, and of that quality of heroism requisite in the absolute monarch. What she set her mind on was made a part of her life. She took no backward steps —she never retreated, for she always burnt her ships behind her.

Love for her husband had gone out in hate; she hated his name, loathed his sin, and despised the man. Any relationship with him, even of a compulsory nature, was an unmitigated evil. She had cast him off forever; and now, to regain her child by forgiveness and reconciliation, was, to her mind, little short of condonement of his sin, and justification of his treachery. The idea of even indirectly palliating his guilt, or screening him from punishment, was, to her, revolting, criminal and impossible.

Of course she was ignorant of the existence of her husband's extra marital son. She was under the delusion that he had taken away his and her son, who was stolen from the cars by the Godardo, and that Charles Tancredi, her son, was now in Italy.

She might possibly have entertained his proposition if his sinning had ceased on his expulsion from her home; but when he super-added to the crime of child-stealing, that of flagrant criminal relationship with the singing woman, his partner in guilt, she rejected his proposition as added insult to injury. Tancredi's letter, instead of mollifying her displeasure, only served to intensify her indignation, and confirm her in her determination to show no quarter to the unscrupulous and shameless villian.

Signor Tancredi, very naturally on his part, was ignorant of the abduction of his own son, Charles Tancredi. By the peculiar construction of his wife's letter, he got the impression that Rosetta Godardo was the " distracted mother " referred to, and that on missing her child, she had gone in her despair to Madam Tancredi, whom she had succeeded in enlisting to intercede for the restoration of the child, Carl Godardo.

If either letter had been less cold and formal, if either had been written with the candor becoming the husband and wife, the mistake would have been prevented, and the evil which befel Charles Tancredi would never have followed. The penalty of the parent's stubborn wrong fell like a blight on the young outcast.

Time with its corroding breath scattered the rust of estrangement through the sombre halls of the Tancredi. The woman sat defiant among the ashes of bereavement, while the man stood among the desolate altars like a stubborn statue of remorse. Pride and guilt allied to roll an ocean between the husband and wife; across the dark waters a mother's love brooded like the spirit of light moving on the chaotic sea of a world just born.

Four years passed away with their ebb and flow of joy and sorrow. During all this time Madam Tancredi had not ceased her importunate demands for the restoration of her child. Nearly every ship bore a request to the father and some token of endearment to her darling boy. But she stubbornly maintained her unswerving opposition to her husband, while he was as unyielding in his exactions as ever. Of course it was impossible that he should have received so many impassioned letters from his wife without having discovered that his and her son was actually stolen and lost. He also knew that it was—must have been—the work of the Godardo, who did it to revenge herself on him.

None but this father can realize what were the fealings that rankled in his remorseful breast when he learned the awful truth. He had robbed a mother of her child, that mother had retaliated by robbing him of his child. And, horrible to think, he must hold his peace! Let imagination, if it likes, complete the harrowing picture.

What could the guilt-stricken man now do to right the wrong? If he told his wife the truth it would be at the further expense of honor already almost bankrupt. His wife knew nothing of the existence of

Carl Godardo; she believed that the latter was her real son. No good, but much evil might result if she were told of the infamous story. He kept his secret.

He wrote to his confidential agent in New York, asking information concerning the Godardo, and instructing him to discover her whereabouts. Gone, no one knew whither, was the answer.

Berta received her instructions, she would keep the secret inviolate. If Madam Tancredi ever discovered the truth about her son, it would be at her husband's option.

After four years of failure to recover her child, and no longer able to endure the pangs of separation, she determined to visit Naples, and try her personal presence and influence on the obdurate father.

She notified him of her proposed journey, to which he made no objection; indeed he rather encouraged her visit, and fitted up his beautiful villa for her reception during her stay in Italy.

At first, for a week or two of her sojourn at the villa, the anticipated joy at meeting and enjoying her child was scarcely realized. She was, however, solaced with the reflection that he had been taken from her at the tender age of three, and had not seen her for four years. Little wonder that he had forgotten her! But she devoted herself so heartily to his service that in a month's time the little fellow came to accept her caresses, and was reconciled to the companionship of the new mamma, who spoke in a language he could not understand. Before two months had passed he was pleased to bestow much of his affection on the gratified mother.

The discreet and disciplined Berta stood by and gazed on the pair with an expression well suited to her office.

"Don't you think, nurse, that my child has grown much darker-skinned since he came to Italy ?" asked Madam Alice of Berta.

"Yes, Madam ; it's the hot climate ; the bright sun it is. Dear Carl! he loves the sunlight so well! Why, he was ever ou doors before you came."

"Don't he know any English, whatever ? He could speak many English words before he left me."

"No one English speak him. He not hear much of that some four years."

"Nurse," said Madam, on another occasion, "tell me, for I have no one else to ask, where is the woman, Godardo ?"

"Madam, I know not. My master has seen her not since from your house in Philadelphia he came away."

"Why will you try to deceive me ?"

"I deceive you not ; I tell you true ; my master thinks her dead."

"Do you tell me that she did not come away with your master to Italy? Will you tell me that it was not she who stole my child?"

"Indeed, Madam, she came not then, nor at any time since. It was I who came away with master."

"You? But it was not you who stole my child from the cars; it was the Godardo. The description I got at the time was too clear to mistake her identity."

"That may be, Madam, but I solemnly swear that Carl came over with master and me, and that the Godardo came not. This I swear; help me all saints!"

The puzzled woman pondered over the new information for days. If Berta spoke the truth, the subject stood in another light, and her harsh judgment demanded revision. If it turned out that Tancredi had not been and was not now harboring the woman who was the cause of all the trouble, then she could believe that, while he was bad enough, he was not so utterly depraved as she had held him to be.

She had not met her husband since her arrival at Naples. She gave him credit for his tact and delicacy in this. She requested an interview.

The Signor came at once.

"I sent for you," said the cold woman, without looking at him, "to ask if you will permit my child to return home with me?"

"Will you return so soon?" he asked, politely, but evasively.

"I prefer to return immediately. Outside my child there is nothing to detain me here."

"Say not that! My sister, Signora Adelaide, will be most happy to meet you. She is absent on a visit to Sicily, but we expect her home at any time, and she may be here to-day. If you depart before she returns she will be sadly disappointed."

"Your good sister and I cannot be as we once were; misfortune such as mine cools friendship."

"My sister will persist in loving you as she ever did, since there is no cause why she should not. Your misfortune—pardon me, *our* misfortune—will not cool her friendship for you."

"But the child—will you give me your answer?"

"My answer you already have; why repeat it?"

"Your answer! I think you mean your terms,— forgiveness—reconciliation."

"Ah, Madam, do you count those terms so hard? And hard they must be when they separate you from your child!"

The wife sat with head bowed down for a long time in silent thought. Tancredi made no move to disturb her reverie.

"Where is that vile woman who stole my child,

the woman who caused all this trouble?" she suddenly asked, gazing for the first time at her husband.

"As God is my judge, I know not. I have not seen her—have not even heard of her since I left New York, and I believe her dead."

"It was she who stole my child."

"Alas that that crime should come between us! Is there not enough without that spectre of the past? Let it be buried from our sight forever. I have expressed my profound sorrow for the wrong done you, and for the grief you have borne; I do so again, and ask you to forgive me."

"Who ordered her to steal my child?"

The husband made no reply.

"Was it you?"

The Signor was silent.

"Since you will not tell me, I shall hold you responsible for the crime."

"I cannot answer your question."

"Then I shall return home, childless, as I came," said the wife, sorrowfully, as she arose and terminated the interview by walking slowly and sadly away.

It has already been shown that Signora Adelaide was not always partial to her brother's acts, although strongly attached to him as a brother. His relations to the cantatrice had always been the cause of dissension between them, and the source of much grief to her. The sister was not aware of all, nor the half, of his heinous conduct, which resulted in the separation from his wife ; she knew nothing of the two boys, and never dreamed that the child now in her brother's possession, was other than he was represented, the child of Madam Alice Tancredi. She knew enough, however, to feel convinced that her brother was almost wholly to blame in the case, and that her sister-in-law was a wronged woman.

She therefore entered the presence of Madam Alice strongly prejudiced in her favor. The meeting was characterized by great tenderness on the part of both ladies. At first the American was cold and cautious, but she could not long withstand the sunny warmth and mesmeric kindness that beamed in the face and thrilled in the voice of Adelaide, and before she was willing, Alice melted down in alternate tears and smiles, which banished all reserve.

Of course their talk was on the subject uppermost in their minds. It is impossible to give their methods or tell how they reached agreement—such was the delicate tact of the one, and the charming complaisance of the other; but they did arrive at a conclusion that was satisfactory all around. They agreed that it would be best for all concerned to terminate the unfortunate quarrel by forgiveness and reconciliation.

The long estranged husband and wife were re-united, and returned to Philadelphia with the child, where they settled down to tranquil content, if not to unalloyed bliss.

CHAPTER XXIX.

"I am constant as the northern star,
  Of whose true, fixed, and resting quality
  There is no fellow in the firmament."

"Taplan, what do you say to a trip across the Alleghenies? I have a friend in Pittsburgh who has been writing to me to come out there, and I've sent him word I'll go. He tells me I'm sure of a good berth at good wages. What do you say, old friend, will you go along, as the spider said to the fly?"

Thus spoke Martin Haley to John Taplan, as they lounged about the Battery one afternoon. The person addressed looked up as if he were not sure the talk was meant for him, and even then he seemed to have forgotten what was said, for he made no reply.

Haley spoke again.

"My friend tells me the coal trade on the Ohio river is a big thing, and growin' bigger every year. It gives good berths for first-class boatman, and he says anybody willing to grow up with the trade will get rich. Now, I'm goin' there; I'm gettin' tired of the sea, an'll try my luck on a western steamboat. Come, what do you say, will you go along?"

"Me? Go along? That's good! Best I ever heard! Couldn't pay my ferriage to the Jersey shore!"

"Oh, never mind the money, as the lion said to the lamb. I've lots, and enough for us both; the thing is, will you go?"

"Yes."

"I want you along to take care of me, for I might get sick, as the monkey said to the sugar. Too many people know me here, and I'm goin' to the dogs. I'm goin' out there to begin life on the new, as Jonah said to the—"

"Didn't I say I'm going along?"

"That's the way to talk, old Jack! I was sure you wouldn't go back on your old mate. You must have a travelin' suit; that jacket ain't fit for a travelin' man; you need a trosser, as the young woman said. We're a goin' on a weddin' trip. Let's see what Moses has in the toggery line; come along."

The two companions entered a clothing shop, where John was fitted to a bran new suit—the "trosser" alluded to by Haley. The new coat on, like the king's shilling accepted, confirmed the bargain between Haley and Taplan. After he had squirmed a few times to familiarize himself with the unusual sensation of wearing a new and complete suit, he announced himself as ready for the "weddin' trip."

"This evenin' at eight sharp, we start; and be on

deck, old man, for I won't go without you, as the thief said to the policeman."

John buttoned up the new coat and nodded, as much as to say, no back out here; I'll be on deck.

"And, Jack," said Haley, in a confidential voice, taking hold of the lapel of John's coat, and drawing him aside, in the most mysterious manner.

Some one came along, and Haley coughed, as if surprised in some questionable trick. He waited till the intruder passed out of hearing.

"See, here, Jack," he resumed, in the same cautious manner of half fear, half dread, as if hesitating to speak of further contingencies of the co-partnership, contingencies unpleasant but unavoidable; "See here, Jack!"

"My, God, are you dying?"

"No."

"What's up, then?"

"Let's understand each other, old shipmate."

"Something bad? Speak out."

"No—more—whis—kee!" whispered Haley in Jack's ear.

"There, I knew it was something bad; I could see it in your face. No more whiskey! Why, that's *worse* than dying."

"No more grog, Jack."

"What! None? No! You don't mean it!

That's too little by a jugful! Can't stand it!" exclaimed Taplan, beginning to unbutton the coat.

"Well, what do you call enough?" asked Haley, with very pale face.

"Sixteen drinks a day," promptly answered the junior partner with the ready air of one who computes by carefully prepared statistics.

"How can you manage to get outside sixteen drinks in one day?"

"By system in your work and strict attention to business."

"What is your system?"

"One for an eye-opener, and one before breakfast. Are you keeping count?"

"Yes; that's two."

"One to settle your hash, and two in the forenoon. Score."

"That's five."

"One before dinner, one after for a hasher, and three in the course of the afternoon. Tally."

"That's ten."

"One before, one after supper, and three friendly social snifters in the evening. That's sixteen Joe-rums, if I understand figures. Is that what you make it?"

"Only fifteen, Jack; but enough."

"Hold on, hold on. There's a cheat somewhere.

I forgot my night-cap. That makes sixteen square, honest drinks, if I've kept a careful account, and none to spare."

"That's too much."

"Just in time! I'm glad you spoke before things went too far; you might have got me into trouble," exclaimed Taplan, pulling off the coat, evidently with the intention of resuming his old jacket and his independence.

"Hold on, Jack; don't go for to make a beast of yourself," exclaimed Haley, growing red in the face, and catching hold of Jack's arm to prevent him from drawing the only arm remaining in the sleeve.

"Sixteen drinks a day don't make a beast. Why, you must think I'm cast-iron to stand such a blow as that would give me. I'm weak enough, now. I'll have the man with the poker after me if you cut off my grog sudden like that!"

"Make it a drink before meals; that's a plenty for a travelin' business man."

"What if I break down, will you bear the blame?"

"I'll take kear of you, as the hawk said to the dove."

John stood for some time looking down at the new coat, partly clinging to his left arm and partly dragging on the floor, as if it were weakly pleading the course of sobriety, and then he cast a briefer glance at the calm old jacket lying on the counter, as if in a drunken sleep. John took brief time with the old garment, perhaps because it was a familiar study. The outcome of his reverie was the offer of a compromise.

"Make it a night-cap in, and it's a bargain," said Jack, very quietly, but earnestly.

"Well, night-cap it is. That's four drinks a day; honor bright, now, Taplan, as the thief said to his mate."

": Honor!" exclaimed the poor inebriate, as he crossed his breast to solemnize his vow. He proceeded to re-adjust the critical coat to his bloated body.

"Here, Moses, is the cash for the trosser," said Haley, counting down the sum. "We come pooty near purchasing elsewhere before we looked at your goods."

The two men, Haley and Taplan settled down at Pittsburgh, where they found no difficulty in obtaining employment on one of the steamers or tugs, used to tow coal barges to and from the south and south-west markets. The boat on which they shipped was owned by Frederick Rellim.

The constant and laborious employment, together with the impossibility of obtaining grog for two and three week voyages, straightened up John Taplan, to

14*

use Haley's expression. He soon looked much improved. Before many months, Taplan attracted the favorable notice of Rellim, who gave him the superintendency of his local business about the wharves and landings in Pittsburgh. He was sometimes required to visit Rellim's country residence on business connected with the coal trade.

While on his way to the latter place on one occasion, and while passing the old mill, he was attracted by cries of distress coming from the direction of the mill race, where he ran and saw a young woman wringing her hands and crying lustily.

He saw at a glance the cause of her distress; a child had fallen into the swift stream, and was rapidly drifting toward the floodgate, through which it would be drawn and broken on the ponderous revolving wheel, unless immediately rescued.

To spring into the water and drag the urchin out from the very vortex of the whirlpool was the work of a moment. He handed the half-drowned lad out to the young woman, who clasped him in her arms and fled to the house, leaving Taplan to scramble out as best he might. He crawled out of the flood, shook himself like a Newfoundland dog, and resumed his journey.

On his return he was intercepted by the miller, who had learned of Jarl's mishap and his rescue by Rellim's sailor, as Taplan was called.

"Give us a shake, my friend?" said Jackman, reaching out one hand, while he held the gate ajar with the other. "You must excuse Prudy; she was so shook up she didn't know which end was up. Excuse her."

John shook hands and "excused" Prudy on the spot; but nothing would do Nate but the sailor's entrance into the cottage, where he shook hands with Prudence, and attempted to nurse the resuscitated Jarl on his wet knee.

Jarl objected to the wet seat—he had had enough moisture in his for a day. This started Nate to hunt up his Sunday suit, and willy nilly, John got into them, leaving his wet clothes to dry. John blushed as he came down stairs with the miller's finery on, and blushed still more at fancying he saw a mischeivous smile in Prudy's eye on behalf of the ludicrous figure he cut in her father's old style garments.

On taking his leave he promised to come back for his clothes on the morrow. After this exciting though pleasant introduction many's the time was he seated by the cottage hearth or leaning on the front gate exchanging weather notes with Prudence. A warm friendship grew up between Taplan and the Jackmans, indeed he monopolized the guest's place at the cottage, for, as we have seen, the neighbors kept aloof.

"How about the grog, Jack?" asked Haley, a

month or so after the time when Jarl was rescued from drowning. "I hav'n't seen you taste a drop—I don't know the day when."

"And, my friend, you never will again, thanks to you for sticking to me even when I had deserted myself."

"You don't mean to tell me! And have you given up whiskey for good?"

"That's what I mean, Haley."

"I'm glad! Oh, but I'm glad! Old Fellow! Now you look like the old Jack I used to know! God bless you, Jack! Oh, but I'm glad!"

It is not easy to wring tears of joy from toilworn, brawny-hearted men. Such tears, when they do flow, are peculiarly ominous of deep heart-soundings. Taplan and Haley stood holding each other by the hands, and looked through tears into tear-brimmed eyes. They looked none the less manly for those tears.

It was true, John Taplan was redeemed from the slavery of the inordinate cup. He gave the credit to Martin Haley, and surely that friend's constancy was above praise, but it was the gentle Prudence Jackman who completed and established the reformation, begun by Haley in the clothing shop in New York. His step was lighter, eyes brighter, actions brisker, tongue readier, brain clearer, manners more social, and dress tidier than ever before.

Taplan had asked Prudence to become his wife and she had consented.

The provident pair waited for the time when he could provide the essentials of a substantial copartnership. But notwithstanding his industry and economy during five years service with Rellim, he made but slow advance in his position, and saved but a small amount out of his moderate earnings. His employer kept him as a drudge on a drudge's pay, while less competent or deserving men were advanced over him in place and salary. In modern times John would have struck for higher wages; in those days dissatisfied toilers struck for the gold diggings of California. John shipped as a sailor on a vessel bound for San Francisco via Cape Horn.

Years passed away without news of John Taplan, the sailor, but Patience Jackman kept his memory and her faith, companions in her true heart.

CHAPTER XXX.

"I have a silent sorrow here,
  A grief I'll ne'er impart ;
It breathes no sigh, it sheds no tear,
  Yet it consumes my heart."

"SEE, here! youngster, let this be a warning to you! Keep out of fights until you are old enough to take care of yourself."

This admonition was bestowed on Jarl on a street in Philadelphia. The person who gave it was a bronzed, broad shouldered stranger, who had rescued the lad from the very midst of a howling, tramping mob of firemen, who, in those days, generally wound up a fire with a riot, in which rival companies and their friends pounded each other with brick-bats and paving stones.

"John Taplan! John Taplan! Hurrah! Hurrah for John Taplan!" shouted Jarl at the top of his voice, and heedless of his recent peril and his present bloody nose he rushed into the arms of the surprised sailor.

It was indeed the long absent John Taplan, just returned from the gold mines of California, and on his route to Pittsburgh.

As a matter of course the information he got from Jarl made the remaining part of his journey superfluous. He was piloted by Jarl to Nate Jackman's house, and was there heralded by his guide shouting "Hurrah for John Taplan!"

Taplan had made his "Pile of dust," but like all the "returned Californians" of those days, he was bound to go back to the "diggings," and only returned to the "States" to carry away Prudence Jackman as his wife. Nor was he long in accomplishing his errand— they were married and off for the Pacific slope before Nate could realize that he was childless. The old miller and Jarl broke up housekeeping and went to live with Mrs. Heron.

This lady took a strong liking for Jarl, and charged herself with every motherly care, superintending his education, mending his clothes, going through his pockets, hiding his pistols, and executing other like duties universally thought indispensible in the rearing of young males. She breveted him her chief clerk, that is, he was to become that official, after some years of schooling to fit him for the place. A part of her plan was kept secret, which was to marry him to her niece, Charlotte Duval.

Nearly opposite to the Heron mansion, where Jarl now lived, dwelt a celebrated tragedian. Jarl had often watched the great man come and go, and regarded him with that awe and admiration felt for a superior being. The kingly tread and grace of the superb, loud-voiced man, impressed the boy with a craving desire to become such a man. The observant actor began to take some notice of the bright and handsome youth, and the casual street acquaintance between the man and boy grew and ripened into the most friendly intimacy. The proud man loved to have Jarl in his sombre home; he seemed to bring with him there the sunshine of country skies and the lark of the blossoming meadows. But the actor also took a practical interest in the lad, and persuaded Mrs. Heron and Nate Jackman to allow Jarl to be instructed in music and elocution, the latter under his immediate supervision.

A year or more had passed in this pleasant manner, during which time Jarl made rapid progress in his studies, especially in music, which art seemed to come to him intuitively. His voice was already phenomenal in its compass, power and richness; besides there was that in his style and presence so thrilling and passionate, as to stamp him with the impress of high talent, if not genius.

With these elements and environments it was natural that he should fall in love with the stage, and he began preparing himself for the profession of the actor. When his tutor, the tragedian, appeared on the stage in Philadelphia, he delighted and encouraged the boy by assigning to him some minor part, or, as was then not uncommon, some by-play interluded into the main drama of the evening's entertainment. On one such occasion Jarl personated a shepherd boy, with song.

In that audience sat Signor Michele Tancredi, looking older, and more sedate, but as distinguished as ever.

On the following day the manager of the Walnut Street Theatre was waited on by Tancredi, who requested a clue to the shepherd boy of the evening before. He was referred to the actor, and the actor took him to Nate Jackman. The Signor was closeted for a long time with the old miller, and came away at last as pale as death.

There can be no doubt but that at that interview he learned the story of Jarl, from the then present, back to when he was left at the old mill by a dying woman. Without doubt he saw and handled the relics kept so guardedly all those years by the miller—the two lockets with the portraits inside of both, and with his first name written by his own hand on the back of one. He must have seen and recognized the defaced picture of his wife.

There was no scene—no outward tumult,—on the occasion when Tancredi identified his long lost son. He was white of face, but he was not the kind of man

to allow his emotions to explode in outward tumult.
Powerful impressions only made him more stoical
because more guarded. On this special occasion he
was as calm as a June morning, as placid as the surface
of the moon. But we who are endowed with lively
imaginations, may enter into his secret feelings and
appreciate what was, or should have been, his remorse.
And, in estimating his inward disquiet and his outward
quiet, we may conceive how possible it was for the
Spartan to make no cry, though the fox dug at his
vitals.

From our knowledge of the man it would be
expected that he would keep his remorseful secret
locked up in his breast, and he did. But the ties of
consanguinity, the prickings of conscience, and, perhaps
most of all, the attractiveness of the youth, prompted
him to take a zealous interest in the youth, and in
everything that concerned him. He, however, dis-
played such clever tact and delicacy, that his attentions,
though marked, excited no remark ; besides every one
who came to know the bright boy felt the same kindly
interest. Mrs. Heron, the Duvals, the tragedian, all
took a practical interest in Jarl ; advising this, doing
that or the other, regarding his training and schooling.
The Signor's known taste and culture, more particularly
in musical matters, gave him extra license to bestow

his patronage on this handsome child of song. No one was likely to suspect the Signor's secret.

It was fortunate for Tancredi, and perhaps for Jarl, also, that John Taplan was in far away California.

It was impossible for Jarl, with his positive, passionate and confiding nature, to resist the influence of the kind partiality shown him by the fascinating Signor. The two became deeply attached to each other, and passed much of their time together, over their music, studying the Italian language, or driving about the city in the Tancredi carriage.

Over five years had passed under the able tutorship of the actor and Tancredi, and it was more than six years since Jackman had left the old mill. Jarl was now twenty-one. He was possessed of such a wonderful voice, and showed such decided love and fitness for the stage, that his patrons determined that he should complete his musical education under the best masters and in the best schools of Europe.

Nate Jackman had hitherto suffered them to do pretty much as they pleased with his foster child, but he drew the line at the proposed European plan. He looked on the new project as absurd nonsense, and he said it was. He had grumbled at the new fangled music (as he termed it) which the boy had practiced. The simple old man loved better the old ballads which Jarl was wont to sing in the meadows, and about the old mill; such songs brought sweet memories to his mind, and affectionate tears to his eyes. But the new songs were to him noise and nonsense, or as he called them "tunes the old cow died on."

The boy's patrons argued so well, however, that Nate's objections were narrowed down to one—the matter of cost.

"Where's the money to come from? That's what I want to know—where's the money to come from?"

"We'll provide for his education while abroad."

"But he can't go by himself, and I can't go along, and Prudy, she's in Californy. Who'll take keer of him among them furriners? and Prudy in Californy?"

"I'm a musician and a native of Italy, and intimately acquainted with the schools and the best teachers in the country," replied Tancredi. "I will undertake to secure for him the best masters and the best care,— I will go along with him, if you will trust him to my keeping."

The old man was well nigh persuaded, but insisted on conferring with Duval before making up his mind. In a short time that gentleman's consent was obtained, and it was agreed by Nate that Jarl, in company with and under the care of Tancredi, should go to Europe to finish his musical education.

Before they sailed, and for the first and only time, Tancredi invited Jarl to pass the evening at his home.

The young man went and met there a young gentleman of about his own age. This person was slight in figure, was not so tall as Jarl, and was darker skinned, with remarkably black eyes. He was always in motion, and spoke rapidly though well. By his manner it was evident that he felt proud of his station as the heir of the noble Tancredi and the illustrious Bannemead. He was, if not as distinguished looking as his father, as proud as Madam Tancredi, whom he called mother.

This young man was known as Charles Tancredi; his real name was Carlo Godardo.

Tancredi and his two youthful companions were seated around a table in the library looking over a collection of rare engravings, and intent on discussing their merits. Jarl sat between the two,—sat facing the library door, and with the soft light of the table lamp shining full on his handsome—how handsome! young face.

A noiseless footfall on the velvety carpet, a silent, proud woman—it might have been a queen—in the doorway, from where she gazed on that beautiful young face. No startled look or movement betokened what may have flashed through her mind; she only stood like a statue with her cold eyes resting on the unconscious Jarl.

"What does this picture represent?" asked Jarl, as he raised his head to look into Tancredi's face.

"The mother and her child, Hager and Ishmael, driven into the wilderness."

Jarl slowly arose to his feet as his gaze met that of the apparition in the doorway.

Thus met the mother and her child after the parting of eighteen long bitter years.

Did the souls of these two beings go out to meet each the other in joyful recognition? Did their spirits, as did their bodies, meet face to face? Did they know each other there?

Does the soul, when it reaches the immortal land, realize that it once suffered in the flesh? If not, then is death practical annihilation.

If the souls of mother and son hailed each other as kin, the brain was not taken into confidence.

Madam Tancredi came forward and gave Jarl her queenly hand. Thus coldly they met, thus coldly they parted for years and years.

Jarl, with Signor Tancredi, sailed for Italy.

CHAPTER XXXI.

"*Xanthus.* For if thou slayest me, thou wilt be thy father's murderer.

"*Ion.* But how art thou my Father ? Is not this ridiculous for me to listen to ?

"*Xanthus.* Not so; a speedy explanation would tell you how I am circumstanced.

"*Ion.* And wilt thou tell me ?

"*Xanthus.* I am thy father and thou art my son."

—Euripides.

"Signor, is it the sea voyage that makes you so quiet ?" asked Jarl, with a playful, bantering air, when they had been a few days out on the sea.

" You give me small chance to show high spirits in your presence, my young friend, for you are almost constantly aloft or among the sailors," retorted Tancredi.

"But I leave you free to enjoy the ladies society. They seem very fond of you, Signor."

" And you, my boy, won't let them make fond of you," answered Tancredi, blushing. " You are different from me in that respect."

" Well, I think when you *are* in my company, you ought to make up for lost time, and talk to me just a little bit; but here we have been sitting for an hour, during which time you have scarcely spoken a word."

"Never fear; I'll make up for lost time when we reach Naples. Traveling always makes me stupid."

Silence again fell on the two companions. Jarl evidently had something on his mind and was bent on making his friend talk.

"Signor, you never told me of your home in Italy."

"The story will be more eloquent when told there. Then you will say that it is the most delightful place in all the wide world. Ah me! I fear you will never consent to return to America."

"You left it for America; why may not I?"

"True; I left it and so may you."

"Of your own free will did you leave Italy?"

"Of my own free will, yes; willingly, no."

"You left it unwillingly; then why should you feel sad on returning?"

Tancredi made no reply.

"You do not answer me, Signor. Have I offended? I meant it not."

"No, my gentle friend, you have not offended; you could not offend me, for I know you would not."

The youth again lapsed into silence, as though the sombre spirit of his companion had cast its shadows over his bouyant thoughts.

The sun was down, the day was dying, and the horizon was disappearing under the fast falling mantle of night.

"Jarl, I have something I wish to tell you; something important and sacred," said Tancredi, in low and solemn voice, after a long silence. "Will you promise to hear what I have to say, patiently, through to the end?"

"I promise," replied Jarl, with a keen look of inquiry and wonder depicted on his handsome face.

"It is a long story, Jarl; therefore you must be patient during its recital. It is a sad story, but do not condemn until it is fully told. It is a true story, reserve your doubts until you try all the facts. The story concerns me; it relates to you."

The wondering look deepened on the earnest face.

"Go on; I listen," he whispered.

"Jarl, look around you. Everything outside this ship is waste and solitude. This vessel alone, at present, constitutes our world, and it contains but one being you can call your friend. I am that friend— your friend, not only here, but everywhere, wherever you are, and whatever you do. I must ever and always be your best friend."

Jarl arose and stood beside the Signor, and placed his hand on his shoulder, a strange habit he had when

15

pleased by those he loved. The Signor held the young
man's hand, and continued :

"Far away beyond that golden barrier of the
twilight, where but now the sun went down in glory,
is the world from whence you came. Toward where
that sun shall rise again is the strange world that
awaits your coming. No kindred will greet you there,
as no kindred mourns your absence from your native
land."

"O Signor! Talk not so bitterly! You forget
my good old foster-father, who will grieve at my
absence, and rejoice at my return."

"I grant that, Jarl; God bless old Nate for his
devotion to you! But I spoke of kindred. The old
miller is not your father; you have no kindred known
to you."

"Alas! Signor, you speak true!"

"Jarl, let me be your father; let me call you my
son. I love you, Jarl, how well, you never can know.
Let me fill the place of father to you."

"How strange that you should ask this, since we
are already the best friends in the world!"

"But, Jarl, a father's place is holier than that of
friend."

"I don't think it will make much difference what
I call you, since you are not my real father, but I
shall try to love and obey you as if you were. Per-

haps as my father I would fear you, and as son give you only respect, where I should give love and obedience. But the story, Signor—you are forgetting the story you promised."

"You are assisting me tell the story."

"But the story we are telling is fictitious, and made up as we go along; besides it is not sad, but jolly. Your story was to have been a sad one."

"Jarl, I know your real father."

"You know my real father!" exclaimed Jarl, withdrawing his hand from Tancredi, and standing before him.

"Yes, I know your father. Look on this picture."

"What, the picture the poor woman left with me at the miller's cottage! How came it in your possession?"

"It has been in my possession for twenty-five years. It is mine, honestly mine, and always has been. It is not the picture left at the mill by the woman, but it is the companion of that picture. Old Nate Jackman still retains that picture in his possession; this belongs to me. Both pictures are the faithful portraits of your father as he appeared a quarter of a century ago."

"And what of him? You know him? Do you know him? Does he still live, and where?"

" I knew him when he was a child, a boy ; I knew him and was with him when he sat for that portrait. He still lives ; I know him as you also do ; he stands before you ; I am your father."

" You, my father !"

" I am your father."

The father stood holding out his arms toward his son.

Jarl turned away and stood gazing out on the placid summer sea glimmering in the phosphorescent twilight. The brightest stars began to shine out one by one like rays of hope and beauty amidst the fast gathering gloom of the night.

Jarl walked aft, as if instinctively turning back home to his old foster-father, who was first in his thoughts, and who filled the largest space in his grateful heart. When he reached the stern of the vessel, he stood and gazed at the evening star, and saw in its beams the fantastic flames that blazed on the cottage hearth on that eventful eve when first he resolved to fly from his enemies. He felt again like fleeing— from what he knew not.

A strange impression came over him, a strange fancy siezed him ; it was not sorrow, or hate, or despair, scarcely even despondency, but a feeling of mingled regret and bereavement—regret that he had ever left the protection of his foster-father, and bereavement at the loss of his society. Somehow he vaguely felt that this elegant Signor, who called him son, had insidiously and cruelly come between him and the old miller. He fancied that the Bohemian life he had hitherto led, and which was endeared to him by usage, was slipping away, and its place filled with family, ancestors, and all the accessories of conventional life. His old life, if solitary, had been independent; in it he had no ancestors to honor, no kindred to copy, no family to humor.

He was jealous of the ambition which lured him from his humble station, suspicions of the Signor with his blandishments and his patronage, and angry with himself for having left his old benefactor. Though weary miles of waves rolled between, yet the Old Miller seemed nearer and dearer than ever before—nearer and dearer a thousand times than the grand Signor who claimed to be his father.

His meditations were interrupted by a light hand on his shoulder; turning round he faced Tancredi.

"Not now, my son, not now; some other time. When we are come to our own beautiful home I shall relate to you the wonderful story of your life."

"As it best pleases you, Signor."

"At present I ask but one favor—do not speak of what I have told you to any one."

"I have no one to tell. But since it is your request

I shall not disappoint you," replied Jarl, coldly, almost bitterly.

Tancredi's knowledge of human nature, and his tact, served him well on the occasion. He realized thoroughly the ordeal to which he had submitted his son. His determination at first was to make no attempt at revealing Charles Tancredi's history until after they were happily established at his home in Naples; and, that there might be no sudden crash, his intention was to slowly and guardedly enlighten the son, that there might be no straining of the regard he had shown for his father. Chance, or fate, had strangely led him to anticipate the opening chapter of Charles' mysterious nativity, but his observant eye had caught sight of the imminent panic in the boy's mind, and his judgment called a halt.

But the secret was exposed, although not fully revealed, and was beyond recall. The story must be completed sooner or later at all hazards; if no one else, Jarl would demand the whole story of his birth and parentage. The Signor, therefore, followed his son to where he stood brooding over the strange story, and sought to allay the storm brewing in his breast.

Jarl, the Miller's Boy, or, as he shall hereafter be known, Charles Tancredi, settled down at Naples to his studies in music. The story begun by his father seemed to exert a great influence over him, at least he exhibited a marked change in deportment, and from the rolicking noisy boy he became quiet, observant and moody. He sought to be alone when not in the conservatoire, and evidently shunned the Signor's company; or if he spent an hour with his father he was taciturn if not answering the simple yes or no to the Signor's interrogatories. His perplexity was a real anguish, which long continued discipline under trials and persecutions alone enabled him to endure with resignation. How often and often he longed for the ignorance, the independence and the content of his days under the guardianship of his dear old foster-father!

One night, at a late hour, Tancredi and Charles sat alone in their beautiful home over-looking Naples. The talk was on the education and the future of Charles Tancredi.

"Charles, you have led me to believe that you are inclined to go on the stage as a public actor."

"Yes, Signor."

"I trust that since you have learned who and what you are, you will give up that ambition."

"What am I, Signor?"

"You are my son. Your relations in almost every particular are materially altered from what they were, and the sooner you recognize that fact the better for you and me. Your family has claims on you which you cannot ignore. You are secure of great wealth which makes a profession no longer necessary; you will, as the head of the Tancredi house—the oldest of the noble houses of Italy—be called upon to fill an exalted station in nation and society, and a professional career would be incompatible with that station. In addition to the noble family of which you are the heir, your mother belongs to a distinguished family, and is quite wealthy in her own right."

"Signor, you speak of my mother; you will please remember that I have not the pleasure of her acquaintance."

"Not know your mother!"

"How should I? You are my father; you tell me so, and I believe you, but I could not have guessed that you are my father. Neither can I guess who is my mother, and you have not told me, hence I do not know her, for it has not pleased you to complete the story you began on shipboard."

"Why, Charles, who should be your mother but my wife, Madam Alice Tancredi, the lady whom you met at my house in Philadelphia the evening before we left America."

"That lady my mother!"

"Yes; who else, pray?"

"No one else, I pray."

"Wherefore, then, your surprise?"

"O Signor, can you ask? What but surprise meets me on every side? I am surprised that she did not call me son ; surprised that you did not present me to her as to my mother; surprised that I never met her before nor since; surprised that she let me suffer all these sorrowful years; surprised that you permitted me to be an outcast without a single tie of blood to cling to; and surprised that my mother coldly let me leave her to come to this foreign land."

"Alas for me, my poor boy, how your words wring my heart! Woe is me! Woe is me! for your true words cut deeper than a knife."

"Perhaps, Signor, I should not feel as I do; but I cannot help feeling surprised at my new and strange surroundings. I seem to walk in a dream—I, who never felt the claims of kindred, am suddenly introduced to father and mother and family. Oh, it is a surprise! I know it is—must be, good news, since it restores me to those endearments held desirable and sacred ; but I have dreaded to hear about my mother—dreaded, oh dreaded it as the culprit dreads to hear the sentence spoken by the judge. For the wrong I have done you I beg your pardon."

"The wrong you have done me! What wrong, Charles ?"

"In my mind I have wronged you, Signor. I have also wronged the lady, your wife—my mother."

"But the wrong, wherein have you wronged your mother or myself?"

"Some other woman might have been my mother, some other woman who had no right to be my mother."

"Forgive me, my poor boy, forgive me for my cruelty, my cruel forgetfulness! Great God, this remorse grows keener every hour! On my knees, I crave your pardon! O, Charles, my son!"

"Signor, listen to me. Of the causes which led to the lot which has befallen me, I am ignorant. You have not finished the story. You speak of remorse; I know not why you should feel guilt stricken. I can only wait until I have heard the completion of the story of my life. How came it that I was an outcast? Why did my family leave me to suffer all those bitter years? Why does no one but you know of my identity, and how came you to discover me? Does my mother know of me? I am not even restored to my family, only to you. Why? These questions must be answered. I feel very bitter and vengeful. I command you to finish the story."

Tancredi then began and told his son everything and every circumstance connected with his own life. The conscience stricken man could not have shown more candor and truthfulness if he had been inside the confessional purgating his sins in his dying hour.

He told everything, and kept nothing back; even where the story blackened with his own perfidy he was the more open and explicit. When he concluded by telling how he had palmed off the son of the woman, Godardo, on his wife—told how Carl Godardo had usurped the place of Charles Tancredi,—the young man sprang from his chair like an enraged tiger and dashed his father to the floor.

For a moment, the angered youth looked down on the prostrate form, for a moment he caught the sight of his father's piteous, terrorized face, and, uttering a wail like that of a man stricken with death, he fled from the terrible temptation.

From that moment Tancredi never saw or heard of his son. For months and months he sought him in every corner of Europe; his son was lost for the second time, this time, forever.

Broken in health and spirits, and bowed under remorse and despair the wretched man returned to his home in Philadelphia. He was bound to give an account of his stewardship to Nate Jackman. He lied to and deceived the old man.

His evil deeds and their woeful consequences swarmed like a troop of noisy demons to shake his pillow with unrest. Keen despair worked a dagger in his heart, scorching memory burnt into his brain, and his form, once so proud and stately, and the step once

so kingly, were bent and halting now. He grew
maudlin in his talk, childish in his behavior, dreaded
being left alone, and followed his wife about the house
like a tottering babe. He gradually lost the use of
his legs, and, unable to walk, sat all day muttering to
himself, or weeping without apparent cause.

"I have something on my mind that troubles me,"
he said to his wife one day while seated in his easy-
chair.

"Ought I to know what your trouble is?" she
asked, kindly.

"My trouble? yes. You must know my trouble—
yes, my trouble. It concerns you more than any one.
I have heard news of the Godardo."

"Ah, indeed? And how can news of her possibly
concern me, unless it is to hear of her repentance?"

"She is dead. She has been dead for twenty
years."

"I hope she is better occupied where she now is."

"She left a message for you."

"A message for me? What message could she
leave me?"

"Concerning your son—our son."

"With whom did she leave this message?"

"With the family at whose house she died."

"Who, and where is this family, and what is the
message?"

"An old miller, called Nate Jackman, who lived in Western Pennsylvania, near Pittsburgh, and at whose house she died, now lives in this city; he has her dying message, and can give it better than you can receive it second-hand."

"I am not interested in any message she could leave. She stole my child; it was not her fault that I recovered him. I have my son, and want nothing of her living or dead."

"I think you should, as a duty to your son, visit the miller. I think you will be surprised at what he will tell you. He has in his keeping a few articles which the dead woman left, and which articles I have seen, and by them identified her."

"What are those articles?"

"Among them a locket worn by our son when he was stolen, and which contains your portrait and mine."

"I have often wondered what became of that locket. I supposed that you took it away with you when you carried Charles to Italy."

"I think the miller would give you that locket. Here is the directions by which he may be found. Go, and hasten back, for I dread being left alone. I feel I shall not trouble you long. I trust it won't be for long."

"Since you are so anxious, I shall visit Mr. Jackman."

Madam found the old man at Mrs. Heron's.

"Mr. Jackman," said Madam Alice, "my husband
tells me that a woman called Rosetta Godardo died at
your house twenty years ago."

"Yes, ma'am, a woman died at my house twenty
years come next November, but she wouldn't tell her
name."

"My husband also tells me that she left a message
for me."

"No, ma'am, she didn't—she didn't leave a message for nobody."

"Are you sure?"

"Sure? Yes; she only left some things and
Jarl."

"Jarl? What is a Jarl?"

"Why, the boy she left with me when she died."

"The boy! What boy?"

"The boy—why Jarl—three years old she brung
with her, and some picters; here's the picters."

He showed her the portraits already described,
which she recognized. Attached to the locket by a
slender chain was a tiny gold charm, marked with the
letters A. B., her maiden initials. She had sat by and
watched the goldsmith fasten this small jewel to the
locket, and, with her own hands, she had placed it

around baby's neck on the first anniversary of his birthday.

"Here's a silk hankercher, it belonged to Jarl, too."

He showed her a handkerchief marked with the monogram, C. T., which she had embroidered with her own hands.

"Whose child was it?"

"She said it wasn't hern."

"But whose child do you think it was?"

"Strayed or stolen! That's what I've been a tryin' to find out for twenty years, yes, for well nigh twenty years. Maybe you know, ma'am."

"What became of the child you call Jarl?"

"I took him and raised him like one of my own. He lived with me till a year ago, when Mr. Tancredi took him away to Itlee, to school, Oh, he's the bravest, and handsomest boy you ever saw! Why, you *did* see him, for he told me so, himself—he told me he saw you at your house the night before he went away to Itlee. But he didn't say nothin' about you bein' his mother. Ax your husband, he knows where Jarl is, for he likes Jarl—everybody likes Jarl."

Madam Tancredi turned deadly pale, and fell on the floor in a swoon. Jackman revived her by dashing water—more than needed—in her face.

"Is that all you can tell me?" she asked, after recovering consciousness.

"That's all. I'm sure the crazy woman didn't leave no message for you nor nobody."

"Will you trust these things in my keeping?"

"What'll you do with 'em? I've kept them to try to find Jarl's kinfolks."

"I think this boy—that Jarl was—O, Mr. Jackman! Do you think that this child was my son? I had a child stolen from me twenty years ago. He was stolen by the woman who died at your house. He wore this locket around his little neck; this was his handkerchief—see, I stitched these very letters with my own hand! O, what if Jarl is my own lost son!"

"Yes, Ma'am, yes, certainly; if you air his mother take 'em, in welcome; take 'em home with you. That's what they're for,—to find Jarl's mother. But mind this—you can't like Jarl as well as I do—mind you, not as well as I do."

She took the relics and went home, where she had a painful and horrible meeting with her husband.

"Well, Signor, I got the message from the old miller, and I ask you in God's name to interpret its meaning."

"Your son was stolen by the Godardo. He is the youth who passed the evening in this house before I took him to Italy. I am as thoroughly convinced of his identity as I am of yours."

"But, the youth we call our son,—who is he?"

"He is not your son."

"My God, can such things be! Then in Heaven's name, whose child is he?"

"He is the son of Rosetta Godardo."

"Who is his father?"

"Alas, Madam, I am his father."

"May God have mercy on your soul!"

"Amen! When I went to Italy at the time of our quarrel and separation I stole the Godardo's child, and carried him home with me to Naples."

"And, in revenge, that mother stole my child."

"Yes."

"And you knowingly and wilfully palmed off her child on me as my own?"

"Now, you know all. I could suffer the pangs of concealment no longer. It was killing me by inches. Forgive me, or kill me!"

"Forgive you! You, the fiend! The child stealer, the traitor, the murderer! God has cursed our union, he may forgive you, I cannot. Begone from this home that you have twice desecrated and desolated! Begone, and take with you your son whom you have fraudulently taught me to love!"

"Mercy! Mercy!" cried the stricken wretch, as

he trembling arose, with the palor of death on his withered face. He convulsively reached out his hands to her and fell forward a corpse.

Too late; he never moved. Too late; he never breathed again. Too late for earthly retribution; Signor Michele Tancredi was dead.

Tancredi's will provided for the young man, Carlo Godardo, who amazed and broken-hearted, went sadly away with his father's dead body to Italy, where he was cared for by the Tancredi family. Madam Tancredi would not see him, she even refused his touching message of farewell. The unhappy Madam Alice sent a messenger to Europe to hunt up her son and bring him home. She only learned that he had mysteriously disappeared from Naples, and was never heard of since. It was renewing and continuing the detective work left off twenty years agone. No trace was had of the boy, lost the second time.

CHAPTER XXXII.

'He left a name at which the world grew pale,
To point a moral, or adorn a tale."

A REMARKABLE phenomenon in the music and dramatic world rocked European society to its depths a year or so after the death of Signor Tancredi. Tongue and pen were busy with praising a new tenor, who at one bound, leaped from total obscurity into unprecedented public favor. His fame was still further heightened because of the mystery which surrounded him. No one knew him, whence he came, or who was his teacher. One day a proud and handsome stranger presented himself before the faculty of the conservatoire in Milan as a contestant for singing in a prize trial, which was appointed for the selection of a tenor for the grand opera house at St. Petersburg. One song from the stranger finished the contest—he was appointed to the place. He seemed to have arisen out of the earth, and from that hour filled the opera sky like a blazing comet, at whose light all stars paled. The unknown tenor, as he was called, had the world at his feet.

The echo of his fame and glory, like a wide-spreading perfume, reached the western world, and America was on the tip-toe of expectation, for the renowned singer was announced for a brief season in the United States.

In New York, where he first appeared, his success was so marvelous, that week after week his engagement was extended, to the no small chagrin of other cities. The audiences went wild over his beauty, his acting, and, more than all the rest, his wonderful voice and singing. His receptions every night were not approval and applause, they were ovations.

At last he was billed to appear in Philadelphia. On the opening night there sat in the packed theatre four of our old acquaintances, Mrs. Heron, Mr. and Mrs. Duval, and their daughter, Miss Charlotte, now grown into a lovely woman.

The opera of the evening was Maritana. When the ragged and rolicking Don Cæsar De Bazan rendered the *Cavatina*, "Let me like a soldier fall," the applause which followed was never equalled in a Quaker city audience. The encore was almost as noisy.

The tribute of Charlotte Duval was tears. Again he sang the last stanza of that stirring *arietta*, while Charlotte followed her libretto with the English words.

"I only ask of that proud race
    That ends its blaze in me,
To die the last, and not disgrace
    Its ancient chivalry.

Tho' o'er my bier no banners wave,
    No martial requiem swell ;
Enough—they murmur at my grave—
    He like a soldier fell !

When the song was concluded, Charlotte was sobbing. What at? Her memory wandered back to the woods and meadows about the old mill when Jarl sang by her side and made the welkin ring with his glad, bird like voice. She thought of Jarl and the gala days of childhood, and wept. There was an echo in the voice of the Don Cæsar of the stage that stirred heart-fond memories of the sweet golden days of childhood ; that was the cause of her tears.

When the tenor next came on the stage in the gorgeous costume of the bridegroom, Charlotte Duval gave a startled cry: "My God! It is Jarl! O father, it is Jarl!"

The whole audience heard, and all eyes were turned toward the excited girl. Her speech was meaningless to that audience. The tenor heard that cry, and he understood those words and what they meant. He stood in dumb astonishment until the frenzied maestro wanded him back to his cue. Charlotte heard no more, but saw only the tenor on the stage.

Mr. and Mrs. Duval saw it and identified it, as did Mrs. Heron, for had she not made it with her own hands?—the Scarlet Scarf with a white heart and anchor worked in white embroidery in either end. That scarf was worn by the Don Cæsar of the opera.

The next morning early an old man with snowy hair and rosy face stood waiting and watching before the theatre entrance. When the doors opened for rehearsal the old fellow pushed past the green door opening into the auditorium. An officer seized him and rudely attempted to thrust him out, but fell sprawling before he knew what struck him.

"I want my boy! I want Jarl! and no one can put me out till I find him. Jarl, I say Jarl!" cried the old miller at the top of his voice.

Other attaches of the place came to the rescue, and, although they pinioned the old hero to the floor, they could not throttle his voice.

"I want Jarl! Hello, Jarl! It's me—it's Nate, the old miller! Hello, Jarl, I say!"

A man leaped from the stage, sprang across the chairs, and in a second the custodians of Nate went flying hither and thither.

"Here I am, father! Here's your boy! I'm Jarl!"

Two men, one old and gray, the other young and proud, were in each other's arms.

"God bless you, my boy! God bless you, Jarl! I know'd you'd come back to me! You won't leave me any more, will you, Jarl? God bless my poor boy!"

"No, my good, dear old father; we shall never part again? I am come back to you—you that I love best in all this wide world?"

Jarl and Nate! They make one prouder of his race.

"Come; let's git out of hear! This place haint big enough to hold us. Come home, Jarl, come home!"

The people along the streets turned and watched and followed the beautiful old man leading home his boy,—for the two grand men held each other by the hand. They talked and they laughed and they cried, and tears so dimmed their eyes that they no more saw their fellow mortals around them than they did the dancing angels that strewed their pathway with ethereal roses. Oh, it was a spectacle more grand and glorious than all the flushing triumphs won by the young tenor on the stage, grand and glorious as were those triumphs.

Jarl and Nate! They reveal the full meaning of the words Honor, Friendship, Gratitude.

Charles Tancredi went home with Nate Jackman; that visit, to him, was as unavoidable as was Gilpin's ride,—Nate would have carried him had he refused to walk. But there was no trouble on that score; the young man was glad and willing to go home.

Arrived there he was the miller's boy, Mrs. Heron's clerk, Mrs. Duval's prince, Mr. Duval's nature's nobleman, and Charlotte's—what was he to Charlotte Duval? What he ever had been—her ideal, her hero, her angel, and her lover, which last rounds the top of a maiden's climax.

On the following day Nate Jackman rang the door bell of the Tancredi mansion on Walnut street, and presently was admitted into the presence of Madam Alice.

"I come to tell you Jarl is found."

"You mean Charles, my son, do you not? Good news, O, good news! Where is he?"

"Here, in Philadelphia."

"Oh, Mr. Jackman! bring him to me. When will you bring him to me? Is he in this house? Will you bring him this minute, to-day—this night?"

"No; I guess not to-night bekase, you see, he is a singin' in the opery to-night, and can't git off. You must know he's the great tinner everybody is a braggin' about."

"What, the great tenor? the unknown tenor, my son? But I care not for that so he proves to be my son. I'm his mother starving to see him before I die.''

"Well, why don't you go and fetch him home, like I did? You've been waitin' for him a good while."

"I'll send you to bring him; you can bring him if any one can. I wouldn't know him if I saw him. You'll bring him to his mother, won't you, Mr. Jackman?"

She rang the bell and ordered the carriage to be brought to the door for Nate.

"He mightn't come for me, Ma'am; just put your hand to a short letter, sayin' as how you air well, and hopes these few lines may find him enjoyin' the same God's blessin', an' so fort. You see I want to curry it along for fear he won't come for my say, don't you see?"

She wrote and sent by Nate the following:

CHARLES TANCREDI.

My darling Son:

Forgive your mother for not writing to you sooner. She would have invited you home on a visit twenty years and more ago, but she lost your address. She might have found your address long ago, but she did not try, for she was deluded into loving a spurious son. And now that she has found you, she claims

16

you all for herself, Come home, my darling, come home to your waiting Mother

ALICE TANCREDI.

Nate returned without the son, but with a note which read:

Dearest Mother: A few more hours cannot seriously add to the long, bitter years of our separation and bereavement. I shall visit you at 3 P.M.

Your son,

C. TANCREDI.

She was disappointed and distressed at his delay, but long experience in both, had tempered her heart to endurance. To while away the time, she got out the relics restored to her by Nate Jackman, and was engaged in a mother's homage to her secret gods, when she felt a footfall on the carpet. Before she could see who it was, a man's figure knelt at her feet, a curly head bowed itself in her lap, and a musical voice uttered the single word, "Mother!"

" Charles, my darling son !"

At last the dark waters lit up with a mother's love. After years of exile and yearning, the lost child was restored to that being most worthy of man's homage, a good mother.

Charles Tancredi and Charlotte Duval were married. They passed a week of the honeymoon at the Duval mansion, near the old mill. The Rellims, and Liftals, and Bowlers, and Tobbys gazed with guilty and mortified awe on the great hero as he passed them unnoticed by; his high lineage and his celebrity had penetrated even their asinine ears.

What more need be said? Only this—Jarl and Nate! They are worthy of imitation.

THE END.

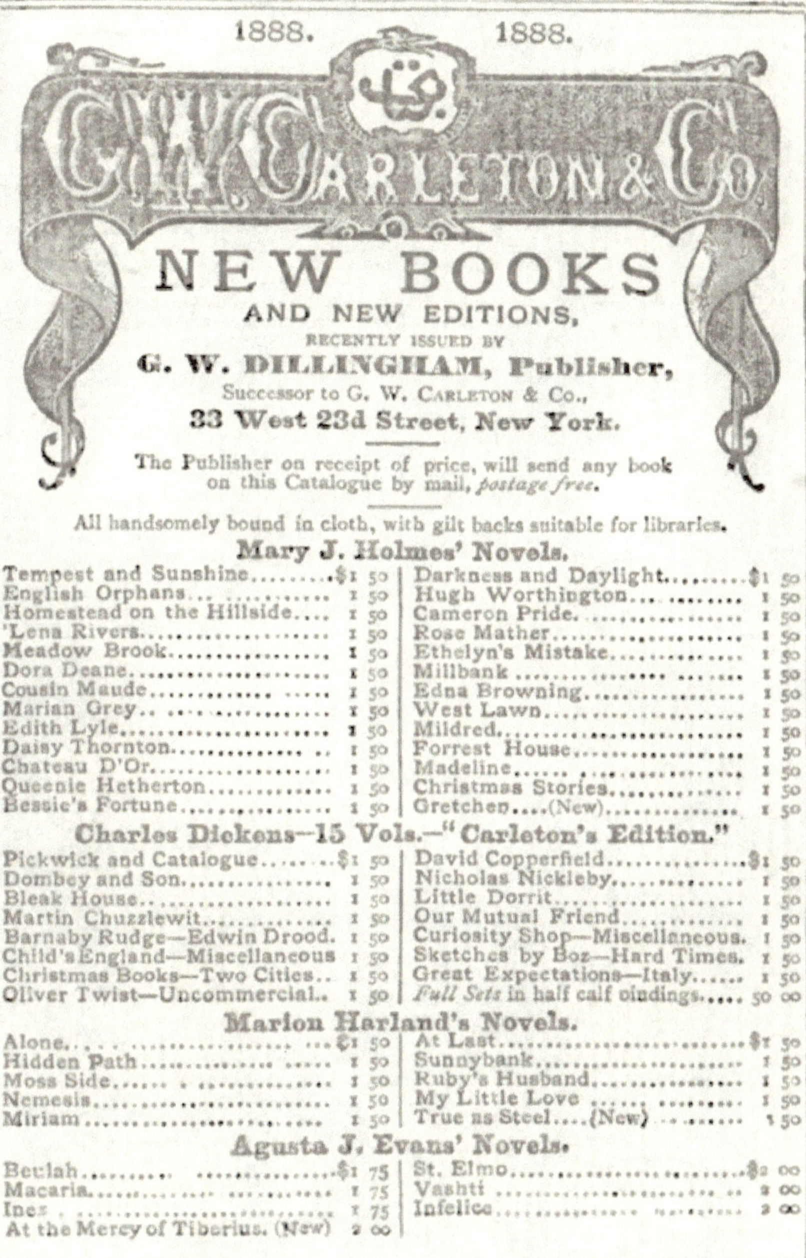

Captain Mayne Reid's Works.

The Scalp Hunters	$1 50	The White Chief	$1 50
The Rifle Rangers	1 50	The Tiger Hunter	1 50
The War Trail	1 50	The Hunter's Feast	1 50
The Wood Rangers	1 50	Wild Life	1 50
The Wild Huntress	1 50	Osceola, the Seminole	1 50

Popular Hand-Books.

The Habits of Good Society—The nice points of taste and good manners. .$1 00
The Art of Conversation—For those who wish to be agreeable talkers...... 1 00
The Arts of Writing, Reading and Speaking—For Self-Improvement ... 1 00
New Diamond Edition—The above three books in one volume—small type. 1 50
Carleton's Hand-Book of Popular Quotations.. .... 1 50
Carleton's Classical Dictionary.. 75
1000 Legal Don'ts—By Ingersoll Lockwood.................................. 75
600 Medical Don'ts—By Ferd. C. Valentine, M.D............................ 75
Address of the Dead—By Charles C. Marble.................................. 75
The P. G. or Perfect Gentleman—By Ingersoll Lockwood.................. 1 25

Josh Billings.

His Complete Writings—With Biography, Steel Portrait and 100 Illustrations.$2 00

Annie Edwardes' Novels.

Stephen Lawrence	$1 50	A Woman of Fashion	$1 50
Susan Fielding	1 50	Archie Lovell	1 50

Ernest Renan's French Works.

The Life of Jesus, Translated	$1 75	The Life of St. Paul. Translated.	$1 75
Lives of the Apostles, Do.	1 75	The Bible in India—By Jacolliot.	2 00

Mrs. E. D. E. N. Southworth.

The Hidden Hand..$1 75

M. M. Pomeroy (Brick).

Sense. A serious book.	$1 50	Nonsense. (A comic book)	$1 50
Gold Dust. Do.	1 50	Brick-dust. Do.	1 50
Our Saturday Nights	1 50	Home Harmonies	1 50

Miscellaneous Works.

Philosophers and Actresses—By Houssaye. Steel Portraits, 2 vols.......$4 00
Men and Women of 18th Century—By Houssaye. Steel Portraits, 2 vols.. 4 00
Fifty Years among Authors, Books and Publishers—By J. C. Derby.... 2 00
Children's Fairy Geography—With hundreds of beautiful illustrations.... 1 00
An Exile's Romance—By Arthur Louis.. 1 50
Laus Veneris, and other Poems—By Algernon Charles Swinburne......... 1 50
Sawed-off Sketches—Comic book by "Detroit Free Press Man." Illustrated 1 50
Hawk-eye Sketches—Comic book by "Burlington Hawk-eye Man." Do. 1 50
The Culprit Fay—Joseph Rodman Drake's Poem. With 100 illustrations... 2 00
Frankincense—By Mrs. Melinda Jennie Porter............................... 1 00
Love [L'Amour]—English Translation from Michelet's famous French work. 1 50
Woman [La Femme]—The Sequel to "L'Amour." Do. Do. 1 50
Verdant Green—A racy English college story. With 200 comic illustrations. 1 50
Clear Light from the Spirit World—By Kate Irving........................... 1 25
For the Sins of his Youth—By Mrs. Jane Kavanagh........................... 1 50
Mal Moulée—A splendid Novel, by Ella Wheeler Wilcox.................... 1 00
A Northern Governess at the Sunny South—By Professor J. H. Ingraham. 1 50
Birds of a Feather Flock Together—By Edward A. Sothern, the actor.... 1 50
The Mystery of Bar Harbor—By Alsop Leffingwell........................... 1 00
Longfellow's Home Life—By Blanche Roosevelt Machetta. Illustrated... 1 50
Every-Day Home Advice—For Household and Domestic Economy........ 1 50
Ladies' and Gentlemen's Etiquette Book of the best Fashionable Society. 1 00
Love and Marriage—A book for unmarried people. By Frederick Saunders. 1 00
Under the Rose—A Capital book, by the author of "East Lynne". 1 00
So Dear a Dream—A novel by Miss Grant, author of "The Sun Maid.".... 1 00
Give me thine Heart—A capital new domestic Love Story by Roe.......... 1 00
Meeting her Fate—A charming novel by the author of "Aurora Floyd."... 1 00
Faithful to the End—A delightful domestic novel by Roe 1 00
So True a Love—A novel by Miss Grant, author of "The Sun Maid.".... 1 00
True as Gold—A charming domestic story by Roe............................ 1 00

Humorous Works and Novels in Paper Covers.

A Naughty Girl's Diary.........$ 50	Miss Varian of New York .....$ 50
A Good Boy's Diary............ 50	The Comic Liar—By Alden...... 1 50
It's a Way Love Has.......... 25	Store Drumming as a Fine Art. 50
Abijah Beanpole in New York. 50	Mrs. Spriggins—Widow Bedott.... 1 50
Never—Companion to "Don't.".. 25	Phemie Frost—Ann S. Stephens. 1 50
Always—By author of "Never.".. 25	That Awful Boy—N. Y. Weekly. 50
Stop—By author of "Never.".... 25	That Bridget of Ours, Do. 50
Smart Sayings of Children—Paul 1 00	A Society Star—Chandos Fulton. 50
Crazy History of the U. S...... 50	Our Artist in Spain, etc.-Carleton 1 00
Cats, Cooks, etc.—By E. T. Ely.. 50	Man Abroad.................... 25

Miscellaneous Works.

Dawn to Noon—By Violet Fane..$1 50	Gospels in Poetry—E.H.Kimball.$1 50
Constance's Fate. Do. .. 1 50	The Life of Victor Hugo........ 50
French Love Songs—Translated. 50	Don Quixote. Illustrated....... 1 00
Lion Jack—By P. T. Barnum.... 1 50	Arabian Nights. Do. 1 00
Jack in the Jungle. Do. 1 50	Robinson Crusoe. Do. 1 00
Dick Broadhead. Do.......... 1 50	Swiss Family Robinson—Illus.. 1 00
How to Win in Wall Street... 50	Debatable Land— R. Dale Owen. 2 00
The Life of Sarah Bernhardt.. 25	Threading My Way. Do. 1 50
Arctic Travels—By Dr. Hayes.. 1 50	Spiritualism—By D. D. Home... 2 00
Flashes from "Ouida.".......... 1 25	Fanny Fern Memorials—Parton 2 00
Lady Blake's Love Letters ... 25	Northern Ballads-E. L.Anderson 1 00
Lone Ranch—By Mayne Reid... 1 50	Stories about Doctors—Jeffreson 1 50
The Train Boy—Horatio Alger.. 1 25	Stories about Lawyers. Do. 1 50
Dan, The Detective. Do. .. 1 25	

Miscellaneous Novels.

Doctor Antonio—By Ruffini.....$1 50	Was He Successful ?—Kimball. $1 75
Beatrice Cenci—From the Italian. 1 50	Undercurrents of Wall St. Do. 1 75
The Story of Mary. 1 50	Romance of Student Life. Do. 1 75
Madame—By Frank Lee Benedict 1 50	To-day. Do. 1 75
A Late Remorse. Do. 1 50	Life in San Domingo. Do. 1 75
Hammer and Anvil. Do. 1 50	Henry Powers, Banker. Do. 1 75
Her Friend Laurence. Do. 1 50	Led Astray—By Octave Feuillet. 1 50
Mignonnette—By Sangrée....... 1 00	Boscobel, a Winter in Florida.. 1 25
Jessica—By Mrs. W. H. White.... 1 50	The Darling of an Empire...... 1 50
Women of To-day. Do. 1 50	Confessions of Two.. .... 1 50
The Baroness—Joaquin Miller... 1 50	Nina's Peril—By Mrs. Miller.... 1 50
One Fair Woman. Do. ... 1 50	Marguerite's Journal—For Girls 1 50
The Burnhams—Mrs.G.E.Stewart 2 00	Orpheus C.Kerr—Four vols.in one. 2 00
Eugene Ridgewood—Paul James 1 50	Spell-Bound—Alexandre Dumas. 75
Braxton's Bar—R. M. Daggett.. 1 50	Purple and Fine Linen—Fawcett 1 50
Miss Beck—By Tilbury Holt... . 1 50	Pauline's Trial—L. D. Courtney. 1 50
A Wayward Life................ 1 00	The Forgiving Kiss—M. Loth.. 1 75
Winning Winds—Emerson...... 1 50	Measure for Measure—Stanley.. 1 50
A CollegeWidow—C.H.Seymour 1 50	Charette—An American novel.... 1 50
Me—By Mrs. Spencer W. Coe.... 50	Fairfax—By John Esten Cooke... 1 50
Ask Her, Man ! Ask Her !....... 1 50	Hilt to Hilt. . Do. 1 50
Hidden Power—T. H. Tibbles... 1 50	Out of the Foam. Do. 1 50
Two of Us—Calista Halsey...... 75	Hammer and Rapier. Do. 1 50
Cupid on Crutches—A. B. Wood. 75	Kenneth—By Sallie A. Brock.... 1 75
ParsonThorne—E.M.Buckingham 1 50	Heart Hungry.Mrs.Westmoreland 1 50
Errors—By Ruth Carter.......... 1 50	Clifford Troupe. Do. 1 50
Unmistakable Flirtation—Garner 75	Price of a Life—R. F. Sturgis... 1 50
Wild Oats—Florence Marryatt... 1 50	Marston Hall—L. Ella Byrd..... 1 50
The Abbess of Jouarre—Renan.. 1 00	Conquered—By a New Author... 1 50
The Mysterious Doctor—Stanley 1 50	Tales from the Popular Operas. 1 50
Doctor Mortimer—Fannie Bean. 1 50	Edith Murray—Joanna Mathews 1 50
Two Brides—Bernard O'Reilly.. 1 50	San Miniato—Mrs.C.V.Hamilton. 1 00
Louise and I—By Chas. Dodge.. 1 50	All for Her—A Tale of New York. 1 50
My Queen—By Sandette......... 1 50	L'Assommoir—Zola's great novel 1 00
Fallen among Thieves—Rayne. 1 50	Vesta Vane—By L. King, R. 1 50
Saint Leger—Richard B. Kimball 1 75	Walworth's Novels—Six vols... 1 75

CHARLES DICKENS' WORKS.

A NEW  EDITION.

Among the many editions of the works of th.s greatest of English Novelists, there has not been until *now* one that entirely satisfies the public demand.—Without exception, they each have some strong distinctive objection,—either the form and dimen sions of the volumes are unhandy—or, the type is small and indistinct—or, the illustrations are unsatisfactory—or, the bind ing is poor—or, the price is too high.

An entirely new edition is *now*, however, published by G. W. Carleton & Co., of New York, which, in every respect, completely satisfies the popular demand.—It is known as

"Carleton's New Illustrated Edition."

COMPLETE IN 15 VOLUMES.

The size and form is most convenient for holding,—the type is entirely new, and of a clear and open character that has received the approval of the reading community in other works.

The illustrations are by the original artists chosen by Charles Dickens himself—and the paper, printing, and binding are of an attractive and substantial character.

This beautiful new edition is complete in 15 volumes—at the extremely reasonable price of $1.50 per volume, as follows :—

1.—PICKWICK PAPERS AND CATALOGUE.
2.—OLIVER TWIST.—UNCOMMERCIAL TRAVELLER.
3.—DAVID COPPERFIELD.
4.—GREAT EXPECTATIONS.—ITALY AND AMERICA
5.—DOMBEY AND SON.
6.—BARNABY RUDGE AND EDWIN DROOD.
7.—NICHOLAS NICKLEBY.
8.—CURIOSITY SHOP AND MISCELLANEOUS.
9.—BLEAK HOUSE.
10.—LITTLE DORRIT.
11.—MARTIN CHUZZLEWIT.
12.—OUR MUTUAL FRIEND.
13.—CHRISTMAS BOOKS.—TALE OF TWO CITIES.
14.—SKETCHES BY BOZ AND HARD TIMES.
15.—CHILD'S ENGLAND AND MISCELLANEOUS.

The first volume—Pickwick Papers—contains an alphabetical catalogue of all of Charles Dickens' writings, with their exact positions in the volumes.

This edition is sold by Booksellers, everywhere—and single specimen copies will be forwarded by mail, *postage free*, on receipt of price. $1.50, by

G. W. DILLINGHAM, Publisher,

Successor to G. W. CARLETON & CO.,

33 W. 23d St., NEW YORK.